TRILOGY OF FATES

THE FATES OF WAR
THE FATES OF SURVIVALS
RENDEZVOUS OF FATE

ERIC MAWSON

TRILOGY OF FATES

THE FATES OF WAR

THE FATES OF SURVIVALS

RENDEZVOUS OF FATE

CITIOFBOOKS, INC.
3736 Eubank NE Suite A1
Albuquerque, NM 87111-3579
www.citiofbooks.com
Hotline: 1 (877) 389-2759
Fax: 1 (505) 930-7244

Ordering Information:
Quantity sales. Special discounts are available on quantity purchases by corporations, associations, and others. For details, contact the publisher at the address above.

Printed in the United States of America.

ISBN-13:   Softcover   979-8-89391-891-5
                      eBook   979-8-89391-892-2

Library of Congress Control Number: 2025918031

TABLE OF CONTENTS

Dedicated to: Patrick "Magonocal" Murphy and all the Murphy Clan whose journeys through life and overcoming serious tragedies has never shaken his faith in God.

And Mena Delaruz who allowed me to use her name and whose warmth, spirit, independence and love of life has warmed the hearts of those who have known her.

PROLOG

Our greatest life changing event was one trillionth of a second after the birth of the universe. Over thirteen billion years later our lives continue to change from intersecting and unsuspecting moments of life. Four billion years ago our solar system evolved, eventually humans inhabited our planet and civilization was created. Each intersection with another human changes our destiny or fate forever. As though one billiard ball strikes another each changing the position of the other never to be in the same static place again until they collide with another billiard ball. Each changing their positions on the billiard table forever.

As history has proven, changes in our destiny can never be undone, but history can repeat itself only similar circumstances, characters and situations have changed with time.

A RENDEZVOUS OF FATES

By Eric Mawsón

PART i

CHAPTER 1

The Philippines, December 1944

Beads of sweat trickled into his eyes, eventually cascading down his face soaking his shirt. Already most of his clothes were damp from his sweat and the stifling humidity as hot sticky humid air emanated from the jungle floor from an earlier morning shower. Vines and thick jungle overgrowth helped conceal his position His rapid breathing and trembling body told him that at any time now he and his two assassins would ambush a Japanese patrol. But for now, he must lie quietly. The muffled silence of the jungle canopy meant only danger to those who knew how to react and read the silence that emanated from their concealed positions. Numerous red ants continued to travel over his body in unison one behind the other. Each one heading for the sweet nectar of orchid plants that had made their home on the Banyan tree that concealed his position. Swatting the red ants from his face he tried to lie quietly concealing his position along with his two companions Ferdinand and Luis. For almost two hours the three guerilla fighters laid quietly well-hidden alongside a small stream strewn with large boulders. For the Japanese patrol it was easier traveling through the jungle following the clearing of a small stream that meandered lazily throughout the jungle. In the meantime, Ensign Ron Garron lay behind the extraordinary giant roots of the Banyan Tree. The jungle was quiet except for an occasional sound of a bird or a monkey. The shade of the jungle canopy gave no relief, it trapped the hot tropical humid heat. Other than the insects that wandered on the jungle floor, not a living thing stirred it was almost sacred, yet he knew very soon it would be loud and violent.

"Ferdinand are you sure they'll will be coming this way? It's been almost two hours. Where are they" Ron said muffling his question as quietly as possible to Ferdinand.

"Quiet Ron," reprimand Ferdinand, "You'll give us away and then we're all dead. Yeah, my sources say the Japanese will be coming this way sometime about noon. Just be patient and lie still," said Ferdinand irritably.

"Hush you two, you'll give us away with your chatter. This is too an important moment in our lives", reminded Luis in a soft voice.

Ron's two comrades Ferdinand and Luis lay quietly about twenty feet away from Ron. Each lying quietly well hidden under the leaves of giant Pako Ferns. Each one tensely waiting for what was about to happen. All had captured Japanese light machine guns that had been seized from unsuspecting Japanese patrols and careless guards by Filipino Guerillas. However, Ferdinand and Luis were low on ammunition and grenades. Perhaps a careless Japanese patrol might have the ammunition they needed to continue the guerilla campaign in the Philippines that Luis had started at the outbreak of the war in 1941. Luis was especially skillful in guerilla warfare and was considered the best leader of a Japanese insurgency group called the "Huk".

How much longer, Ron wondered? Had Filipino intelligence been correct, that a small Japanese patrol would be coming this way towards the small coastal village of Loay, Bohol and then onto the Japanese Garrison at Tagbilaran City. Luis's small band of freedom fighters desperately needed Japanese ammunition, grenades and anything else that could sustain their jungle insurgency against the Japanese. Help from the United States' Far Eastern Command did not provide the needed necessary weapons for Luis and his freedom fighters to fight effectively in jungle warfare. Luis was committed to the communist party and had sworn to continue a peasant uprising against rich landowners at the conclusion of the war. Ferdinand had other ideas about forming an independent government in which he would play a major part, but that idea was on hold for the time being.

What was it that brought Ron to this point in time? Why was he here now with Luis and Ferdinand? By all rights he should be on a USS Naval ship as an officer somewhere with the US Navy in Leyte Gulf. But for now, he was lying in wait hidden on the jungle floor ready to ambush a Japanese patrol. How did he get into such a predicament? Was it a fate of war that Ensign Ron Garron an officer aboard the destroyer USS Abner Reed was here in the jungle with his two companions? By all rights he should be dead or fighting from the deck of a U.S. naval ship. The Abner Reed was sunk three months earlier. Now, he was deep in the jungle fighting with a small group of freedom fighters on the Island of Bohol, Philippines Islands

Three months earlier he was a naval radar intelligence officer on board the American destroyer Abner Reed. In an apparent act of redemption, the Japanese super destroyer Shimakaze (Island Wind) was sent to the Leyte Gulf to report on any lingering allied American and Australian shipping that may be lagging in Leyte Gulf. A week earlier a fierce and historic naval battle had just occurred. The naval battle of Leyte Gulf was considered as perhaps the greatest naval battle of all time as Japan assaulted the allies with everything the Japanese Imperial Navy could muster. Despite suffering heavy casualties, the allies eventually repulsed the Japanese naval force by the American Navy's 3rd and 7th fleets, but in doing so the American Fleets paid a heavy price in losing many ships and thousands of sailors and airmen. So, on one fateful day on November 1, 1944 the super destroyer Shimakaze along with Kamikaze attack planes were looking for easy stray targets and found the Abner Reed. The Shimakaze had spotted Abner Reed and radioed the ships position to its aircraft carrier to launch an Aichi D3A class Kamikaze bomber plane. As the plane began its final approach towards the ship, the Abner Reed fought for its life as every available gun thundered at Lieutenant Ryoji Imahara's dive bomber. The kamikaze plane's cowling was awash with fire but flying officer Ryoji Imahata's was determined to strike Abner Reed. Lieutenant Imahara was a young officer; and by an unfortunate fate of destiny, he received his white slip of paper from the Emperor ordering him to die for his country by crashing his plane into enemy's shipping. Outfitted with a single bomb and enough fuel for a one-way flight he guided his plane towards his quarry. Lieutenant Imahara did succeed and fulfilled his personal mission for the Emperor of Japan. He was one of hundreds who blindly gave his life without question to the Emperor of Japan. In his final letter to his mother, he did not wish to be a Kamikaze pilot, nor did he wish to blindly sacrifice his life. However, his loyalty to Japan and duty to his emperor was without question, he did not wish to bring shame to his family. Before his bomber plane crashed into the Abner Reed's main deck, Lieutenant Imahara skillfully maneuvered his plane close enough to deliver a single bomb down one of two smokestacks on the Abner Reed. The bomb exploded in one of the engine rooms while at the same time Lieutenant Imahara 's plane crashed and cartwheeled in a fireball diagonally across the main deck. The deck turned into an inferno from the aviation fuel that had spilled out onto the deck. However, its only bomb had done its damage below decks. The fireball consumed Lieutenant Imahara's plane killing him immediately. After the initial assault on the Abner Reed, succeeding explosions cascaded throughout the ship's superstructure eventually igniting its magazine stores and fuel tanks. The explosion of flames and black putrid smoke quickly took the lives of the crew on the Abner Reed. The beleaguered ship was awash in flames with belching heavy dark smoke that could be seen by sailing vessels from the distant horizon. Explosions from below decks bellowed loudly from all directions. Ron had no time to help his shipmates. The Abner Reed was listing alarmingly close to the waterline and going down fast. Sailors were screaming from every part of the ship for help from injuries sustained from the concussive explosions of white-hot fire and dense toxic smoke. There were dead sailors still at their general quarter's positions as well as floating in the sea. Before the attack by Ryoji Imahara's, dive bomber Ron had ventured top side to evaluate the weather and the Shimakaze's position. However, one explosion after another cascaded throughout the hapless ship, prevented the naval vessel from firing any of its initial salvos at the Shimakaze. The Abner Reed began to tremble with convulsive seizures as its death throws marked the end of its life. The concussion waves from the explosions stunned everyone who was topside forcing Ron to lie flat on the deck and escape the fireball from the Kamikaze plane. He was lucky to be wearing his orange-colored Mae West life preserver. How he made it overboard he did not know, perhaps he jumped, or was he pushed by someone, or perhaps the concussion waves of the magazine compartments propelled him into Leyte Gulf. Bobbing up and down as though on a roller coaster, Ron watched in disbelief as he rode the crests and troughs from each wave drifting away from his stricken ship. He had to splash and paddle furiously to avoid waves that were on fire which had ignited from a thick coating of gelatinous bunker oil that was spilling profusely from the Abner Reed. His naval ship rolled over on her side and sank stern first forty five minutes later after the initial attack of flight officer Imahara's dive bomber. 'The Abner Reed lost its engagement with the enemy and was sunk a week after the battle of Leyte Gulf. Of a crew of three hundred thirty-six sailors there were only a handful survivors Ron was one of them. What was left of Abner Reed was a sea covered in fire, floating debris and a coating of dirty sticky thick bunker fuel. Ron's upper body and face was covered in a black coating of gelatinous bunker fuel. He gagged and choked as he swallowed some of the oil causing him to continuously cough and vomit, wrenching his body in spasms of pain. A strong current pushed him away from his stricken ship, far enough out to sea away from the smoke and fire but also far away from other American destroyers which were responding to Abner Reed's distress calls. He did not see any of his shipmates floating on the surface of the crests and waves of Leyte Gulf. Ron was too far out to sea to be rescued by other US Naval ships.

The naval engagement was witnessed by a small fishing boat. Sailing in the small vessel were two Filipino freedom fighters masquerading as fisherman. It was Ron's. orange-colored Mae West life preserver that caught their attention. Their small sailing boat came along side Ron as he waived for their attention. He had been drifting alone for several hours feeling seasick from riding the swells and troughs of Leyte Gulf. It had occurred to him that he might never be found and that he might die out here drifting helplessly and alone with no land or ship in sight or any other means of life support available to him.

Five hours after the sinking of his ship and by the grace of God Ron was rescued by a small Filipino fishing boat manned by two fishermen. On board were Ferdinand Marcos a well-educated Filipino Army officer on special assignment, along with his partner Luis Taruc. Luis was the peasant leader of a communist group of freedom fighters called the ""Huk"". Both were observing Japanese naval movements and troop positions on Leyte Gulf. In order to make their identities as authentic as possible they had fishing gear and several crates of fish, they had caught to give them the appearance of simple and poor but authentic Filipino Fishermen. Catching Ron was not a part of their plan but now they were stuck with him which prevented them from continuing on with their covert military mission. But they could not leave him bobbing in the water either, so they aborted their mission. Hauling Ron into their boat they were amazed that he was an American sailor. Ron's face and arms and chest were coated in black oil.

"Who are you" asked Ron. "Are you Japanese?" he asked cautiously. He had not expected to be picked up a by a small Filipino fishing boat.

"No, we are not, we are Filipinos, I'm Ferdinand Marcos and this is my companion Luis Taruc. We saw the thick black smoke and heard the heavy fighting from several miles away. So, we navigated towards it to see what had caused such a disruption on the horizon. We saw you bobbing in the water but no one else from your ship. It was the orange color of your life jacket that gave you away it was easy to spot you against the deep blue color of the sea swells. It saved your life in more ways than one." Ferdinand said with quiet resolve.

"Thank you for rescuing me, I'm Ensign Ron Garron of the naval vessel USS Abner Reed. My ship has just been sunk by a Japanese Kamikaze plane. I'm afraid I did not see any survivors. I'm not sure, but I may be the only soul who survived. It seems I was incredibly lucky; however, I've lost my ship and my shipmates," he said in quiet resignation.

"It is an incredible fate that we were able to rescue you to be here at the right time and this place in this vast ocean so we can save you from drowning. But for now, we must get you to a safe place. I know a quiet little harbor town not too far from here maybe two days sailing time, we can reach the little town of Consolacion," said Luis. "I know these waters very well my father is a fish broker he used to take me fishing as a boy to see if I would like to learn the family trade, that's how I know how to navigate these waters. Ferdinand and I must abandon our current fishing expedition. Our immediate concern is to find a place of safety for you."

With fresh water on hand, and after eating dried fish and day-old rice Ron felt a little better. During his two days on the sailing boat, Ron's mind wandered to his childhood days growing up in Lahaina Maui. How he had loved to take his skiff out to Molokini Reef to snorkel with the turtles and underwater creatures in the warm crystal-clear water of the Molokai Straights. This was his home; his parents let him go as he was skilled in the ways of the sea. A strong swimmer, he was at home in the warm seas that surrounded Maui He was independent, tall, dark, jet black hair with dark piecing mischievous eyes. Well-tanned from the elements, his lean body and strong muscles made him an excellent swimmer. The locals from Maui thought perhaps he was a native maybe half Portuguese maybe half Asian. His father was an American Seaman while his mother stayed home and took care of the family. Earlier the Navy re-assigned Ron's family to Pearl Harbor in Honolulu from Alameda Naval Air Station in California during the early 1930's. Ron's father eventually retired in 1935 preferring to settle and retire to Maui instead of returning to the mainland. Be it so, Maui was the home he loved more than anything else. Ron had learned to hold his breath for almost three minutes at a time while free diving amongst the coral reefs. He could identify almost every variety of fish that swam in these Hawaiian waters. Above all he loved to hand feed a Zebra Eel with squid, it almost became his pet. Ron believed it was a special gift from God. Each time it recognized Ron it came out of its hole in the coral reef to swim to Ron's outstretched hand to take the easy sample of fresh squid. In his mind he called it "Jackson" because he had read somewhere that the meaning of a person named Jackson is easily loved and a pure joy to all who meet him. He felt privelged to have this quiet communion with a dweller of the deep. He never disturbed any of the creatures who dwelled here in Molokini Reef. He felt it brought him luck and good fortune. The coral reef was spectacular. Its warm sparkling pristine clear waters surrounded this lovely little horseshoe shaped remnant of an old volcano was just sublime. He respected and loved nature, he left it as he found it. He did not wish to disturb the creatures that dwelled on his ocean doorstep merely to interact and enjoy observing the rhythms of underwater life. It was a value that he would pass on to his future children. Perhaps his water survival skills as a youth in Maui kept him alive after the sinking of Abner Reed. Ron had just finished his marine biology degree at the University of Hawaii when the Navy began enlisting officers and enlisted men after the attack on Pearl Harbor in December of 1941. It was the outbreak of World War II when Ron's life was about to be radically changed forever.

"Hurry! Hurry! We must get you off this fishing boat before the Japanese patrol boats find us Ron." yelled Luis After two days and very late at night the fishing boat came to the small secluded quay in the small coastal town of Consolacion on the island of Cebu. They had docked in the dark of night on one of the quiet, calm quays of Consolation. Ron had recovered enough to function and moved as fast as he could. However, still covered in bunker fuel and very stiff and tired he disembarked slowly and gingerly from the fishing boat.

"Hurry! Hurry! Ferdinand pleaded, "Get off the boat as fast as you can Ron."

The fishing boat and its occupants could be easy targets for any lurking Japanese patrols either on land or water. Ron was just off the gang plank and standing on the quay when the fishing boat was lit up by powerful lights. The dark silence of night was broken as a harsh white spotlight began dancing on the quays from fishing boat to fishing boat. The bright lights from the gun boat eventually spotted their small fishing vessel, lighting up the boat and its two crew members. Ron had just alighted from the boat and was standing on the dock away from the boat. Only his two rescuers were highlighted in the bright spot lite as they were still putting away the sails and fishing tackle. It was a Japanese gunboat almost fifty yards away running at high-speed heading straight for the boat.

"You there! tumigil o shoot kami," (stop or I shoot you) came a loud mechanical stern voice in broken Filipino and English from a Japanese officer as he addressed the fishing boat from a bull horn. The two fishermen froze in stricken terror and stood very still as they were silhouetted against the harsh search lights from the Japanese patrol boat against the backdrop of a dark night. The patrol boat could gun them down at any moment without reason. Ron knew the only thing he could do and without endangering the lives of his rescuers and himself was to quietly slip back into the water between the boat and the dock and hold his breath while submerged as he had done some many times before at Molokini Reef. Submerged he held on to the keel for dear life without having to surface for as long as possible in order not to give away his position.

"What are you doing so late at night?" yelled Captain Hideki Funakoshi.

"We have just returned from fishing sir" replied Ferdinand.

"Where is your catch?" demanded Captain Funakoshi. Luis carefully removed the canvas tarp and fishing gear from the crates of fish they had caught several days before. The Japanese officer saw the catch and demanded the two fishermen give their catch to the Japanese sailors. Their ruse as fisherman was authentic enough to fool Captain Funakoshi. They reluctantly gave their fish to the Japanese crew; it was meant for the people of Consolacion. It was lucky that Captain Funakoshi did not wish to interrogate them anymore. He was more interested in eating fresh fish than thirty day old dried out Japanese war rations. Had Captain Funakoshi known that Luis and Ferdinand were freedom fighters and spies they would have been immediately arrested.

"Who else is with you?" Demanded Captain Funakoshi.

"No one sir", replied all two together as though a small child had been caught in a lie. A sweep of the boat revealed no one else on board. But Captain Funakoshi knew they were lying they had probably done something illegal or were involved in hiding contraband. Ron could no longer hold his breath, so he silently surfaced behind the stern of the boat and held on to the large rudder. Taking a deep breath, he submerged silently again under boat's keel. The Japanese sailors were more preoccupied with the two fishermen standing in the bow and did not hear or see Ron surfacing and submerging.

"We will give you a going away present. Shoot at the boat's waterline!" shouted Captain Funakoshi to his sailors. With a burst of the patrol boat's fifty caliber machine gun the Japanese sailors fired at the water line as they had been ordered to do so. Wood, spray, and smoke coursed everywhere; the noise from the guns were deafening and cascaded throughout the town of Consolacion. Ferdinand and Luis were too terrified to move, thinking they would be gunned down. However, it was their little fishing boat that took the gunfire. Riddled with bullet holes it would never sail again as it began taking on water and began sinking very rapidly. But Luis and Ferdinand were spared and did not incur any injuries Their deceptive disguise as simple and poor fishermen worked very well. Captain Funakoshi had no idea of the value of the two big fish that had escaped from his net. Shaken and relieved that they were alive they watched from the dock in despair as their boat gurgled its last breath from below the waterline. They stood on the quay wondering if Ron was still alive. Ron did not understand what was happening above the water. Streaks of turbulent bubbles had buzzed like angry bees throughout the water narrowly missing his aching body, hearing gunfire only meant one thing his two companions maybe in trouble. Aching for air, his lungs bursting, once again he had to surface very silently to get a breath of air and take a daring chance to look around hoping that he would not get caught. As he surfaced, he could hear the sound of the patrol boat slowly puttering away with laughter from the Japanese crew mocking and jeering the two fishermen and gloating over their ill-gotten gain of fish. Ron had surmised that the trouble was perhaps over for now and that his two friends were still Alive. Using an old wooden rickety ladder that was nailed to the dock he climbed out of the water and onto the quay. He did not realize that the chain that held his dog tags had snagged on the ladder, slipping off his neck and had fallen silently on the quay, as he climbed out of the water.

"Those bastards, we have no fishing boat now," said Ferdinand. "They call us Asian Brothers, and they tell us how they have defeated the Imperialistic white American race, but the Americans do not steal our fish or sink our boats or kill our people. Those Japanese bastards even force our women to be comfort women for their soldiers."

"No countered Luis, the Americans do it in different ways, they take our minerals, copra and guano from our small islands without paying for it. They utilize our cheap labor on our haciendas for rich American land holders. There is nothing for us except small pesos and now they do not give us weapons that we need so badly so we can fight the Japanese on our own terms. It is because we do not follow nor obey their commands and orders of the Far East Command. The Americanos will not give us weapons we need. One day we shall remain independent and not be ruled by the Japanese or the Americanos. We are Filipinos who need a homeland of our own, communism is the best way to do it. Equality for everyone in a classless society, it is our best bet my friend," while looking sternly at Ferdinand and Ron.

The question now was what to do with Ron? They had no boat of their own. The answer was to take Ron to the nearby town of where Father Salvador Silva was the standing Filipino priest at St Joseph The Patriarch, Catholic Church he would know what to do with all of them.

When Father Silva and Sister Catherine saw Ron for the first time in the Church of St Joseph the Patriarch they were taken aback as Ron looked like the Devil. Half-naked he was still partially caked in oil from the sinking of the Abner Reed. Only the whites of his eyes and the pink of his lips on his face showed that he was a white man.

"God have mercy" cried out Father Silva. "Is this a black Devil?"

"Only a white Devil." replied Luis. "He's an Americano sailor. We rescued him from his sunken ship, he was drifting in oily water and so we brought him here. We didn't know where else to go. Ferdinand and I had to abort our mission. The Japanese sunk our boat, so we decided to come to your church. We were nearly caught by a Japanese patrol boat as we tied up at one of the quays, but this Americano hid in the water below the water line and did not give us away. The Japanese didn't see him. We didn't get caught but we lost our catch and our fishing boat. The Japanese sunk it," continued Luis. "We don't know what to do father, can you help us? We're stuck now with this Americano devil."

"Ah, that was you guys the Japanese were shooting at, we could hear the noise of the machine guns inside the church. We were praying that it was not a firing squad killing innocent civilians. Of course, we will help you," replied Father Silva,

"Sister Catherine, can you help get this Americano get cleaned up, so he does not look like the Devil and help take care of any wounds he might have. In the meantime, we will figure out what to do with all of you."

Father Silva introduced himself To Ron, Luis and Marcos.

"My name is Father Salvador Silva; I have completed my seminary work at St Vincent Ferrer Seminary close to Manila. I have come here to be the temporary parochial vicar because we have no one else who is available to serve the needs of the church here at the Church of St Joseph. During times of war, it is exceedingly difficult to manage the affairs of the church. But I will do my best to help my people and anyone else who requires my services even if it puts us in danger. After the war

I hope to return to my home province of Aklan near Bataan. You can stay here for two or three days but no longer. The Japanese have regular patrols that often burst into my church at any time looking for people who are on their wanted list. They are also very fascinated about the large crucifix behind our alter and will point and laugh at it gleefully but strangely enough they do not go near it."

Ron was grateful for the care he received from Sister Catherine and Father Silva, he and his companions were fed bowls of rice porridge or Lugau and drank fresh coconut milk. Cleaned up and no longer looking like the Devil he felt much better. He was extremely anxious; he had inadvertently may have put his two companions in extreme danger as well as Father Silva's. church. They and their families could be executed while trying to save his life.

Sister Catherine also attended to the two fishermen as well as she was able to with the meager provisions that lay in the church. She made sure they were fed and drank plenty of coconut water.

"You had better hide out in our church" said Sister Catherine. "Father Silva will provide you with safety for as long as he can without endangering us and our parishioners," she said very quietly and politely.

At the outbreak of World War II, the Japanese made their triumphant entry to Manila. Sister Catherine was teaching at St. Scholastica's College for women in Manila. She had come all the way from Ohio as a missionary of the Benedictine Sisters. Eventually e Japanese seized St Scholastica's college as "property of the Japanese Imperial Forces. Parts of the school were converted into a hospital. The Sisters opened the school gates to welcome people who sought refuge in the concrete buildings of the school. But on one fateful day, an incendiary bomb accidently set fire to the college. The buildings were razed to the ground. St. Scholastica's buildings were all gone. But by God's grace, Sister Catherine and the remaining staff who lived on the campus were spared. She was only twenty five years old when she was reassigned to the Church of St Joseph's the Patriarch to assist Father Silva in the small town of Consolation in the island of Cebu in the central Philippines. Father Silva had the administrative duties of the church during wartime conditions Ron was grateful for being sheltered and safe for the time being.

"Father Silva, if I am still alive and I should return here, then I promise to do something to repay you. I don't know what it will be but I thank you for helping me and my two companions. I know I have endangered their lives as well as yours and Sister Catherine's life as well in order to help me survive and escape the Japanese."

"Sister Catherine and I are only servants of God" replied Father Silva. "We would do it for anyone who needs our help. However, for the short time you and your two companions will need to look after yourselves. You cannot stay here for too long," he warned. "We have a cellar behind the alter where we keep our important documents, it is under the alter rug so that hopefully we can conceal our cellar for safe keeping from the Japanese." All concerned knew it would be a matter of time before they would be caught.

"Go down into the cellar and hide there, we'll give you food and water until we decide what to do with you." And so, for two days, Ron and his two Filipino companions whose military mission had to be aborted stayed quietly and gratefully in the small cellar under the alter at St Joseph's. Two days later Father Silva talked to the three hideouts.

"I know who you two are and what you were doing, but don't worry, your identity will be safe with me. At this point the Japanese don't know that you are hiding here, but it's only a matter of time before they find you and then all of us will be executed. They are looking for the two fishermen whose boat was sunk in the harbor and perhaps hiding an American Sailor. If you are caught, they will torture you and then shoot you and probably your families as well. There are Japanese posters being circulated regarding the fisherman who have helped an American Sailor. There may be bounty on your heads for someone to turn you in to the Japanese authorities.

"How do they know I am here?" asked Ron in amazement.

"I think they must have found your missing dog tags Ron, as you may have dropped them or snagged them while climbing on the wooden ladder. You will leave when the time is right, until then we willl provide you with a small sailing boat. Do you know where Bohol is?" Father Silva said rhetorically,

"It is the next largest island over from Cebu." He answered to himself. Luis said he knew how to get there from Cebu as he had fished these waters as a boy with his father many times.

"It would be four days journey traveling by night for safety all the while hiding from the Japanese patrol boats. Go to the little seaside town of Loay, find my cousin Ligaya on my mother's side, and tell her I sent both of you and Ron. Have her find shelter and safety for as long as she is able." Father Silva knew it would be difficult for Ron it would be near impossible to hide him for too long, but his two fishermen friends could blend into the community without too much difficulty. Waiting in the cellar in temporary security of the church, Ron began asking Luis many questions.

"What did you mean about the guano asked Ron curiously? I've never heard anything about stealing or taking guano from other countries."

"America is always in our hearts Luis replied we will always bleed for America we will sacrifice ourselves and wear our hearts on our sleeves. We have always supported America even if we sacrifice our hearts for our homeland. It is a small opportunity for us to leave the poverty of the Philippines and go to America to start a new life even if it means being separated from our families. We hope that eventually we could send our families later and be reunited as families again. Hopefully, we can come one by one to America. It has been that way for us for many years. But the Americanos have come here and exploited our natural resources. Your government allowed commercial contractors to come to the many small islands of the Philippines and take the bountiful bat guano that exists in the many caves in our country. They use it for fertilizer in your country for your corn and wheat fields. We are powerless to stop them we do not even receive any compensation from the Americanos. We need it also for our own crops also, but we cannot stop your country from coming here to exploit us. Our farmers who work in the fields are very poor and are often being taken advantage of our cheap labor by the rich landowners. The landowners get rich, but our agrarian brothers remain in desperate poverty. I was born into poverty; I will probably die a poor peasant as well." He said sadly. "In the meantime, during this war I have formed a group of guerilla fighters to fight the Japanese."

" Yes, that is true", Ferdinand chimed in. "America is always in our hearts it is a chance to start a new life if we can make it to your country. But sadly, for my relatives who have left the Philippines to start a new life in America they do not do well. Even with a high school education or some college they wind up working picking apples in the Yakima Valley in Washington or picking lettuce in the Salinas Valley in California. Even picking grapes and asparagus in the San Joaquin Valley where they are exploited by laborer contractors for piece meal work. They will probably never earn enough money to be reunited with their families or see their homeland again. They will never have enough money to send back home to their families or even return back to the Philippines. They never can live the life in America that they have always dreamed about. So, they work hard, receive poor pay and make American ranchers and farmers rich in return. After the war when we defeat the Japanese, it will be our turn. We will have the country we have always dreamed about. It will be similar in concept like America, but free and independent and very prosperous." Ferdinand boasted.

"If life has been hard for you here and even tougher in America then why don't you side with the Japanese, after all they are your Asian like you," asked Ron?"

"Yes, it is true." Ferdinand said, "The Japanese are Asian like us and the Japanese have defeated the Americanos at Corregidor. MacArthur had to flee from the Japanese to Australia and General Wainwright had to surrender his American-Filipino command to the Empire of Japan and march his defeated troops to Bataan. They showed us that the white race could be defeated by our Asian brothers, but the Americanos have always treated us fairly with law and order and the promise of democracy and freedom. They do not brutally attack and slaughter our people. Americanos gave our people a sense of justice for law and order, not blind obedience to an emperor."

"But do not forget Ferdinand," Luis said, pointing his finger at Ferdinand, "The Americanos have exploited our lands in many other ways without giving back to us," said Luis accusingly. "They do not even give us guns and ammunition to fight the same common enemy because we do not take orders from the allied command. We want to fight the Japanese in our own way on our own terms. For several years since the war began in 1941, we have begged the Far Eastern Command to give us guns and ammunition to fight the Japanese, but they have turned a deaf ear. They want us to obey Americano commanders who know nothing of the guerrilla fighting we must do in the jungles of our own homeland. We do not trust the allied forces ordering us about when they know nothing of Filipino culture, language, or customs. Often the intelligence they give us is faulty or the weapons they had given us were bulky and heavy, often outdated, and useless for the kind of fighting our people need for guerilla fighting. So, it us up to us our own independent freedom fighters who must fight the Japanese on our own terms. I call it the "Hukbalahap" meaning "The Peoples Anti- Japanese Army" we call it "Huk" for short." It was clear that Luis Taruc disliked the Americans but hated the Japanese even more.

"In 1935, I became a member of the communist party in order to help my poor countryman to help them get out of poverty from the abuse of rich landowners. I encouraged insurgency during our agrarian revolt to reform the rich landowners to give our peasants a better way of life. But when the Japanese invaded the Philippines, I stopped my agrarian revolt and formed the "Huk". I am wanted by the Japanese. I am incognito acting as a spy hiding as a simple fisherman until I decide where to strike next. Right now, in 1944 we have almost thirty thousand independent freedom fighters in revolt in almost every island fighting the Japanese,

"And what about you Ferdinand, are you also a "Huk"?" said Ron curiously.

"Oh, my goodness no" he replied. "I am an officer with the Philippine armed forces. By trade I am a lawyer. I received my law degree from the University of the Philippines. I am working with Luis to understand how guerilla fighting is being carried out and report my information back to allied command. Before the war I was a trial lawyer. When my islands were invaded, I became an officer in the Army and was sent on special undercover assignment to work with "Huk" guerillas and to report back to the Far Eastern Allied Command. Right now, our enemy is the Empire of Japan. Luis and I have put aside our political differences in order to fight our common enemy. Once the war is over then I am sure we will resume our own political interests again. And, perhaps one day, we will have a homeland of our own free of any foreign interests and pressures. Yes, one day we will be independent with our own president, constitution and freely elected officials not dictated by the U.S. or anyone else" said Ferdinand Marcos wistfully. "But I am afraid that somehow we still need the United States in many ways yet to come" he said while taking a big sigh of resignation.

"Are you all from here?" Ron asked Ferdinand.

"No, we are from the northern part of the Philippines Luis is from Pampanga and I am from Ilocas north of Manila that is where our homes are. We pretend to be fisherman in the Gulf of Leyte disguised as fisherman to recruit guerillas and spy and report on the Japanese naval and army movements. We endanger our families and friends if we stay close to our barrios back home, so we must be careful. By coming south to Leyte Gulf, we lessen the chance of getting caught and keep our families and friends safe from Japanese reprisals. But we will return home very soon, one of these days when the war is over," said Ferdinand. "I have plans for my people and my country if we can survive this war."

Ron was amazed how much his two companions knew so much about America and yet he knew so little about the Philippines. Both were intelligent and articulate people; both could speak English well. One being born into poverty with a little bit of education and the other having influence and position with a college education and a practicing lawyer in Manila. They were all so fluent in English speaking English well and yet he did not know a single word of Filipino.

"How did you learn to speak English so well?" inquired Ron.

"Tagalog is our national language." Ferdinand replied, "With so many islands and each island having its own dialect we found it was easier to speak English. It is the one common language that unites all of us. Sometimes we are too proud to speak Tagalog, instead we would rather speak our own regional dialects. There are too many dialects perhaps as many as eighty. So, we Filipinos cannot communicate with each other, so we choose English. When Commodore Dewey engaged and destroyed the Spanish squadron in Manila Bay, well from that day on, we learned how to speak English."

For three days they stayed in the Church under the care of Sister Catherine and Father Silva, but on the third day it was time to leave and make the dangerous crossing to Loay, Bohol. It would be only a matter of time now that they would be caught if they did not immediately leave. Sneaking out of the church at night to one of the quiet quays with three days provisions they sailed only at night in order not to be seen. During their crossing to Bohol, they found refuge in the quite inlets of each tiny atoll. In doing so they were able to elude Japanese patrol boats. During this crossing Ron never forgot his promise to Father Silva. Loay, Bohol would be a sense of relief. They knew they would be safe for the mean time if only the Japanese did not find them in this quite back water of World War II.

Bohol is an island that lies about one hundred miles east of Cebu in the central part of the Philippines. It is smaller than Cebu, but large enough to have several large towns and multiple small fishing villages scattered throughout island. The interior has a dense lush tropical jungle with several large hills and for some unknown reason the locals called them "Chocolate Hills. Loay is a tiny seaside town on the coast relying heavily on fishing for its staple food from the Bohol Sea just south of the Cebu Straights. The Island of Bohol is engulfed by a warm gentle crystal-clear tropical sea with white languishing sandy beaches not unlike the Hawaiian Islands. The Bohol Sea is pristine, warm and with an incredible inexhaustible fishery of every kind that Mother Nature could display.

Ligaya Marapao was twenty-five and stunning. She was small and petite. Her soft smooth dark skin was very sensual. Her long black hair was neatly tied into a ponytail. She simply was beautiful; she did not need to use make up of any kind to reveal her natural beauty. Western women used too much make up hiding their natural qualities Ron thought to himself; She often wore a "Yankee" baseball hat when the Japanese were not around. Her white teeth complemented her luminous brown eyes. When Ron first saw her, he was reminded of the Hawaiian Aboriginals in Maui. Yet she was unlike Hawaiians as she was small, petite, diminutive but very shapely in her T shirt and blue jeans. She was intelligent, courageous and without question she willing to risk her life for Ron and his two friends. She was widowed but Ron did not know that, nor did she tell him. She knew her cousin Father Silva, would not have sent them to her unless it was urgent and important. And when she wore her white pukka shells necklace against her dark skin, she was stunning. She took Ron's breath away.

In the meantime, he stayed as much as he could inside the small wooden house of the Marapao family. Due to occasional typhoons and heavy rains Ligaya's house was made of wood and raised on stilts to avoid the high floods that bad weather brought with it. Being raised on stilts it allowed for goats, chickens, and ducks to live underneath to avoid the heat of the day and also eat the scraps of food that were pushed through the gaps of the wooden floorboards. It was also covered with a corrugated rusty tin roof but leaked badly when it rained. Ron stayed with Ligaya's mother and father and her two sisters. He was afforded temporary shelter and safety. It was at great risk to the Marapao family, but they were willing to shed blood for Ron, after all he was an Americano, now living in their midst on their terms.

Ligaya had an older brother by the name of Vicente who had been killed at the outbreak of the war during the Bataan Death March along with her husband. She remembered her older brother when she was a young girl how he could skillfully climb a coconut tree. With his bare feet and without the use of ropes, he could climb any tree no matter how high without fear. Using his Bolo Sword that was used for hacking and cutting tucked under his belt he could find the youngest and sweetest coconuts cut hem down and send them hurling to the ground. He had earned the nickname of "cowboy" from his friends who envied his courage and skill. When occasional American landowners would come to Loay, to see if there was any money to be made, they would often see Vicente and other Filipinos bravely climbing the coconut trees in their bare feet to harvest fresh sweet coconuts or mangos. Crudely they would call them " little brown monkeys" as a racial slur at Vicente and other Filipinos who were similarly harvesting coconuts or mangos, Ligaya had never forgotten the racial insults she heard from the Americans how it had denigrated her brother unfairly from a daring, brave and skillful Filipino man to the level of a monkey. She was uncomfortable being around Americanos. They said racial epithets insulting her country men, but her country men were so eager to leave the Philippines to go to America. Why would her countrymen wanted to leave the Philippines and go to a country that denigrated them and subject them to the level of a monkey? She thought this was very bewildering she did not know what to make of it. She would rather stay in Bohol than go to America. She began to distrust Americanos and so she kept her distance from Ron.

Before the beginning of the war, Vicente had trained a long-tailed Macaque to climb coconut and mango trees to harvest the fruit to earn meager living. Tethered to a long rope Vicente could give commands and signal the Macaque whom he called "Puti" meaning "white" to find the best coconuts and throw them down to the ground they worked very well as a team. Often local villagers would hire Vicente and his Macaque to harvest coconuts, bananas or papaya from their small plantations. They could often be seen together, Vicente riding his bike and" Puti" squatting on the handlebars tethered by a leash. Before he was killed in Bataan, Vicente did have the last laugh though. While taking a break during the noon day sun Vicente and "Puti" were sitting in the shade against a wall of a house with "Puti" beside him still tethered to its leash. There came three groups of husbands and wives, missionaries from Salt Lake City to see if they could spread the word of the Latter-Day Saints in the Philippines. They had taken the ferry from Cebu and decided to spend the day sightseeing in a large, rented van and driver. Riding around Bohol Island they came to Loay. Perhaps they could establish a mission here similar to the ones started in Hawaii many years ago by similar missionaries.

"Oh look, dear, look at the darling monkey man and his pet monkey," said Mrs. Iris Ridley, to her husband Earl. Iris Ridley was very corpulent and not accustomed to the tropical heat of the Philippines. She was in no shape to be a missionary she was not of much use but nevertheless she was here with her husband Earl and two other couples. All-expenses were paid by their church since she and the others had donated quite gratuitously to their church. As a reward they were sent to the Philippines on a working vacation to find a mission site for their church.

"Can he do some tricks for us? He is so darling. I hear all these Filipino guys are like monkeys they can climb any tree. Please make the cute little monkey man have his monkey do some tricks for us." Not moving, Vicente and "Puti" did nothing but stare at Mrs. Iris Ridley.

"They don't seem too eager to work he looks kinda lazy; they just seem to sit there," whined Mrs. Ridley. "I wish they would do something to entertain us we have come such a long way. We deserve some entertainment on this dreary island," she continued to complain to Earl.

Mrs. Ridley was corpulent, bored, and very uncomfortable; she was wearing a loose-fitting green and white flower print summer dress similar to a Mumu with a hem line just above her ankles. It was the only thing she could wear to keep herself cool. She was uncomfortable being in the tropics or anywhere else outside of the United States. Being ignorant, she assumed that Vicente did not know how to speak or understand English.

"Puti, pumunta ang babai at umakyat and kanynag mga binti" (climb up the lady;s leg) he said softly to Puti.

With amazing speed and alacrity. Puti ran to Mrs. Ridley, got under her dress, and climbed up her large fleshy white leg pulling on her underwear and pubic hair. It continued to do so until her underwear was down below her knees. Mrs. Ridley screamed in sheer terror as she felt Puti's hairy claws and feet climb up her leg with its long hairy tail thrust and coiled around her other leg. It pulled and tugged on her underwear and pubic hair with its nimble fingers. Mrs. Ridley thought she was going to be raped, as she kept on screaming in terror as Puti" returned to Vicente.

"What the hell did you do with that damn gorilla you god damned fucking son of a bitch!" yelled Earl Ridley, as his suppressed racism came blurting out of his mouth.

Calmly Vicente replied:

"I understood every word you said about me. I am extremely poor; I cannot afford to buy fancy equipment to harvest coconuts, bananas, or mangos. We Filipinos make do with what we have including the use of Macaques and any other natural resource we can find. They are not pets; my trained Macaque doesn't do tricks for the entertainment of tourists. We work awfully hard every day and toil in the hot sun with little pay. I don't like being called a monkey man. And during the hottest part of the day, we take a break. Only tourists and mad dogs come out in the mid-day sun." He had once heard the phrase from a musical he had heard on the radio and substituted the word tourist for "Englishmen". Getting up and turning around he and Puti quietly walked away, mounted his bicycle with Puti squatting on the handlebars in its accustomed position and calmly rode off to their next job site. All the while chuckling as he could hear Mrs. Iris Ridley screaming while trying to pull up her underwear and regain her composure under extreme embarrassment and complaining about being raped by a monkey. The missionaries were in stunned silence by Earl's foul mouth and how Vicente had quickly denigrated the group to the level of mad dogs.

"I'm never coming here again. These people are so rude and backward!" she screamed at Earl. They could never understand the word of God. This is not a place for our mission for God."

"You god damn right Iris, these fucking people are backwards", said Earl as his suppressed racism continued to spew out of his mouth in front of his religious colleagues.

And that was the last these missionaries ever set foot in Loay.

In their ignorance of Filipino history, Earl and Iris never knew that in1596 The Roman Catholic Church established The Immaculate Conception in Baclayon, Bohol where it still stands today not too far from Tagbilaran City and the fishing village of Loay.

Chapter II

Loay Bohol, Philippines 1945

Sargent Akira's patrol could no longer think about the rigors of War. Fighting the Americans and Filipinos was not on their minds of this small Japanese patrol. The Japanese garrison at Tagbilaran City was an oasis for respite for war weary Japanese soldiers. The soldiers thought of nothing else but drinking Filipino coconut wine, eating fresh fish, rice, luscious tropical fruits and best of all just rest and relaxation for weary soldiers. It was paradise compared to the subsistence life deep in the jungles of the Philippines. Slogging daily through jungle covered mountains enduring tropical thunderstorms and hordes of mosquitoes. The humid tropical heat became unbearable. The search for insurgents to the occupying Japanese forces was intolerable. Fresh food was not readily abundant, Japanese food was scarce and limited, the Filipino freedom fighters hindered and sabotaged the Japanese supply lines so that fresh supplies of food and equipment were becoming more and more scarce. But best of all on their minds perhaps the taste of beautiful Filipino comfort woman who were forced to consort with troops of the occupying Imperial Japanese. The patrol was heading for Tagbilaran City where the Japanese Garrison was quartered, not too far from Loay.

Sargent Akira Takahashi was deep in thought. He knew following this meandering stream through the forest was dangerous and a good set up for an ambush, but it was the quickest way through the jungle to reach the warm refreshing beaches of the open sea, away from the sweltering heat and mosquitoes that resided in Mongolian like hordes under every leaf and water hole deep in the jungles of Bohol. He wondered about the Japanese population living in America. Why were they in internment camps? What had they done other than being of Japanese ancestry? They were not fighting for Japan. Japanese newspapers had spread and propagandized how American Japanese had been interned in relocation camps for being Japanese and how poorly the Japanese population was being treated by the American Government. What about American Germans and Italians? Why punish only Japanese he thought? He was puzzled about the war and why he and his troops were here. His mind continued to wander and thought about his wife and 2 children in Yokohama, how were they doing he thought to himself? It had been a month since he had received a letter from back home. He knew things were not going well. The Japanese were slowly losing key islands in the Pacific to General MacArthur. It was December 1944; it was only a matter of time before the Philippines fell. Maybe the war will quickly come to an end and then what? He was very depressed; things were not going well for Japan. He was impatient and too eager to get away from his daily rigors of military life. His guard was down and became careless while leading his patrol. The patrol was weary and eager to arrive at the small fishing town of Loay and then on to Tagbilaran City which was not too far away. They were not suspecting an ambush; they were just eager to get out of the jungle and spend time away from the routine of war. Within moments the jungle canopy became noticeably quiet not a bird of any kind squawked, whistled, or moved. Macaque Monkeys had now become a silent audience. Without warning Sargent Takahashi knew there was trouble.

"Quiet you bastards!" ordered Sargent Takahashi. "Stop talking! Listen to the jungle, there is no noise, get your weapons ready now" whispered Sargent Takahashi. In doing so, his soldiers stopped, crouched very low and came to the ready, pointing their weapons aimlessly into the jungle without seeing the enemy.

"Shit" he cursed. "Without thinking I have led my men into a trap."

The time was now!

Ron fired his machine gun first; the noise was deafening immediately hurting his ears. Luis and Ferdinand also fired on the frightened Japanese soldiers. Smoke and the smell of gunpowder clouded the scene as Japanese soldiers screamed out in pain and fear during their onslaught. Their screams quickly filled the air taking the place of the startled Macaques jeering cries. Sargent Akira Takahashi could not see the enemy and could not fire his weapon quickly or shoot it accurately. Moments later, multiple bullets splayed his neck wide open. Another burst of gunfire blew off half of his head canvasing the green foliage with bright red blood and pieces of his pink and white brain still throbbing on the leaves of a huge Elephant Ear plant. Within thirty seconds it was all over. The ten-man patrol had fired wildly into the jungle not knowing where their enemy was hiding. When the smoke had cleared not one solitary Japanese soldier had survived, they were all gone. The three freedom fighters did not suffer a single scratch. Remembering his shipmates on the Abner Reed, his two companions also remembered their many countrymen being executed for siding with Americans felt justified. They felt vindicated in slaughtering the Japanese Patrol. There was no guilt or shame in what they did there was no time for remorse. It was war and a matter of survival until at least the war ends. Leaving the soldiers where they had fallen, the three fighters stripped the soldiers of much needed weapons, ammunition, and several dozen grenades. Ron, Luis and Ferdinand carried what they could and returned to the safety of Loay.

"Ikaw ay ang lahat crazy!" screamed Ligaya at the threesome. (Are you all mad?) she screamed again. "Do you know what you have caused?" she shook her finger at the three of them as though they were being addressed by the headmaster of a primary school. "There will be reprisals now. We have been able to survive and live with the Japanese. Yes, they have taken our food and supplies, even some of our young women, but we have been able to survive without getting shot or having our heads cut off. Our small fishing village is still as it is; it has not been burned down to the ground despite the war. And now! You, you three desperados, have gone ahead and wiped out a Japanese patrol. We have warned you not to do this. We have all met with the pangulo (president) of our village we pleaded with you not to do this. We are still able to survive these terrible times despite the personal tragedies we have suffered. We have given you shelter and hidden Ron from the Japanese patrols when they come into Loay and now you bring deadly danger to all of us. Despite our warnings not to ambush the Japanese patrol you went ahead and killed ten Japanese soldiers. There was no need for you three desperadoes to do this."

"Yes, we knew of the consequences." replied Ron, "But the thought of my shipmates on the Abner Reed dying a horrible death and I might be the only survivor. It's too much for me to carry on without doing anything. All of us had a sense that we needed to do something. Luiz and Ferdinand are guerilla fighters, fighting for the freedom of the Philippines. I wanted to do it to avenge my shipmates. We knew if we could capture Japanese weapons and ammunition, we could fight the Japanese on their own terms."

"And now we have weapons; we can fight and protect your home. We can even get more weapons and more freedom fighters for the people of Loay" said Ferdinand.

"I agree." said Luis "We can now fight the Japanese on their own terms and defend your village" he said very quickly without too much thought to his words.

"Ikaw ay ang lahat crazy!" screamed Ligaya again, how can you fight tanks, planes, and ships, they can bomb us any time now, have you thought of that? The bloodshed of that Japanese patrol is now our death sentence. And soon we will bleed for America again. We will soon be dead and Loay will no longer exist. Our small village will be wiped off the face of the earth." She left them alone she was in tears and visibly frightened. Ligaya's family said nothing they were all stunned about the current state of affairs. Ligaya's father and mother were afraid for their family and for their peaceful fishing village. The thought of advanced mechanized warfare destroying Loay and killing everyone in the village did not occur to the three combatants. They just wanted to kill Japanese with blind vengeance and continue with the "Huk" freedom campaign. A feeling of dread spread throughout the Marapao family and eventually spread throughout the seaside fishing village. The inevitable was about to happen, there was nowhere to go. Bohol was a smaller than its neighboring island of Cebu it was quiet and relatively peaceful and had escaped most of the atrocities and ravages of war. Ron went to his quarters in Ligaya's family house and laid down on the thatched mat made from palm fronds and thought about how Ligaya had scolded all of them. Ferdinand and Luis went into to the town and disappeared with the local fisherman to have a few drinks of coconut wine and rum.

Several days went by, Ron wondered what todays date was? Later at supper of rice and fish stew he asked Ligaya what is todays date? He had lost track of time since the sinking of the Abner Reed. By this time, Ron had remained in the shadows of his hut, he dared not show himself too frequently less he would be spotted by an enemy agent. And so, he stayed close to Ligaya's home going out at night to help gather food and pick vegetables. He had often wondered how he could get word back to the Navy that he was still Alive. There was no electricity for a radio nor were there any runners or dispatches that could be sent to allied headquarters telling them of his whereabouts as well as his two companions.

"I've been wondering what's todays date?" he asked Ligaya while eating a meal of bitter melon, rice, onions, and fried eggs.

"It is January 9th, 1945" she replied, "Why do you ask?"

"Thank you Ligaya. Since the sinking of my ship in Leyte Gulf, time has stopped for me. I didn't 't realize almost three months have passed. I've been living and surviving day to day without any thought of time while I've have been hiding from the Japanese. I've also known that I've put you and your family in constant jeopardy," he said very slowly under a deep breath. "I'm very grateful."

"My cousin Father Silva felt it was important to take care of you and so it is my family's respectful duty" she replied very respectively.

"Where's your husband?" he finally asked her. He was hoping she would reply that she did not have one. However, she was still wearing her wedding ring, perhaps he was a soldier somewhere in some far-off place.

"He died along with my oldest brother in the Bataan Death March in April of 1942 defending General Wainwright's command." She said steadily in a low voice. "We were living in Manila at the time. We didn't have time to have children; it was my cousin, Father Silva who married us in Manila. On the news of my husband's and brother's death, I returned to my barrio and live the rest of my days with my friends and family here in Loay.

"And what about your family, are you married?" She asked in respectable politeness holding back her anger at Ron, Ferdinand and Luis who had without thinking had put Loay in the cross hairs of the inevitable Japanese reprisals. He told her how he had grown up in Maui graduated from college and joined the navy as a naval officer after Japan bombed Pearl Harbor. He had no time to get married.

The next morning as Ron was having breakfast of dried squid, rice and a fried egg with Ligaya's family, when Ferdinand and Luis wildly burst into the house.

"Ron" they shouted loudly, "It's time now we must go hurry; hurry get your things we should leave quickly."

"No! I'll stay here with Ligaya's family; since we are guilty of putting them in harm's way, we should stay to defend them and if needed I'll die for them. We have guns and grenades. We can hold off the Japanese attack for as long as we can until we get Ligaya's family out of danger while they hide in the jungle. "

"No! No! Ron." Ferdinand shouted. "Haven't you heard the news?"

"No" Ron replied. "Are there Japanese ships training their heavy guns on Loay or tanks rumbling down the streets to tear this village apart while killing all of us?" he said moronically.

"Yesterday American Armed Forces Radio, announced that MacArthur has invaded the main island of Luzon, the Japanese have begun pulling out all of their troops and sending them to Luzon to fight Macarthur" Luis shouted in breathless eagerness. "One of our fisherman friends has just returned from Cebu and heard it on the radio. He just arrived to tell us the good news. They'll probably no longer bother a small town like this they'll need to send all their troops and resources to Luzon. Your fishing village will be saved Ligaya, there will be no reprisals from assaulting the Japanese patrol."

The news was electrifying to the Marapao family and to the small village of Loay. There was great joy everywhere. And it was true, the Japanese garrison at Tagbilaran City had been abandoned, not a single Japanese soldier could be seen.

"We must go now and leave Loay as quickly as possible," replied Ferdinand and Luis in eager unison. It'll be safe for us to travel and report back to our commands".

"I must return to my command and then go to Ilocas Norte and help my people vanquish the Japanese, they will not be looking for us, now we can rejoin the war." said Ferdinand. "We can start a new government and greet our American comrades. The war will soon be over."

"And I will return to Pampanga to continue the Hukbalahap and resume the campaign to continue to lead the farmers in an uprising against the local governments and landowners in order to gain greater economic freedom. I am determined to solve the problems of our poor agrarian Filipinos." Luis stated defiantly. "I know it's my destiny and calling in life. I started this before the war broke out, now I can finish it".

"After the war Luis If you decide to continue your peasant revolt you will be in great trouble Luis, you may even go to jail," warned Ferdinand.

"Then it will be up to God" answered Luis defiantly." And what about you Ron, are you coming with us?" Luis asked."You are now free to go to join your command"

"Not yet, I'll stay a little longer to see what I can do before I leave. The Marapao family and this village have done much for me. Hiding me from the Japanese all this time has placed them in reprisals from the Japanese. I've to do something for them before I leave. I owe them my life," while constantly contacting Ligaya's eyes.

"Then may God go with all of us," said Ferdinand. "The war is almost over it's finally coming to an end."

By a fate of war MacArthur began his campaign in Luzon two days before the Japanese garrison at Tagbilaran City was ready to amount an all-out assault on this tiny fishing village as a reprisal for the ambush of the Japanese patrol. Had MacArthur waited a day or two more to launch his campaign then there was a good chance this small fishing village of Loay, Bohol and its citizens would have been decimated and wiped off the map of the Philippines. The Japanese Imperial Army had hurriedly re-deployed all its divisions and resources in defense of Luzon. There was no time for reprisals to this small fishing village. .Loay was spared as was the rest of Bohol Island.

The town celebrated their good luck by butchering a pig to roast it and gathered the pigs' blood which made for a savory dish out of the intestines, pig's blood, vinegar, and a healthy amount of chili peppers. Ron tasted it for the first time. He liked it. For his sake they called it "Chocolate Meat",

"And now we can finally shed blood for ourselves," Ligaya said proudly as she began cooking a dish of pig's blood called Dinaguan.

Most tropical islands in the tropical Pacific Ocean consists of miles and miles of white, sandy, pristine beaches. Where waters are so warm and gentle that it is often difficult to remind yourself to get out and dry off. The shallow shores are teaming with colorful tropical fish that can often be found in the clear blue sparkling waters usually inside a reef. Under a full moon, you can watch giant sea turtles exiting out of the ocean to lay their eggs in the soft white sandy beaches that is illuminated like pristine snow. The exotic display of plants, flowers, and fruits can overpower your senses. Standing on the white sandy beaches on the island of Bohol is no exception. The aroma of exquisite fragrances of thousands of Night Blooming Jasmine, Arabian Jasmine and best of all Sampaguita, are intoxicating. The aroma of the Sampaguita flower is so alluring and seductive that once you smell the intoxicating fragrance you cannot leave this beautiful white flower alone. The aroma of hundreds of orchids of every kind will come wafting out of the jungle as the evening wind shifts from landward to seaward. It infects your senses and never leaves your memory. The rich aromas and fragrances that drift out of the jungle to seaward at night are unforgettable. There is nothing as romantic and exotic as the gentleness of an evening breeze after a hot day on a cool night lit by a brilliant full moon. Watching the full moon delicately reflecting its own light dancing and shimmering gently on the incoming waves is mesmerizing. It is a moment of nature one can never easily forget. The quiet rhythms of gently breaking waves on the shoreline disturbing the bioluminescent algae lighting up each incoming wave. Each breaking wave enabled the shoreline to capture its own universe of shooting stars and miniature moonlight. It is breathtaking if you have never seen it before. The backdrop of a beautiful tropical evening can easily provide the stage for an alluring prelude.

She was ashamed how she had scolded Ron and his two companions. They were probably right and she was scared and probably wrong. Her attitude towards Americanos had changed after meeting Ron. She no longer distrusted them. He was willing without question to shed his blood and perhaps give up his life for her family and also the village of Loay. It was usually the other way around that Filipinos were sacrificing themselves for Americans. And on a full moon in February, she asked Ron to join her for a walk to the beach to gaze at the full moon and discover the amazing enticing natural wonders that could be found on the beaches of Bohol.

"Ron I am so ashamed for the way I yelled at you." she said softly.

"No need to apologize Ligaya," Ron said, "I'm the one who put you and your family in danger. I didn't want to leave for Manila with Luiz and Ferdinand, I stayed because of you. I wanted to help you and your family in any way I could." As they walked hand in hand on the sandy beaches of Loay she told him that she had fallen in love with Ron and that he was a good person with a good soul. Her opinion had changed about Americanos. She moved closer to Ron as he felt Ligaya's intimacy for him.

"I have always wanted to kiss you. The first day when I saw you, you took my breath away. I wanted you, but I dared not go any further with my feelings." Ron said breathlessly.

"Why not." she asked shyly.

"Because of the war, at any moment you and I could be shot dead by a Japanese firing squad. There was too much uncertainty in our lives to risk any emotional moments with you. We've both suffered enough. I was living day to day while all the time Luis Ferdinand and I were putting your family in danger. And how could I even escape? Take a boat to Manila? It didn't seem probable. There was no time for romance. But now I want you more than ever. The war will be over soon, I want to start a new life with you Ligaya."

Pulling her gently towards him he kissed her on the lips and then moments later with great passion and eagerness kissed her as heatedly as he could. She did not resist, entwined they fell on the soft sands of this quiet beach and made love between the twinkling of the stars and the full moon in the night sky above. The brilliant display of shooting stars and moonlight that were now illuminating the shoreline on the incoming tide of the Bohol Sea only complimented this tender moment.

Luis and Ferdinand were correct; the war did end quickly in the Philippines. By April 1945, the Japanese surrendered all hostilities in the Philippines, and General MacArthur set up his command at the Manila Hotel in Manila. Two months later in June of 1945 Ensign Ron Garron reported to his command at the Manila Hotel. He had been reported missing in action since the sinking of the Abner Reed. No one could confirm that he was alive or dead and so was listed as a MIA. There were only a handful of survivors on the Abner Reed, Ron was one of them. He had left Ligaya, with the promise that he would return with permission from the Navy to marry Ligaya as a war bride. She reluctantly did not go with him. She waited patiently for his return all the while fearing he may not come back to her. Her feeling of insecurity with Americanos still lingered in her head. But as she analyzed Ron's personality and promises, she was right; he was a good person with a good soul and a good heart. He would not let her down. It was this moment she realized that not all Americanos are racists or ignorant. Her attitude changed considerably.

His amazing account of survival, fighting as a guerilla and ambushing the Japanese patrol after the sinking of his ship earned Ron a Navy Cross for bravery while engaged in action against and enemy of the United States. He also received a field promotion for his initiative and his concern for the citizens of the small fishing village while he took refuge in eluding the Japanese. His parents in Maui were informed of Ron's survival as he was Alive and no longer listed as MIA.

Ron returned to Bohol as he had promised in July of 1945 with his request granted to marry Ligaya Marapao a citizen of the Philippines. With Ligaya and her family, Ron took the ferry back to Consolacion and returned to the Church of St Joseph The Patriarch on the Island of Cebu. Ron and Ligaya had only one thing on their minds and that was to quickly seek out Father Salvador Silva.

"Well bless my soul, if it is not the White Devil!", exclaimed Father Salvador Silva. "Sister Catherine come here quickly." shouted Father Silva excitedly at the top of his lungs. "And Ligaya and my family, what a wonderful surprise we thought you might be all dead by end of the war. I put you and your family in grave danger in sheltering Ron, Ferdinand, and Luis. It was all I could think of at the time Ligaya, in order to save the lives of those three fugitives."

"It turned out well for all of us in the end," said Ligaya happily.

"For goodness sakes," said Sister Catherine recognizing Ron. "What brings you back to the Church of St Joseph's here in Consolacion?" she said curiously.

"If you remember father and sister, I promised both of you I would like to repay you one day for keeping us out of danger while hiding us in your church. Well, I would like to marry Ligaya here in your church as soon as you can. I would like Ligaya's father to be my best man and her mother to be the maid of honor, her two sisters can be our bridesmaids. This is the best gift I can give to you and Ligaya's family. It would make me incredibly happy as well I am deeply in love with Ligaya. Would you marry us father?" Yes indeed, Ligaya was right; Ron did have a good soul and a big heart. He had demonstrated that before with love of the sea creatures that lived in Molokini Reef.

Both Father Silva and Sister Catherine were stunned at Ron's sincerity and willingness to marry Ligaya. Americans did not usually do this. And so, it was, Ron's promise was fulfilled on August the 27thth 1945. That Ron Garron, an American citizen, married Ligaya Marapao in the Church of St Joseph The Patriarch, on the Island of Cebu, Visayas, Philippines. Before leaving for Manila, Ron asked Father Silva,

"Does Ligaya have an English meaning or translation he asked inquisitively?"

"Yes, it means happiness," replied Father Silva joyfully.

Ron resigned his commission after the end of the war and returned to Hawaii bringing Ligaya with him. Settling down with Ligaya, he found a small apartment near the Marine Air

Station at Kaneohe on the Hawaiian Island of Oahu. However, on summer vacations they often returned with their children to Bohol in order to spend time with LIgaya's family and friends. Ron loved the Philippines but felt his family could have a better life in Hawaii. April 23, 1946, Jackson Garron was born at Kaneohe Marine Air Station. In 1948 saw the birth of their second child Tanya Garron. Ron finished his work in marine biology with the State of Hawaii and contributed to forming a Hawaii State marine sanctuary at Molokini Reef as well as other marine sanctuaries on other Hawaiian Islands. Ligaya obtained her nursing license and worked at Tripler Army Medical Center in Honolulu. It was there sometime later in the early Sixties she began taking care of wounded service men that been shot or injured in the war in Southeast Asia. Jackson Garron would make his own mark in South Viet Nam. Those events are yet to come.

Chapter III

The Philippines,

The Island of Luzon, 1946

After the surrender of Japan, Luis Taruc was able to get himself elected as a Jr congressman in the Philippine House of Representatives Luis was angry andwas shouting at Colonel Williams at the US Army Command Center in Manila.

"We are asking for reparations and payment to our veteran freedom fighters. If the Philippines is a commonwealth of the United States so why can 't we get benefits from America for our freedom fighters. We fought the Japanese as you did. We spilled our blood, fought side by side with Americano soldiers. We aided and harbored Americans to avoid capture by the Japanese at the risk of our own lives. Why can't we be compensated the same as your veterans? Without us you would not have won the war in the Philippines. Your soldiers get benefits from the GI Bill so why can't we get the same benefits?"

"Luis, I know you are a member of the House of Representatives, but we have told you before, the US

Government is not going to give you anything for your veterans. We have been over this before." Colonel Williams said in resigned frustration."As far as I know your "Huk" freedom fighters are acknowledged communists. Secondly you did not fight with us; you led your own band of independent freedom fighters without consulting us. Thirdly you would not take orders from us or trust your command to our cadre at our Headquarters. You fought independently without keeping us informed of your whereabouts and tactics. If it was not for Captain Marcos, we would have been clueless as to how you guys operated in the field and where you were. And most of all you know damned well that President Truman signed The Rescission Act in 1946 which reversed all promises made to Filipino Soldiers. So why should we compensate your "Huk Freedom Fighters.? We're not going to pay you one single peso Luis and that is final, tell that to your communist party friends."

Luis slammed the door as he left Colonel Williams's office. He was furious and angry especially at the post war government of the Philippines. The new government of the Philippines was not giving in to his requests for land reform. He had authored an amendment to oppose andprevent American businessmen parity rights with Filipinos in exchange for US rehabilitation funding but was voted down. The current president at the time Manual Roxas, arranged for Luis and other oppositional members to be ejected from congress on the grounds that Luis Taruc and his party had committed terrorism.In addition, the American government would not contribute any compensation to his "Huk" Freedom Fighters or to any other Filipino veteran. He was boiling mad. Luis was determined to show the government of the Philippines his anger and his vow to uplift the lives of his fellow countryman that put a yoke of poverty on his peasant brothers by rich landowners.It was the lack of land reform that made him the angriest. He vowed that one day he would see peasant farmers have some political and economic power to better themselves to lift them out of poverty. He had enough and was fed up with the lack of concern his government showed to poor farmers. There was no other way but to go underground.Luis Taruc went underground in late 1946, following failed negotiations with President Roxas, the "Huk" guerillas soon numbered ten thousand armed fighters. Subsequent negotiations with President Aquino in June and August 1948 also failed.By the presidential elections of 1949, the "Huk" guerillas had abandoned electoral politics and rule of law in favor of armed insurgency. The "Huks" controlled most of central Luzon's "rice basket" of the Philippines, including two provincial capitals. However, the rich upper class. were driven by fear of losing their power and their social privileges. Early in 1950, the "Huks" were reorganized as the HMB, "Hukbo Mapagpalaya ng Bayan", (People's Army of Liberation) or the HMB, with Luis as a Politburo Supervisor. The HMBhad almost fifteen thousand armed men, and the country was embroiled in a miniature civil war. Murder, mayhem, looting, arson and ambushes on the major highways were common tactics used by the HMB coercing money and power through violence. They continued their campaign of terror into the early "50's

"Jesus! God Damn it," said President Manual Roxas to Ferdinand Marcos. "That bastard Taruc is tearing up the countryside in Luzon. The local governments there are terrified of him and are asking me to stop his campaign of terror. I am fed up with The People's Army. You know him well enough, you both fought together during the war. Go find him and ask him to negotiate a peace with us, this uprising has got to stop. I know he will trust you."

"Yes, I do know him, we fought together side by side during the war, but since then I've been elected to congress and I have lost touch with him. I wouldn't know where to find him," said Ferdinand Marcos with resignation in his voice.

"Go see Ramon Magsaysay, he would know how to sniff out those communist bastards."

Shortly thereafter, Ferdinand made an appointment to meet with the Secretary of Defense of the Philippines, Ramon Magsaysay.

"Ramon, President Roxas has asked me to find Luis Taruc and put a stop to this violent insurgency in Luzon. Can you help me find him?" Ramon and Ferdinand were shrewd politicians and both recognized a potential political wind fall if they could put a stop to the terrorism created by Luis Taruc.Both had designs on the presidency of the Philippines but being elected president depended on eliminating The People's Army of Liberation and having Luis Taruc surrender his position. Ramon was the powerful Secretary of Defense while Ferdinand was still a junior congressman.

"Of course, he has been on my mind for a long time now. His insurgent communist guerillas have now controlled Luzon long enough. They have been demanding excessive payments and extortion in the form of taxes from landowners in order for them to sell their rice. I have spies all over Luzon I have just received fresh reports that our spies seem to know where he is hiding and how to approach him. We can work together."

Ramon Magsaysay and Ferdinand Marcos sent independent emissaries to Luis to give up his command as Politburo Supervisor of the "Hukbo Mapagpalaya ng Bayan". It was not easy; Luis distrusted the governmental emissaries who offered unconditional terms for peace. In 1953 it was Ramon Magsaysay who ran for the presidency on a platform that stated he was the one who enabled Luis Taruc to surrenderand was able to cease all hostilities in Luzon.But what Ramon did not know that Ferdinand went secretly to Luzon prior to Ramon being elected as president. Under a white flag Luis agreed to meet Ferdinand face to face. Ferdinand came without the aid of emissaries, so as to appear as a poor peasant riding on the back of a carabao brazenly rode into Luis's headquarters. To help consolidate his appearance he wore a familiar white shirt, blue jeans and sandals. His ensemble was convincing enough to allow Luis Taruc to meet with him on his terms as though he was also a simple peasant. Ferdinand's tactics was able to assuage Luis distrust of emissaries, jeeps, or weapons.

"Luis my old friend," said Ferdinand. "It is another fate of war, here we are again, fighting and hiding and now once again in search for peace.Please give up your position here, and return to Manila, Luis. It is hopeless, it's a matter of time before Magsaysay will have government troops down your throat. Eventually the military will undermine your organization and it is just a matter of time before you and most of your guerillas are killed or sent to prison. Luis knew it was true. His rebellion was running out of money and at the same time was being undermined by government troops. The extortion tactics that he used to raise money was becoming increasingly unpopular with the local peasants of Luzon. The violence had gone on far too long. However, there was some control of the rice belt in Luzon, but overall, there was no noticeable improvement with the quality of life for the peasants of Luzon and elsewhere in the Philippines.

"I promise you Luis, that one day I know I will be president. I know it will be my turn and when I do become president, I will make changes and make land reforms one of my top issues but until then you must give yourself up to the government troops that is the only way you can make the changes you want Luis."

"If what you say is true, then sing the song I taught you while we were fighting the Japanese together, prove it to me so I know you are not lying and that I know your intentions are sincere, only then I will take my chances with the government."

"I do remember." said Ferdinand.

"Then sing it to me, prove to me your words are true and that one day when you become the president, you will honor your words to me."

And in a slow and quiet shaking voice Ferdinand Marcos recalled the song that Luis sang for him while hiding in the church cellar in the town of Consolation so many years ago.

"We are what they call mere peasants.

Who were created by God in sincere love;

We who live by our own will;

We who live by our own toil,

We are those peasants; always in poverty; always sacrificing.

No rest from work, suffer more and more.

While others depend on us.

We are peasants who always wear shorts,

We work in rain or shine without resting.

We are the planters who show no fear.

Who prepare the land with carabao, plow, and rake.

We are those planting with bended bodies,

Mud to our knees on rainy days.

When we peasants quit working...."

"Stop! stop! You do not need to sing anymore," said Luis with tears streaming down his face.

"I believe you and I will cease and desist my campaign. I will no longer encourage my comrades to continue their uprising I will surrender my campaign to the Government."

Being Secretary of Defense Ramon Magsaysay received the credit for stopping the "Huk" civil rebellion which helped him win him the presidency of the Philippines.He was known as the man who stopped the "Huk" rebellion. No one knew about the secret meeting between Luis and Ferdinand until long after the death of Ferdinand Marcos. Taruc surrendered unconditionally to Benigno Aquino Jr then a journalist assigned by the president's office as a personal emissary. Later he would be assassinated on the tarmac at the Manila Airport as he returned from the United States to run against President Ferdinand Marcos.

In Jan. 1953, Luis gave up his position from the Politburo. Representatives from President Ramon Magsaysay's met with Luis Taruc. After four months of negotiations, Taruc surrendered unconditionally to the government, effectively ending the Huk rebellion. On June 15th 1954, Luis met with President Magsaysay and General Eulogio Balao at Camp Murphy in Quezon City just outside Manila. Luis agreed to a trial, was found guilty in which he was sentenced to prison for twelve years. Ferdinand Marcos did not become president until December 1965 in which he served almost for 20 years by declaring martial law. In bad health he fled the country to America in February 1986. However, he did pardon Taruc on September 11, 1968 and Ferdinand Marcos gained the former "Huk" leader's support.After his release, he continued to work for agrarian reforms. As fate dictated in earlier times, President Marcos kept hispromise to Luis Taruc and persuaded local and national leaders to strengthen the legal rights of farm workers which led to a more equitable distribution of farmland.

(n.b. Author's Note: In 1996 the US government reversed its decision and granted Filipino Veterans compensation for fighting in WWII. Luis lived long enough to see his wish come true before he died at age 91 in 2005)

Chapter IV

Zamboanga, Mindanao, Philippines 1969

Commander Ali Razak hated the Marcos Government. Living in the small town of Zamboanga City in the southern province of Mindanao he was determined to find ways to overthrow President Marcos and his Christian Regime. He wanted Malaysia to annex Mindanao and become a part of the Malaysian Federation of States. He wished he could have the political power in order to change the lives of fellow Muslims and to follow a political style similar to the Muslims in Malaysia. However, Mindanao was mainly Christian and fifteen percent Muslim. The Marcos Government kept a strict eye on non-Christians in Mindanao and prevented them from obtaining national and local political power. But Commander Razakhad observed and learned from Luis Taruk and his Huk movement's use of violence, extortion and murder in order to fund Luis campaign of political terror. Commander Ali Razak felt he could use similar methods and tactics in Mindanao. There were plenty of Muslim Filipinos in Mindanao that could be persuaded to revolt against President Marcos and give their allegiance to Malaysia. After all it was only six hundred and fifty kilometers or a little over four hundred miles from coast of one country to the coast of the other. But he needed money to purchase weapons for his fighters to enrich the population of his small unrefined, raw recruits. He belonged to a new chapter of subversion In the Philippines, a new order called the "New People's Army" or NPA. The New People's Army or NPA as it was called became the armed wing of the Communist Party of the Philippines (CPP) was formed and founded by Bernabe Buscayno A.K.A. "Commander Dante". Commanders Dante and Razak needed weapons, guns and anything they could use to begin their campaign of terror against the Marcos Government.

In the spring of 1969, several businessmen from Saudi Arabia came to Zamboanga Peninsula to meet with two of the commanders of the newly formed NPA movement. One Saudi who was incredibly young, lean and hawkish looking about eleven years of age was a part of the party from Saudi Arabia. He came with the group of businessmen and relatives to learn about selling arms to the Muslim fighters in Mindanao. He was escorted by his uncle Abdallah Bin Laden.

"Watch and learn Osama, one day you will have the same responsibility." As they sat down in a small house in Zamboanga with along with Commanders Razak and Dante. Speaking in English, "As-salaam alaykum to all," as Commander Dante addressed the entourage from Saudi Arabia carefully looking at Abdallah Bin Laden and the young man accompanying him.

Commander Razak quickly blurted out before even drinking any customary tea or exchanging ideas and pleasantries about the state of the Muslim world.

"We want to buy arms and munitions," said Commander Razak to sound like he was the leader of the local NPA movement. "We wish to start a revolt against our present-day government and Align our political wishes with the Malaysian.

Federation" It was a blunderbuss mistake to open negotiations to immediately lay on the table their main negotiation point.

"And how will you raise the money to buy arms from us and have them shipped to Zamboanga?", while ignoring the rudeness of Ali Razak. "Yes, we have plenty of weapons to sell you but how will you pay for it?" said Abdallah brashly while pointing a finger at Ali Razak.

"Can you loan us the weapons until we can get enough money to pay you back?" Commander Razak said eagerly as a neophyte who had never negotiated before.

"It is possible, anything is possible if Allah wills it" said Abdallah Bin Laden," but we will extract a heavy price from you."

"Such as?" said Commander Dante curiously. Abdallah Bin Laden said in a very stern voice.

"We will send you all what you need may be even more than you expected to meet your needs. The Americans sell us weapons and then we can sell the same weapons to you. However, all our future payments to us must be in American Dollars delivered to a bank of our future determination. There must be strict observance of Sharia Law in Mindanao. You must give up your alliance with Malaysia" Abdallah recognized the NPA commanders were going to pledge their allegiance to Malaysia and not to Saudi Arabia.

"However, you cannot give your allegiance to Malaysia. You must pledge your allegiance to King Faisal."Malaysia does not follow strict ultra conservative Sharia Laws. Malaysia has a more open, democratic progressive form of Islamic government. The Saudis knew they would lose political and religious persuasion of Mindanao if Sharia law was not imposed.

"In addition, you must pay us back the principlethe amount of the cost of arms in less than five years, however, we will not charge you interest. It is the Muslim way, but you must send annual tithings to our sovereign highness King Faisal. Let's say five hundred thousand pesos per year for five years."

"And what if we could not pay you back what we borrowed to buy arms or could not send tithings to King Faisal?" said Commander Razak boldly.

"Well then," Abdallah continued slyly "then our political channels will inform the U.N. or perhaps the U.S. embassy in Manila and probably the Marcos government of who you are, where you are, and what your intentions are. Your plans would be finished in less than a month. All of you will be shot or in jail." Commander Dante was shocked at the harsh terms, he spoke in Visayan to Ali Razak about his concerns. He realized they were being blackmailed and coerced in following the dictates of Saudi Arabia and eventually they would lose political and religious control in Mindanao and could no longer ally themselves with Malaysia.

"Sheikh Abdallah, thank you for coming all the way from Saudi Arabia to talk to us," he was re- taking charge of the meeting away from Ali Razak. "You and your party have made a very long journey for nothing. I think my comrade and I will pursue other methods of finding weapons. "Wa-Alaikum-Salaam" Peace be with you as well. Would you like some tea now?" After tea and minimal chit- chat the meeting dissolved as quickly as it started. No one seemed to like the deal. As they were returning to Saudi Arabia, Abdallah said to Osama, "What did you learn today Osama?"

"I learned they were not serious negotiators they were not sincere in buying weapons from us. Not once did they counter back with an offer. That Ali Razak! He was as rude as a pig; he does not have the intelligence or the manners to be the leader of this group. We cannot and should not trust him. and Commander Dante as welll think you were testing them Uncle to see if they would be loyal business and political allies. They were not; they did not even try to shake the palm tree to see if any dates would fall down. Did you see how both squirmed when you mentioned you wanted Sharia Law to be enforced in Mindanao and to break their allegiance from Malaysia?"

"Ah! Osama you will go a long way, your destiny has been ordained. And so, it is written. May Allah bless you and your family and give you a long and happy life to the end of your days."

Commander Dante said to Ali Razak, "I don't like these Saudi guys; we will go the Chinese and see if we can get our weapons from our communists' brothers. Can you imagine they want Mindanao to observe Sharia Law? We do not want to go backwards like the Saudis; we want an Islamic government and rule of law similar to Malaysia. At least I think the Chinese will not black mail us," he thought.If we help them, they can go to Malaysia and start their revolution there for communist rule they can hide in Thailand as a base of operations." However, he distrusted Ali Razak even more now and became more suspicious of his intentions and how he had deliberately tried to usurp control of the meeting with the Saudis away from himself. It was he who had made the original overtures to the Saudis to begin with. However, Commander Razak had other dangerous ideas of his own. He knew now how to get the money necessary to raise the weapons necessary for his own style of insurgency and in his own way. Luis Taruc had previously demonstrated how to do to raise money by coercion and intimidation. The "Huk" insurgency in Luzon and elsewhere showed Commander Razak that extortion and violence could be an easier method to get money and power instead of negotiating with the Saudis or Chinese Communists

"In nominee Patris et Filii et Spritus Sancti, bless you Sister Catherine," Bishop Amado Paulino y Hernandez said. He was the auxiliary bishop of Manila who had come from Manila to Cebu in order to do official church business with Sister Catherine.

"My dear Sister Catherine," he said. "Since we sent you to Cebu from St. Scholastica's College for Women in Manila your work and devotion here in Consolation for the past twenty years here at St Patrick's has been truly inspirational for all us in the clergy. Your work with the orphans and providing medical care to the poor whoever needed it the most, is truly carrying on God's work. Your faith in God and Jesusin troubling times has been truly inspiring. However, I have come here to see you of the utmost concern. I must ask you to give up your post here at St Patrick's. Your knowledge of some of the Visayan dialects and Filipino culture is remarkable. We need you to go to Zamboanga to work at our Church of the Immaculate Conception. You will have three sisters from your order arriving from Germany to assist you. They'll need training in cross cultural differences, languages and social mores. They all speak English; you don't need to worry about speaking German. However, there is some risk to your assignment, there is social unrest in Zamboanga. The population is about fifteen percent Muslim who are mainly hostile to Christians who want to break away from the Philippines. In doing so, they' have created social chaos for President Marcos. President Marcos has declared martial law and has asked me if we could send additional Christian and social support to the citizens in and around Mindanao. I replied that I would see what we could do. I've contacted your order requesting you to be reassigned to the southern Philippines near Zamboanga City, in which they have agreed if you should choose to do so and are willing to leave Consolation and travel to Zamboanga City.

PART III

CHAPTER V

South Vietnam, Bien Hoa December 1972

Colonel Quan Minh screamed at Jack, "Pull up, pull up Jack! You are too close to the deck we are taking on enemy fire. "Cut Khoi day" (get the hell out here,) he screamed at Jack through the Jacks head set. Colonel Minh was sitting in the rear seat in tandem as a copilot. Jack was piloting the craft in the front seat.

"Did you see where the incoming fire was coming from colonel?" Jack replied.

"Yes, about twenty meters to the left of the bridge on the north side of the Dong Nai River, by those palm trees now let's get out of here fast before we're shot down."

First Lieutenant Jackson Garron could fly an AH-1 Cobra attack helicopter better than anyone. Without letting Colonel Minh know, he arced his attack helicopter in a high almost a steep vertical climb, and skillfully using his collective pitch control, swung its nose down very rapidly to almost vertical again at break neck speed then hovering to a stop one hundred meters above the ground. With his nose at a forty-five degree down angle, Jack emptied his 9mm machine gun at the clump of palm trees that colonel Minh had previously spotted. Dirt, dust and broken palm trees flew in all directions.

"You should have told me that you were going that" yelled Colonel Minh through Jack's headset. "You scared the nuc mam (fermented fish paste for eating) out of me."

"Do you think we hit the target Colonel?" replied Jack, "I could not see anything through the dust and dirt being kicked up when I sprayed the area with our 9mm."

"Probably not" replied Colonel Minh because we're getting beau coup ground fire again," as AK 47 rounds" began pinging off the protective bullet proof Kevlar that embraced the outer skin of the cockpit area of the attack helicopter. "Now let's go home!" ordered Colonel Minh.

Jack knew the Colonel was right and orientated his craft to Bien Hoa home of the First Air Cavalry Army Base about 35 kilometers north of Saigon.

Bien Hoa sat on top of a slow rising hill that overlooked the airport at Bien Hoa. What was once heavy jungle were now just acres and acres of bare low-lying grass. At one time it was a dense jungle, but now it lay nude from deforestation. The town of Bien Hoa in itself was a typical war-torn town that had once suffered horrific damages and casualties. For now, it could not be rebuilt however the citizens of Bien Hoa did what they could with what they had to work with. Ram shackle shacks, barbed wire, tin roofs, open stalls selling everything one could buy items both legal and illegal. There was little if any law enforcement. During the rainy season mud was everywhere there were no sidewalks or hard top roads to evade the ever-present red mud. The smell of rotten and decaying garbage and a dipping ng sauce of fermented rotten fish paste called "Nuoc Mam" when cooked in open air stalls it permeated throughout the town. It is an aroma Jack could not get used to, sometimes it was so strong it made Jack want to vomit. The town itself was not clean like Loay Bohol when his family used to take him there for their family vacations. But "Nuoc Nam" was considered and still is considered a staple of Vietnamese cooking. During the day time there were groups of young wandering GIs strolling throughout the town sightseeing and taking pictures with their expensive cameras all the while looking for whore houses or the best places to get laid to tell the buddies back at their bases. During the nighttime, the same events occurred when the Viet Cong wandering around Bien Hoa doing the same thing that American GIs did earlier that day. The GIs had to return to base before night fall. Motorcycles with whole families two small children wedged between their father and mother all riding on one small two-cycle Suzuki or Honda. Motorcycles had become the most popular and cheapest means for local transportation. As the motorcycles moved with dare devil speed, they belched acrid blue smoke into the hot humid sticky air. The air was already foul from rotten, decaying garbage and fermenting rotten "Nuoc Mam" fish paste. The mixture of unburned oily blue exhaust smoke only added to the foul air of Bien Hoa. For westerners it was hard to take in and breathe the air, for the Vietnamese it was a way of life. However, the drivers of these motorcycles could skillfully navigate the dusty roads that meandered through the town without apparent difficulty. The roads were marked with craters and potholes. A motorcycle could navigate the roads well but a jeep or a deuce and a half had a tough time getting through the crowded streets of Bien Hoa.

"This is not the Philippines," Jack muttered to himself.

"No use in taking chances Colonel," he said to Colonel Minh, despite having superior weaponry and protective armor. Jack had introduced Colonel Minh's incredible first lesson on what an attack helicopter can do. Jack was sure he would be back for more training.

The Cobra attack helicopter was a two-man helicopter sleek, slim, fast could fly at ten thousand feet at two hundred thirty kilometers per hour miles per hour with a range of over three hundred kilometers. Its armament was as sophisticated as it could get. The pilot could move its automatic machine guns through sensors on the pilot's helmet, so all that pilot needed to do is to visually see the target and squeeze the trigger. The Cobra's battlefield roles went beyond simply escorting air cavalry birds for they also offered Close-Air Support (CAS) service through a mix of weaponry options. They could loiter over contested regions and attack exposed enemy infantry or targets of opportunity as needed necessary was to look at his quarry and his guns would I follow his eye gaze.

Colonel Minh had received permission from General Nguyen Cao Ky of the South Vietnamese Air Force to train and learn how to fly the Cobra AH-1G attack helicopters for the Army of South Viet Nam. Previously he had been flying The Grumman F85 Bearcat fixed wing planes leftovers from WWII which provided limited attack sorties on Vietcong positions in South Viet Nam.

"Jack! You're a crazy papa san," said Colonel Minh as they landed at Bien Hoa..

"How did you know how to make that incredible maneuver at the Dong Nai River?"

"It comes from knowing my aircraft Colonel, how did you like your introductory lesson in flying the Cobra attack helicopter?"

"It was incredible I did not know it could do some many things, but those incoming rounds scared me to death beau coup (plenty) we were so low, we were easy targets for ground fire. I thought the rounds would hit something vital in our craft and we would go down in flames," said the Colonel.

"It is always possible Colonel; we always have to be careful and know what we are doing. Think it over if you still want to continue make sure you decide with General Ky. How about a cold beer Colonel?"

For those who knew Jack, he was a skillful pilot and could fly and maneuver his helicopter with amazing ability. He was first in his class at Fort Rucker Army Aviation School. In many ways he resembled his father, lean, dark haired, and dark piercing mischievous eyes. He had a love for nature that he learned from his father and mother during their family vacations to the Philippines as well as living in Hawaii. He had learned how to speak fluent Tagalog. He was easy going, affable and good natured. When on missions he was very serious and also inclined to take risks that gave him a nickname of "The Lone Ranger"

Morris met Colonel Minh. Warrant Officer Morris Broom from Dallas Texas was Jack's co- pilot in the two-seater helicopter and had flown with Jack as a team for about three months.

"Good afternoon sir" said Morris as they were being seated for a cold beer at the First Cavalry officers club in Bien Hoa." How did you like flying with the "Lone Ranger" Colonel? At times he is some kind of a daredevil, but I am getting used to it."

"You know if my country's air force could learn how to fly a hundred of these amazing helicopters the Vietcong could have no place to hide. But your pilot I think he is a little "beau coup dinky dao (plenty crazy). We almost got our asses shot off."

"How well I know Colonel Minh, I have flown with him for three months now and each time is an adventure, but we always come back alive and intact," said Warrant officer Morris Broom in apparent sympathy. Jack knew Colonel Minh was teasing him and decompressing from the prior mission. Jack laughed at the conversation and was glad he was back safely at Bien Hoa downing a cold Schlitz. The next morning Jack and Morris had not anticipated being called into the CO's office the next morning.

"Good morning gentleman, we want you guys to fly to Dau Tieng District near Phuoc Long. We have unofficial reports of increased North Vietnamese Army activity in the area and we want you guys to do a reconnaissance for us, scout the area and take pictures of anything unusual," said Colonel Martinez. "Do not engage the enemy we just want to know what's happening there since the First Infantry Division, and 11th Armored Cavalry Regiment, did operation Atlas Wedge about a year and half ago and cleaned up all the VC activity in the area."

Dau Tieng District is about seventy-five kilometers north of Saigon in the Phoc Long area. Jack figured that he and Morris could be back by lunch for a cold beer and listen to the Cowboy vs the 49ers game on armed forces radio.

"Sure, thing Colonel" said Jack.

"Oh, Jack I heard you scared the piss out of Colonel Minh yesterday, but he wants to come back for more, are you up to it again? He thinks you're a "numbah one chopper pilot but plenty dinky dau."

"No problem Colonel, it was kind of fun watching Colonel Minh shit his pants."

At seven am the next morning Jack and Morris climbed into their Cobra attack helicopter and lifted off from Bien Hoa towards Phuc Long in Dau Tieng District. Jack loved flying; the air was cooler at thousand meters and felt good to be away from the sticky humid heat at ground level. He could also pick-up U.S. Armed Forces Radio from Saigon very clearly. Away from everyone he was the boss of his aircraft. Unlike his visit to the Philippines, Viet Nam was different. Although a humid tropical climate, the lush tropical jungles had been denuded by chemical spraying. The land looked like it had been raped. Pock marks from bomb craters and artillery rounds covered huge swaths of land destroying the natural beauty of this once pristine landscape. The chemicals used as a defoliant not only destroyed the plants that it was intended for but also crippled and destroyed living beings that came in contract with these toxic chemicals. The deforestation of the land caused major flooding and soil erosion during the rainy season. Unlike the Island of Bohol's beautiful unblemished tropical seas, Viet Nam's beaches, coastline and estuaries were clouded in a dark sea of red inky mud.

"It's a shame," Jack thought to himself, "I know what this place could have looked like before the war."

"Say, good buddy," Morris piped into Jacks headphone. "The shutter on this camera is kinda sticky sometimes it works and other times when I press the shutter It does not work; I think it is from the humidity. do you want to abort the mission and get pictures another time?"

They were more than halfway to Dau Tieng District; Jack felt they could just do a visual reconnaissance, taking visual notes on what they saw. Besides, there had been hardly any VC or NVA activity in that area since the 11th Armored Cav was there a year or so ago.

"No, we'll continue, you can listen to the Cowboy 49er game when we get back in another hour and half or so. Then we'll be back at Bien Hoa suck on some cold suds and we can relax and listen to the game."

As they got closer to Dau Tieng District Morris Broom excitedly yelled out over Jack's headphones.

"Holy, son of a bitch! Jack, do you see what I see? It looks like there are several NVA trucks and armored personnel carriers parked in an open school courtyard," he said amazingly. They were all emblazed with a yellow star on a red background all were quartered in neat rows in what looked like the local school yard.

"Damn, according to intel they were not supposed to be there let's take a closer look-see," replied Jack.

"Jack, don't you think we should abort and return back to base. Colonel Martinez will need to hear on what we saw?"

Jack thought he could get better intelligence by getting closer to the NVA vehicles and ignored Morris's advice He pushed the nose of his Cobra down to about one hundred meters above the deck for a better view. Instantly Ak 47 rounds began pinging off the nose of his craft.

"Jack we're getting incom...." Those were the last words Morris Broom ever said as a hand held soviet designed anti-aircraft missile exploded with a loud and thunderous roar. It was almost a direct hit close to the rear canopy where Morris Broom was seated. Shattering Morris's window. Gravely injuring his head, he was killed instantly. Jack's cockpit filled with smoke and splattered blood. His vision was partially obscured he could not see clearly. His controls became less responsive it became difficult to steer his craft. Flying blindly, he pushed his controller as hard as he could to fly his Cobra up and away from the incoming rounds. His Cobra had also sustained irreparable damage. He flew his craft as best as he could, however he could not attend to Morris's catastrophic head wound until he was able to land in a safe landing area.

"Morris! Morris! Speak to me can you make it? How badly are you hurt" he yelled loudly into his headset. Jack had no way of knowing that Morris was killed instantly. As he gained some distance from the incoming rounds, he began losing altitude and speed his cockpit was filling up with smoke from his damaged craft.

"May Day! May Day! Come in base. This is "Lone Ranger" I've been hit and I think I am at Dau Tieng District can you read me?" Jack yelled his position into his radio several times, but his equipment was not working well, His transmission went silent. There was no answer he had ran out of time. His shattered wrist watch told him he had crashed at 1:30pm December 24th, 1972 somewhere in Dau Tieng District. Crashing belly first into a swampy area took all of Jack's flying skill to keep his craft level he was lucky to crash into such a soft-landing area otherwise he would have been seriously hurt. Everything stopped working but his rotor blades remained intact without puncturing his canopy. Fortunately, there was no fire, probably the swamp's waist high water put out the fire, but there was a huge plume of white and black smoke indicating where Jack had crashed. Unbuckling his safety harness, he was able to get a good look at Morris. His head was a mess of blood and white gelatinous goo, there was nothing he could do to help Morris. Before he could get Morris out of the helicopter, he saw human movement in the strand of strange looking trees. The trees had buckets nailed to the to the trunk of each tree what looked like white oozing thick fluid draining into each bucket. Four humans were coming straight at him about twenty meters away. Pulling out his sidearm he stood quietly by his helicopter and waited for the attack to begin.

"Christmas Eve and my day has gone to hell in a handbasket. I lost my co- pilot, my ship and could not even report our sightings of enemy troop movements in time back to headquarters, I failed my mission and now this is my last day on earth," he said to himself. "Well let's get it over with and I don't want to be captured nor do I want to become a prisoner of war. Maybe I will save one round for myself."

"Don't shoot GI! Don't shoot GI! came a woman's voice shouting at him. We help you; we help you."

She was close now and Jack could see she was a young woman along with her came three men. They were not VC or NVA, they were wearing civilian clothing and did not bear any weapons instead they were carrying gardening tools.

"Bon chance you crashed here,." she said rapidly in English with a heavy French accent. "We get you out to safety.". Other than bruises and bumps he was in good shape with no open wounds or broken bones.

"What about my dead friend I cannot just leave him here."

"Non! Non! You must leave him here. The VC and NVA soon will be here they find you; they shoot you "se depecher" (hurry) Come with us we hide you." So, with the lady and her three companions they led Jack away very quickly from Morris and his ship and away from the swamp, it was the last time he saw of Morris and his crashed helicopter.

"Who are you, and where am I, and where are you taking me?" Jack kept asking her but there was no time for explanations. A half mile later they came to a beautiful two-story French Colonial House perhaps built in the late 1800's.

Made entirely of what looked like gray limestone, complete with a covered outside porch and several verandas on each upstairs bedroom and a garden on the side. A gravel driveway circled up to the up to front door. During French Colonial times its must have been a splendid house.

"Go inside "attendez" (wait) for me I will be back in five minutes." She said to Jack in a hurried voice. He complied, as he did not know what else to do.

"Deplacer le corps vers le siege avant." (move the body to the front) She said to her three companions. They understood what she meant and without saying a word they returned back to the swamp.

"Where are your friends now?" he asked.

"I sent them back to the marais (swamp) to move le corps (the body) from the back seat to the front seat of your helicopter. I am Francine Chang; my brother François and I manage this rubber plantation for the Michelin Rubber Company."

"Why did you move my co-pilot to the front seat?"

As she slowed down her speech her English became clearer. Jack understood her better and could decipher her words as she spoke despite her heavy French accent.

"Because the VC will be here very soon looking for you. They know by now your helicopter crashed in our marais They will ask me where the pilots are? I will tell them that there was only one pilot, we left him as we found him."

"I'll be damned" said Jack in disbelief and amazement, "but for sure they will come inside of your house looking for me to confirm your story. What will you do then?"

"It is simple," said Francine. In the kitchen I have a moveable false wall that opens up like a closet. It is large enough for one person to hide behind the wall and then I close it again it's built into the house. No one can see it unless I show them where it is. I have used it before to hide foreigners who wish to do business with me and hide from the VC. When I tell you, go and hide behind the wall I will open it for you and close it. You are not to come out nor make a sound until it is only me that will open it again. Do you understand?"

"Yes, but don't you have a cellar for me to hide in?"

"Yes, but the Vietcong know that, and they always check my cellar when they come to my house for payments. They are always suspicious and think that my cellar is the best place to hide someone. So, I let them come in to check around in my cellar. Bon chance they never think of checking my kitchen for secret rendezvous."

One of the workers burst into the house. He yelled out in Vietnamese that five Vietcong and one North Vietnamese Army officer are quickly approaching on the driveway in a truck to probably look for Jack's helicopter.

"Go quickly now, and remember my instructions, or we will both be dead."

She opened the secret wall. Jack could barely get inside; but there was enough room for him to stand erect in the dark. He could hear everything in Vietnamese but did not understand what was said between the officer and Francine. The only foreign language he knew was Tagalog, and that was no use to him here.

"Where is the helicopter we shot down," demanded the North Vietnamese political officer in a very harsh voice as he met Francine at the front door. The political officer was small no more than a hundred pounds wearing a sweat stained crumpled North Vietnamese Uniform. His narrow eyes and black teeth from chewing betel nuts and lime, his receding hairline made him look like a weasel.

"It is in the swampy area replied Francine in perfect Vietnamese. "Go see for yourself," as she pointed her finger in the general direction of the crashed helicopter.

"No! You come with us now! You show us," he demanded in a loud curt voice.

As they neared the downed helicopter the political officer demanded where is the other pilot? There should be two pilots one in front and one in back.

"There was only one pilot when it crashed; there was no one in the back seat. We left it as we found it knowing you would be coming," said Francine innocently enough.

"Yes, I can see that, but why is there so much blood splattered in the back compartment instead of where the dead pilot is sitting. If the pilot is in the front with little evidence of blood, then who was sitting in the back seat that had lost a lot of blood and some of his brains?" This pilot has been moved he surmised.

Francine knew her cover story was not holding up.

"I do not know what you are talking about. Perhaps he jumped out with a parachute, or perhaps he ran away when the helicopter after it crashed" she said fiercely. "Anyway, how should I know where he is?" she shouted at him in false bravado.

"Let us go back to your house, we have much to discuss. My men will burn and destroy the helicopter with the dead pilot in it so that it cannot be seen from the air. Their search parties will not be able to find it," he said with clipped finality to his voice. "I will search everywhere inside and outside if it takes all day and all night. If you are lying, we will drive bamboo stakes through your heart."

Good to his word for ten hours his men searched inside Francine's colonial house including the cellar, every bedroom, living room and lounge. All the outbuildings were searched over and over again. Not once did they bother to look for a hidden wall in Francine's kitchen. Ten hours was a long time for Jack to be standing behind a hidden wall. He needed to urinate until he no longer could hold it anymore. Bladder spasms caused him to lose control. The amber liquid trickled down both of his legs and slowly seeped to the bottom of his hiding place slowly oozing into Francine's kitchen. Francine noticed the urine slow pooling from the bottom of her secret compartment. The political officer continued his lecture and railed on about the values of communism and the peoples fight against the South Vietnamese regime and the American invaders. He was so intense in his lecture he did not notice Jack's urine seeping out on to her kitchen floor. Quickly she grabbed her mop and bucket from the kitchen closet and began mopping the floor.

"What are you doing demanded the political officer?" He was annoyed at stopping halfway through his political diatribe to Francine.

"Your troops have dirtied up my kitchen floor with their dirty sandals," as she snapped back at him. "What do you have to say about trying to keep a clean house is there anything wrong with that? Hurry up and finish your search, by this time the pilot has escaped and has gotten far away from you. What will you tell the commandant of Dau Tieng that you let him slip through your fingers? And besides he will be here tonight for his regular payment. You had better leave before he gets here."

Begrudgingly the political officer and his troops left Francine's house without finding Jack's hiding place.

"I will return to look for him. I know the missing pilot is here. I will be back when you least expect it and remember I will kill you If I should find him here."

For the time being Jack was safe.

With fresh clothes similar to men's' Vietnamese dress, Jack was able to slip out of his wet flying fatigues. Francine's workers hid them in them in an outside shed at the back of her house.

During Jacks free time when he was not hiding from the NVA or Vietcong Francine began to explain things to Jack. She and her family fled North Viet Nam at the French surrender of Dien Bien Phu. Her mother being French, had married into a Chinese family that had owned a large rice plantation. Francine's family had to flee with their lives as the Vietminh did not wish anyone that had consorted with Europeans or were of mixed race. It was the new political order. So, the Vietminh drove Francine's family as she and her family fled from North Vietnam to the south. With only their valuables she and her brother, mother and father slowly made their way to the Michelin Rubber plantation in Dau Tieng. The Michelin Rubber plantation needed managers that could speak French, English and Vietnamese. Eventually through hard work and their resourceful skills in negotiating contracts her family became plantation managers for Michelin's Rubber plantation in South Viet Nam. Sadly, her mother and father were both killed during the Tet Offensive of 1969, while her brother was in

Saigon negotiating a rubber deal with representatives from the Michelin Rubber Company and the Japanese Toyota Company. She was twenty-seven and of mixed race she was beautiful, but for the Vietnamese she was an outcast and undesirable. The Vietnamese disliked women of mixed races, and therefore she had not attracted any suiters. She was tall and had large bones. Her skin was not white but not dark brown either. Her face was soft and tender with almond shaped dark eyes, but her hands showed that she was used to hard work. Her dark brown hair cut short; it was not true Asian black. It was long enough to be neatly tied in a bun behind her head revealing large ears and an intelligent face. Her white blouse and back silk pants and shapely appearance gave her an elegant appearance. Vietnamese men found her ugly because of her mixed race and Chinese men did not care for her because she had large facial bones and large feet, but Jack felt she was a real beauty.

"My plantation is the largest rubber plantation in Viet Nam," she explained. "However, the Saigon government demands beau coup taxes from us for their war operations against the Viet Cong Also the Vietcong receive payments from us to pay them off so they leave us alone. The Vietcong realize it is a source of revenue for them. as well. So, to keep the plantation operating during the war they leave us pretty much alone. We use the money from the Americans as compensation to Michelin Company for damages caused to our rubber trees during their military operations. In turn we use the money and pay the Vietcong not to bother us too much so they can go on and buy their weapons from China or Russia and we continue to pay taxes to Saigon." Jack realized now what those funny looking trees were when he crashed his helicopter.

It had been three weeks it was January 1973, and now needed to get word back to Bien Hoa. First, he could not stay here forever. He needed to report back to his base in order to report his observations regarding North Vietnamese troop movements. He also realized, he had to get away from Francine's house to lessen the danger to her home. Francine suspected her house was being watched on all of her routine activities and did not dare to send letters to Bien Hoa Army base in order to acknowledge, that Jack was still Alive. She did not have a two-way radio or any other form of communication. The Vietcong confiscated whatever forms of communication she had from her plantation. She did not wish to send her workers to Bien Hoa as they had been through numerous violent and traumatic retributions from the Vietcong. She did not wish to risk their lives.

"What about your workers are they Vietcong?" Jack asked.

"No, they hate the Vietcong and their communist friends as I do. That political officer is a rat, he keeps coming around representing the Vietcong. All they want is money, power and control. All my workers have had family members or close friends tortured or killed by the VC. They are grateful to be working here in relative safety because I pay protection money to the VC. If I pay, they leave us pretty much alone. I trust my workers with my life. Tonight, you must hide in my kitchen again the district commandant is coming to pick up his monthly protection payment from me."

"How is it you can speak several languages?"

"When we lived in the north my father and mother taught my brother and me English, French as well as Vietnamese, Chinese. They felt languages in this part of Indo China would be an important asset for future success since we traded with the Chinese and Europeans, we were governed by the French and made our home in Viet Nam. To be useful we had to learn many languages.

"Why did you leave the North, why didn't you stay?" he asked.

"After the fall of the French Provincial Government at Dien Bien Phu, we did not wish to stay and be bullied by the communists to be dictated by China they would tell us what to do and when to do it. So, we fled to the South. We dug up the floor boards in our house where we hid our gold, precious stones and cash and carried them with us to the South Vietnam" She said matter in a matter-of-fact fashion.

"Under the floorboards of your house you kept your valuables there?" he said in amazement. "Why didn't you put your money in a bank?"

"Because we do not trust banks the communist government could seize those banks did at any moment," she replied. "Eventually we found our way to the Michelin Rubber Plantation here in South Vietnam. They were looking for plantation managers, and with our language skills my family was hired immediately. Before the war we did business with European countries, Asian countries and anyone else who wanted to buy raw latex rubber for their tires from the Michelin Rubber Company."

Her workers rushed in and interrupted her conversation with Jack. The obnoxious political officer was returning in a hurry with some of his troops it was time for Jack to hide behind the hidden wall again. Rudely the weasel looking political officer burst into her house.

"Where is he?" he demanded shouting at Francine. "I know he is here. Where is that criminal pilot of the downed helicopter, we shot down three weeks ago?"

"I do not know what you're talking about?" replied Francine,

He threw the soiled flight fatigues of Jacks pilot uniform in her face. His soldiers must have found them in the shed behind the house. Francine had forgotten that Jack's flight fatigues were still there.

"Here you ill-bred bitch what are these?"

He began punching her and slapping her face as hard as he could.

"Where is that American bastard?" shouting as loud as he could into Francine's face.

She screamed as he began striking her with his fists and kicking her, eventually knocking her unconscious.

Jack, hearing Francine's screams, opened up the secret wall and jumped onto the officer's back piggyback style putting him in a strangle hold. He did not remember more than that as he was knocked unconscious by the butt of a Vietcong rifle.

"Go! Get the district commandant," yelled the political officer to one of the Vietcong soldiers, "Tell him, I have the American pilot we shot down three weeks ago and also the criminals who have been hiding him."

Several hours later the district commandant arrived at the colonial house. Jack, Francine, and all of her workers were kneeling on their knees on the driveway. All had been blindfolded, their feet bound together, and their hands tied behind their back with a painful bamboo pole wedged between their hands and backs. They were trussed up like turkeys ready for dinner. The political officer acted in a flamboyant manner as though he was General Giap himself and began parading in front of his troops as though he had supreme power over his blindfolded hostages. Taking an AK 47 from one of his cadre he was ready and eager to execute each one of his prisoners. He was eager to show his troops why he became the regional political officer.

"I have them now," he said confidently to his soldiers. The district commandant showed up in his chauffeured French Citroen automobile. Smartly dressed, in a clean pressed uniform with a sidearm holstered by his right hip he was much more elegant and professional looking than the weasel looking political officer. He had an air of intelligence and aristocracy about him.

Shouting to the commandant in a gleeful manner, "Watch me, I will blow each one's head off one by one slowly so each one can squirm in their own shit as they wait their turn to die." he said to the commandant. He deliberately chose Francine first; in his mind he wanted to kill this ugly bitch. He put the rifle that he had taken from one of the soldiers and placed the muzzle next to Francine's temple, squeezing the trigger, it clicked. It misfired. In his haste and eagerness to impress his troops and the commandant he had forgotten to chamber a round.

"Stop!" demanded the district commandant as he came closer. "Put away your rifle."

"What!" in incredulous indignation said the political officer. "What are you mad? We have caught the enemy. I need to execute these people until there is no one else that can prevent us from achieving our final victory for the good of our revolution," he blurted out.

"Let me show you how to do it more efficiently." The commandant replied quietly as his chauffer assisted him as he exited from his Citroen automobile. Pulling out his pistol he quickly chambered a round. Cocking the hammer, he carefully put his pistol behind the left ear of the political officer's head.

"There you see, this is how it is done, it is more efficient, so you do not need to use your rifle and waste a more expensive bullet that the party has bought for you, do you understand?

"Yes sir, it'll be a pleasure to shoot them this way," said the officer.

"Good then, I want you always to remember this moment in time," said the commandant.

Squeezing the trigger of his pistol it fired with one loud retort smattering Francine's and Jack's blindfolded faces with the political officer's brains and blood. Smoke curled out of the gaping hole in what was once the officer's temple area as he lay dead on the driveway. The commandant had never liked him anyway and now this wretched looking political officer had become a liability. He hated political officers they always got in the way of military solutions he was a career soldier-diplomat. Political officers always were an unnecessary nuisance. He turned to the small cadre of stunned and confused Vietcong troops that came with the political officer.

"Yesterday Le Duc Tho and Henry Kissinger have signed the Paris Peace Accords. As of yesterday midnight, all hostilities in Viet Nam must come to a stop. The Americans will withdraw their troops and leave Viet Nam and we will settle the differences between North and South Viet Nam in a negotiated manner. This is a direct order from Ho Chi Minh and the commanding general of the liberation of Viet Nam, and General Giap. Anyone violating these orders will be shot. We want the Americans to leave Viet Nam as quickly as possible; we do not want to give them any excuses to stay longer than necessary for violating the peace accords. Let these prisoners go, there will be no more retaliation." He said it loud enough for Francine and the others to hear. "Now go and bury this man, he is of no use to us anymore." Secretly he still wanted to receive his monthly protection payments from Francine's rubber plantation. The political officer or anyone else was not going to get in his way he enjoyed spending most of Francine's protection money.

A week later Jack was sitting in Colonel Martinez's office.

"Jesus Christ Jack, we thought you were dead," said Colonel Martinez in amazement. "We could not hear any of your distress call so we couldn't find your craft anywhere in Dau Tieng District. We had sent a letter to your parents Ron and Ligaya that you were MIA, but we were still continuing the search for your downed helicopter. I am sorry to hear about Morris though; I'll do what I can for his family. Did you find any personal effects from your ship?

"No sir, the VC did a good job in destroying my craft. I think they buried Morris and his belongings somewhere on Francine's rubber plantation. There was nothing left of my ship for you to see. That is probably why you couldn't find me. Is it true we will be going home soon?"

"That is what it looks like Jack, we're winding this thing down, and hopefully we will be all stateside by Christmas 1974."

Those where the words Jack did not want to hear, thoughts wandered to Francine's Rubber Plantation. The thought of nearly being executed with Francine and her workers took several days for them to decompress and accept the idea they were still Alive. The idea that the war in Viet Nam was changing and perhaps coming to an end in a year or so was incredulous news. A week ago, he and Francine were facing a firing squad together and now circumstances have changed hundred eighty degrees degrees in less than a week.

"Why didn't the rifle discharge, he had heard the click of the trigger" he wondered to himself?

"Oh Jack, Colonel Minh still wants to learn how to fly your Cobra, General Ky still wants to modernize the South Vietnamese Air Force. He wants Colonel Minh to give and assessment on the Cobra's performance capabilities Are you up to it"?

"Yes sir, no problem when do I start," Jack said eagerly as he quickly hatched out a plan to see Francine.

"Take some R and R and spend two weeks sightseeing in Saigon or Vung Tao before you come back to work. You can use the company jeep; the war is beginning to wind down so you shouldn't have any trouble from VC cowboys. And Jack, please be gentle with the Colonel Minh he has not recovered from his last fight with you."

"Thank you, sir," Jack replied grinning and thankful he had two weeks to himself without having to report for duty.

Of all the cities in South East Asia, Saigon can rank as one the most incredible exciting cities to visit and spend time sightseeing. A mixture of elegant French Colonial Architecture and wide tree lined boulevards made you feel that you were in Paris. Vietnamese hovels were strewn anywhere there was space to shelter, bars, restaurants and roadside shops of every kind dotted every street selling everything and anything that was usually found on the black market. Along with the Lunar

New Year came. thousands of motorcycles spewing out acrid blue smoke as each family prepared for its festivities for the Lunar New Year. During the Lunar New Year or Tet, Saigon never slept it had the energy of New York City. But Saigon or the beach front town of Vung Tao was not on Jack's mind. It was how to get back to Francine's plantation.

Jack was able to take the jeep as part of his R and R and drove back to Francine's plantation in the company jeep. As Colonel Martinez predicted there was no incidents of hostilities as he drove his jeep to Francine's plantation.

"Jack you're back I never thought I would see you again after we said goodbye to each other," Francine said happily as Jack drove up to the front door of her house with his jeep.

"Listen I could not stay away. I do not have much time Francine. Things will be changing rapidly. I came back because of what we went through together. That moment in time when I thought we were going to die brought me closer to you any other person I have known. I want to come and see you at every opportunity I can. Would you let me stay with you tonight?" Jack said with quiet anticipation. "I have two weeks to spend with you, please say yes," as he held her closely in his arms.

Francine had never had a suiter before because of being an outcast of her mixed European and Asian ancestry. Jack was the first one who had showed interest in her for what she was: a very brave and intelligent, beautiful woman. Jack realized about her social position of being of mixed race in Viet Nam. He had similar experiences while attending flight school at Fort Rucker Alabama. There were no helicopter pilots being of Filipino- American ancestry. So often he was racially taunted deliberately or in humor as a" Mexican or

Puerto Rican" when drinking with his friends. Or the Army would classify him as "Other". Racism, bravery, and death were common denominators that both of them had together. Being almost executed together, established an unbreakable bond between them, making love to Jack certainly was a much better alternative.

"Yes, you can," said Francine coyly, "For as long as you don't hide behind the wall."

For two weeks Jack stayed with Francine and forged a romance with her that would not let him get her out of his mind. He could not stay longer; being AWOL was a grave offense that could land him in the Army Jail at Bien Hoa or the federal prison at Fort Leavenworth. During the coming year Jack saw Francine at every opportunity. He would even illegally fly his helicopter on false training missions to Francine's plantation without Colonel Minh. He would ask for supplies from the commissary especially cases of canned fruit. It was a luxury item for Francine; she had never tasted canned peaches, or pears. It was on the pretense he was donating them to a local orphanage. He wanted to do what he could to please Francine. As Jack and Francine became more involved with each other he began making plans about their future. He wanted to stay with Francine and help her manage the rubber plantation. He was scheduled to leave and rotate back home in April of 1975 at the end of his enlistment period. He volunteered to stay as long as possible to help American personnel leave Viet Nam. He told Francine that his six-year commitment to the Army would be up in April of 1975. He would not re-enlist and would like to stay with her after his tour of service was over. As a helicopter pilot he would be the last to leave Viet Nam and would be needed to ferry out troops, equipment, supplies and passengers out of Viet Nam to Ton Son Nuht Airport by that time his service to the Army would be over and once discharged he could come and stay with Francine for as long as they wanted. It was not until December of 1974 that Francine told him that she was carrying his child.

"Ambassador Martin!" as Captain Winchester continued to plead. Captain Winchester was a special advisor at the American embassy in Saigon. He provided current intelligence information to Ambassador Martin. Captain Winchester was assigned directly to Saigon from the White House.

"We have to evacuate now sir! he said emphatically." Viet Nam is beginning to fall to the invading communist troops. Please issue the evacuation order for all civilians contracted with the US Government to be evacuated now to our waiting ships just off the coast, before it's too late. We promised them and their families we would safely evacuate them if the communists should over run South Viet Nam."

"No! damn it! I will not surrender Viet Nam we will stay here and support the Vietnamese troops as we had promised. I am not giving hope for this country, and that is final."

"But sir, please reconsider, I beg you, Da Nang, Hue and the Mekong Delta are all in North Vietnamese hands now. The communists have broken the treaty signed in Paris a year ago. Vietnamese troops are fleeing for their lives there is no more resistance to the invading communists. Please Issue the order to begin evacuating our Vietnamese civilians as we promised them. We need to evacuate them and their families to safety now before the communist attack Saigon. Our embassy and Saigon will fall in less than a month," shouted Captain Winchester. As a special advisor, Captain Winchester was attached to the State Department with links to the CIA as a special advisor sent by President Ford 's office to help Ambassador Graham with the remaining American contingent in Viet Nam. "We need the order now, please Mr. Ambassador."

"Once again no! Now get the hell out of my office I will not issue an order to evacuate our contracted and vetted civilian workers."

Ambassador Graham Martin was the final American authority in South Viet Nam. He had lost a son several years earlier in Viet Nam and was determined that his son's death was not in vain.

It was late February 1975 when special advisor Captain Winchester called together as many pilots as he could muster to the American embassy one of which was Jackson Garron.

"Listen you guys, that chicken shit ambassador won't issue the order to evacuate our contracted civilians. It's only a matter of time now that we will lose Saigon, and thousands of our loyal civilians will be slaughtered. I want you to begin flying out our civilians and their families as quietly as possible to the waiting ships just off the coast. We will start a Black Ops operation without the ambassador knowing about it. I will tell him later and take full responsibility should there be any repercussions. I am sure President Ford will back me up."

Jack immediately knew that Francine was in danger; he calculated that communist troops and tanks were less than a day's march from her plantation. However, she was not a contracted and vetted civilian and would not be evacuated as she did not do any work for the American government in Viet Nam. Returning to Bien Hoa Army base he quickly wrote letters to Francine and his grandparents in Loay Bohol. Grabbing a small suite case Packed his bags, knowing he would not be coming back to his home base. Firing up a larger Huey helicopter that could carry a half a dozen or so passengers and their supplies, he lifted off to find Francine. Jack took off without filing any sort of flight plan or notification as to where he was going. He had no time to waste filling out paperwork. Already the civilian population of Bien Hoa and Saigon were beginning to panic as the realization that communist troops would soon over run South Viet Nam. Thousands of Vietnamese soldiers were taking off their uniforms and throwing away their equipment and gear in the streets to look like regular civilians. No longer wanting to stand and fight they deserted by the thousands. Knowing what the consequences would be if captured by units of the North Vietnamese Army, the Army of the Republic of South Viet Nam fled in terror. There was no longer an army to protect South Vietnamese Civilians it became a huge rabble of South Vietnamese civilians fleeing for their lives

Landing his Huey in a small open field between her house and the rubber trees he set his Huey down at Francine's rubber plantation. With his rotors still turning, Jack jumped out of his Huey and rushed to her house.

"Francine! Francine!", he shouted as loudly as he could. "We must leave now get your things and get your workers and their families ready to leave now in my helicopter. The communists are less than a half days march from here probably closer, there is no time to waste," as he shouted in a panic-stricken voice.

She delayed her decision to move.

"Why are you waiting?" Hurry up, hurry get your things" he cajoled her. "We don't have much time".

"Non! I'll stay here Jack, this is my home, and this is where I will stay. Where will I go in America what will I do there? I do not know anyone there. I will deal with communists when they get here. They need my rubber also. And what about my brother François he is in Hong Kong putting a deal together? I will need to stay here." She said in defiance of Jack's orders.

"Francine why are you so stubborn is it your French blood taking over your thinking?" he said angrily. "Your brother will have to take care of himself at least he is out of the country for now. The communists will take you to a relocation or a re-indoctrination camp perhaps somewhere in Cambodia, probably even take away our baby from us since it will be of mixed race. Listen to me!" he shouted.

"Here is my plan. I'll fly you and your workers to one of our waiting ships just offshore. About an hours' flight from here. From there, the ship will take you to Manila in the Philippines. Once you are in the Philippines find a ferry that will take you from Manila to Cebu. From there find my grandparents at a place called Loay, Bohol. I have written a letter explaining everything you need to know and to my grandparents also. Put the letters in your bag for safekeeping. Follow my instructions in my letter. Take only your jewelry and gold and I've several hundred Dollars to give you to help you find your way. Vietnamese money will be worthless throw it away. My grandparents will understand and protect you and their future great grandchild. Now hurry. Wait for me in Loay, Bohol somehow, I will find you perhaps in a month or so. I still have work to do here."

"What about my workers?" As she began to see the logic in Jacks plan.

"I will fly them out also and their families but once onboard the naval ship they are on their own."

One of her workers came running up to Francine and Jack. Breathlessly stating that there was a long column of large North Vietnamese tanks accompanied by armed NVA troops less than a fifteen hundred meters away were slowly and cautiously approaching the plantation's driveway.

"Francine, get inside my helicopter now never mind your belongings it's too late," as he shouted above the noise of the turning rotors and the whine of his engine."

"Non I will not leave without my workers they are my friends."

Fed up, Jack grabbed her by the waist picked her up and threw her inside his waiting helicopter. She resisted vigorously but acquiesced once inside Jack's waiting helicopter.

As if on cue the workers came running with their families as Francine grabbed them, she hoisted her workers and their families one by one inside Jacks trembling helicopter.

Jack could now see huge amounts of black diesel smoke emanating from the exhaust pipes from the numerous North Vietnamese Tanks. He could hear the clanking and banging of the iron treads as the tanks cautiously drove up the plantation's driveway.

"Francine, we have to leave now, I can't wait any longer" he shouted at Francine.

"Non! Wait Jack there is one more family." She shouted at the top of her voice over the roar of the engine and rapidly whirling blades. A father, his wife and their five-year-old daughter came running to Jacks helicopter. But Jack had wound up his rotors to a fever pitch in order to take off. The downdraft from the turning rotors caused the five-year-old child to be blown down from the ferocity of the downdraft. Quickly picking up his daughter, her father had enough time to throw his wife and daughter inside the rising helicopter. However, Jack was almost three meters off the ground. In desperation the father jumped onto one of the landing skids and held on for dear life as Jack lifted off with the dangling worker hanging on to his skids. Francine pleaded for Jack to set down and rescue her worker, but it was too late. The roar of the turbine engine, and the high-pitched sound it created, the rush of the down draft was deafening. It was impossible to hear Francine. The communist troops began shooting at the dangling worker as if it was target practice. He was holding on for dear life as he tried to wrap his legs up and over the landing skids. The first burst of weapons instantly killed the worker that was hanging onto the skids. As multiple rounds tore holes in his body. He fell to the ground in a lifeless lump. Jack's helicopter was being pelted with incoming rounds Francine and her workers including the child and her mother were lying as flat as they could on the floor and were huddled next to each other for protection. The mother and child were killed instantly as incoming rounds penetrated their torsos. Another round found its mark and lodged itself into Francine's right arm shattering her bones. In desperation Jack flew his helicopter within three meters off the ground and aimed his helicopter towards the approaching tanks. By this time, the tank's fifty caliber machine guns began shooting at the hapless helicopter. Having no armaments of any kind, Jack instantly decided to aim his helicopter's landing skids at the tanks gunners who were situated topside next to the turret. By diving as low as he could the chances were good that he could probably try and spear one or two of the machine gunners with his landing skids otherwise his craft was going down with everyone aboard. The angle of the tank's guns could not be adjusted in time to fire at him at such a low position. All he needed to do was to stop those machine gunners and disperse the ground troops even for a fleeting moment. The noise of his helicopter, the speed it generated, the ferocious downdraft, the deafening whine of the high-pitched turbine engine at ground top level was intimidating. The site of this behemoth helicopter three meters above the ground aiming straight for the tank gunners was enough to make the machine gunners and ground troop's dive for cover. His landing skids did not spear anyone from the gun emplacements, but they did cause a momentary stop to the shooting as the NVA soldiers found cover for themselves. Jack was so low to the ground as he passed over the tanks voluminous, black, and sooty exhaust smoke engulfing his cabin and his passengers with its foul black exhaust. However, it was the time he needed to fly away safely with his passengers both dead and Alive. Francine had stopped the heavy bleeding from her wound with a pressure pad from the Huey's first aid kit, but she had gone into shock she was not responding well and slowly became unconscious.

It took Jack almost an hour to find the USS Kirk and land his helicopter on the ship's landing pad. Francine had lost a lot of blood, but she was still Alive. She was quickly rushed to sick bay for immediate X rays and a plasma transfusion. The dead mother and child were quickly taken away, and the rest of Francine's workers joined the milieu of thousands of refugees already on the USS Kirk.

"I am First Lieutenant Jackson Garron of the First Air Cavalry stationed at Bien Hoa Army base," he said to the ship's executive officer. "I know I am not supposed to be here, but I had no choice." Jack proceeded to tell the ship's XO of his narrow escape from the communist tanks that had rolled into Francine's plantation.

"I did not know we had anymore Army personnel in Viet Nam mostly Marines from what I here," The XO said in a slow southern drawl as he fingered the numerous bullet holes in Jacks' helicopter.

"I was scheduled to leave last month sir, but I volunteered to stay on for as long as I was needed. I was flying American and

Vietnamese personnel to Ton Son Nhut International Airport to prepare them to be ferried back to stateside.

"Well lieutenant, for your information Ambassador Martin has finally given the order to evacuate only contracted Vietnamese civilians who have worked for the US Government to our waiting ships. It looks like you and your girlfriend made it out just in time. Oh lieutenant, you had better go below and clean up, you look like the devil with all that soot on your face."

After cleaning up, Jack went below to sick bay to check on Francine, she was still unconscious. Her emergency wounds were addressed by an IV drip and a heavily bandaged right arm. He told the doctor she was maybe three or four months pregnant. The Navy doctor acknowledged this and said he would keep an eye on her. She also needed surgery to repair the broken bones in her right forearm. He would have to schedule it later until her vital signs were stable and that she and baby could tolerate surgery. For the next two days Jack watched as helicopter after helicopter ferried South Vietnamese Nationals who had worked for the US Government either at the American Embassy or any of its affiliated bases. Waiting ships just off the coast of Viet Nam, not too far from Saigon received as many Vietnamese civilians as they could safely accommodate. Jacks helicopter had been scuttled and pushed over the side into the sea to make room for the incoming helicopters that were flying back and forth between the ship and Saigon. The USS Kirk had already received the maximum number of refugees it could safely accommodate and was ready to leave Vietnamese waters and proceed to Subic Bay Philippines. Before getting under way the ships executive officer found Jack and told him about orders the ships communication department just received. He handed Jack a cryptic message from U.S. Military Command South East Asia Saigon, USS Naval vessel Kirk It read the following:

"…Lieutenant Jackson Garron US Army Viet Nam, to report to the American Embassy ASAP in Saigon. Assist the Marines with the final evacuation of American Personnel. Proceed ASAP on the next available flight.…"

"Holy smokes," he said to himself, "just when I thought I had felt the war was behind me I am back in it again, shit!"

Realizing his predicament, he went back to sick bay to talk to Francine.

"Francine, I have bad news I have been ordered back to Saigon to help Ambassador Martin's final request for evacuation plans of Saigon. I will not be able to go to the Philippines with you."

She was awake now but still slightly groggy from the morphine the doctor gave her to alleviate her pain.

"How long will you be gone?" she asked as tears began to flow down her cheeks.

"Probably no more than two weeks, and then I will be out. I will be at the American Embassy in Saigon helping to evacuate American personnel; Bien Hoa has already fallen to communist troops."

"Lieutenant Jackson Garron your flight is ready to leave. Please report to the landing pad area for takeoff in fifteen minutes," as a mechanical sounding announcement over the ships intercom system sounded throughout the ship.

"Francine I must go now; do you remember our plans once you get to the Philippines?"

She nodded her head yes.

"Do you remember the name of the fishing village I will meet you at?"

"To Manila, then to Cebu and the ferry to Loay, Bohol." She replied.

"Good I will leave you with as much money I have. Safeguard it you'll need it so you can get to Bohol safely. The Filipinos there will help you and look after you; they will be your friends. Make sure you look up my grandparents and wait for me there I will join you soon."

They embraced and kissed passionately for as long as they could, as they both realized the dream of living together as man and wife while raising their child at the beautiful French Colonial House for the Michelin Rubber Company was no longer attainable. He went to his quarters and retrieved his flight bag as the second announcement came ordering him to his waiting helicopter back to Saigon.

As Jack flew over Tan Son Nhut International airport on a marine helicopter it was obvious it had been under attack. The night before, communist troops had fired numerous rockets at the airport. Buildings were on fire; planes had been destroyed and the runway was pock marked with craters rendering the airport as unserviceable. It was clear Saigon would fall to the North Vietnamese Communists in less than a week. The enemy was already at the gates.

Not far away was the American Embassy with two serviceable landing pads, one located on the roof of the embassy and the other in the courtyard close to the swimming pool. The swimming pool was dirty and cluttered with debris and confiscated weapons that the Marines threw into the pool from the Vietnamese Nationals that were being evacuated to the waiting American ships. Jack's marine helicopter landed in the courtyard of the American Embassy. Waiting there for him were two American civilians and a two well-armed Marines. He immediately recognized one of them as being Captain Winchester who gave the order to begin flying civilians out of Viet Nam a week or so ago unbeknown at that time to Ambassador Martin. It was Captain Winchester who greeted Jack as he alighted from the marine helicopter.

"Lieutenant Jackson Garron, I am Captain Connor Winchester on personal assignment for President Ford and the State Department and this gentleman is Mr. Morley Warbuton. He is from the CIA," as he greeted Jack without a handshake.

"Lieutenant you are under arrest! Gunnery Sargent, arrest Lieutenant Garron and put handcuffs on him. Take him away to the holding cell and keep him there under armed guard.

Jack could not believe his ears; he had dutifully come to the American Embassy to carry out Ambassador Martin's order to evacuate personnel from South Vietnam presumably because of his excellent flying skills and now he was in handcuffs being led away to holding cell.

"Why are you doing this, what have I done?" as Jack cried out to Captain Winchester and Morley Warburton while being led away by a two-man marine guards.

"You will find out soon enough son," replied Morley.

For two days he was confined in a non-ventilated locked holding cell. It was unbearably hot and uncomfortable, with time out to eat, drink and use the bathroom. Already he could hear nearby explosions from the approaching communists, maybe three days away from the American Embassy. After his two days of being confined he was summoned to an office in handcuffs under a marine guard where both Captain Winchester and Morley Warburton were seated.

"I do not know what I have done you must have the wrong man and mixed me up with someone else." Jack blurted out before he was even seated.

"We will see," said Mr. Warburton.

Morley Warburton pulled out a dossier labeled First Lieutenant Jackson Garron and began reading its contents:

"...Jackson Garron born Kaneohe Marine Air Station Honolulu Hawaii, Father Ron Garron WWII hero. Received the Navy Cross, Mother, Ligaya Garron born in the Philippines in Loay Bohol works as a nurse at Trippler. At age sixteen received your pilot's license. Fluent in Tagalog. At age eighteen, entered the University of Hawaii Army ROTC program. On graduation at age twenty-two, qualified for helicopter flight school training At Fort Rucker Alabama. Graduated top of your class. Do I need to go on"? ....

"Yes, that is all true," said Jack in a puzzled voice. "But what has any of that got to do me with me being arrested?"

"Look lieutenant, we do not have much time perhaps we have no more than ten more evacuation flights left to get the hell out of here before the communists are knocking on our front door," Captain Winchester said sourly. "We have compiled a list of serious charges against you.

"Such as?" Jack said inquisitively.

"First of all: unauthorized flights to visit your girlfriend in Dau Tieng District."

"Secondly: taking military supplies under false pretenses that you were supposed to be giving to an orphanage. For all we know you were selling canned food items on the black market."

"Thirdly: not fulfilling your training missions with South Vietnamese flight officers. We met a Colonel Minh at the officer's club. Over a few friendly beers he began talking about missing training flights that you were supposed to have given him. He said you were one crazy pilot."

"Fourth: evacuating civilians: who are not contracted or vetted employees of the US government."

"Fifth: Taking unauthorized civilians to American ships that were off limits to you and your passengers without proper authorization."

"We have enough criminal activity here to put you away for 20 years at Fort Leavenworth. I probably could go on and find more charges against you." Morley Warburton said seriously as he put down his dossier on Jack.

"How do you know all of this?" said Jack in amazement. And besides it was Captain Winchester who gave the order to flight out civilians to our ships." Jack said in trying to defend himself on the spur of the moment.

"It is my job to know everything," said Morley Warburton slyly.

"Your girlfriend was not vetted by us; she did not work for us nor did she do any business with the US government. So, she was not entitled to be airlifted out to safety. Hell, lieutenant her father was Chinese, for all I know he was a communist and you were aiding abetting a communist sympathizer lieutenant." Said Captain Winchester as Jack's argument rapidly fell apart.

"Lieutenant as we see it, you have three options open to you," continued Morley.

"First, we leave you here for the communist troops who will be here probably in the next day or two. You felt what it was like when we put you in that holding cell. If the communists don't kill you first, then they'll probably put you in a holding cell like that one you came from as an American prisoner of war for the rest of your life."

"Secondly, he continued "we take you back stateside give you a military UCMJ court-martial. You can take your chances with a court-martial, but we have overwhelming evidence against you. Lieutenant you would not stand a chance. You will be found guilty as charged and probably get dishonorably discharged after serving a ten to twenty-year sentence at Fort Leavenworth. Or thirdly we want you to listen to this closely lieutenant," said Morley Warburton slowly and slyly.

Captain Winchester began.

"Mr. Warburton and I are putting together a black ops elite commando team. We need a hot shot helicopter pilot to get us in and out of a dangerous world hot spot, who can keep his mouth closed and his lips sealed," he said calculatingly.

"What kind of dangerous world hot spot?" Jack said dejectedly as though Viet Nam was not enough to satisfy the world.

"President Marcos of the Philippines has requested our government to provide him with an elite American strike team to covertly and quietly fly into a place called Zamboanga and extract several civilian hostages that are being held for ransom by several local terrorist groups. If they do not get their ransom from the Marcos Government then one by one, they get their heads cut off. These insurgents are led by a local chief called Commander Ali Razak. He is part of a larger terrorist network called the NPA led by a guy nick named Commander Dante. We've about a month to work with. Your knowledge of Filipino customs, flyting ability and language skills would make you a valuable asset for this mission Jack. We want you to come with us instead of spending time in Leavenworth or leaving you to the communists." Captain Winchester said with finality.

"The choice is yours Jack," said Morley Warburton in a friendlier tone.

Jack realized his charges against him were probably correct, except he was not selling items on the black market. He was giving canned fruit to Francine because she enjoyed eating the canned fruit. The options were clear enough as to which one to choose. Francine Chang had no communist connections; she hated them more than we did and would be waiting for him in Loay.

Slowly considering the consequences Jack spoke to Morley.

"If I team up with you, all charges will be dropped and expunged from my record?"

"Perhaps we'll have to see what happens. Maybe after five years your record will be expunged of all charges, there is one more thing though, your enlistment ends next week, we need for you to re-up again for five more years to keep us on the same team so to speak, otherwise we have no deal. We have very little time lieutenant we need to make a decision now so we can get the hell out of here", said Morley Warburton in desperation as he heard distant explosions getting closer to the embassy,

With a long painful sigh of resignation, Jack Garron realized the situation, he was in dire straits.

"Oh shit! Gentleman," he said in a deep sigh of resignation and not wanting to stay in Saigon for as long as he had to, "you've got me by the balls, where do I sign?"

"Great Jack, welcome to the team, Sargent take off his handcuffs." said Captain Winchester enthusiastically. Two days later he, Captain Winchester and Morley Warburton, and some of the remaining marine embassy guards were the next to last flight to be evacuated from the American Embassy. Ambassador Martin had already left earlier a week ago.

"At least I can see Francine," he thought, "The Philippines has to be a much better place than being a prisoner of the communists or to be jailed in Leavenworth. "

As they lifted off, he could see the familiar green colored communist tanks that he had so narrowly escaped from with his life at Francine's plantation. Each tank hoisted the flag of North Viet Nam a bright yellow star on a red background. They were no more than hundred meters from the American Embassy announcing final victory on their loud speaker systems. The last evacuation flight from Saigon left shortly after Jack's evacuation flight. It was the last time Jack Garron ever saw Viet Nam. It was April 30th, 1975 as the North finally reunited the South into one country.

CHAPTER VI

Malacañang Palace, Manila

Philippines, May 1975

"**G**ood morning Mr. President how are you and the first Lady doing today?" said Admiral Taylor to President Marcos as they met for morning coffee at Malacañang Palace. Being President of the Philippines had changed Ferdinand Marcos remarkedly since his days as a young idealistic captain during WWII. Now corruption and greed fueled his desire to be President instead of altruistic idealism.

"I am doing like hell Admiral. My life is a mess. I have the "Thriller in Manila" coming up in October with all the worlds' reporters and news teams coming to Manila to see Muhammad Ali fight Joe Frazier. What am I going to do if Manila presents itself in a bad light? Mrs. Marcos seems to want to spend more time with Muhammad Ali rather than with me. I have the American State Department on my back demanding an audit and accounting to see where all their money has gone that they've sent me? I have this Commander Dante in the south demanding that Mindanao secede from the Philippines and become a part of the Malaysian Federation. He is raising hell with my troops down there. I am not sure if I can even pay my troops right now. Now I have this new fanatic called Commander Ali Razak who is demanding ransom money from me to release civilians he's locked up somewhere in Zamboanga. I've requested assistance from your government to help me settle this problem with these two insurgents Commanders Ali Razak and Commander Dante. My troops can't find them and will no longer do it because I can't pay them on time. And now your government is bringing me thousands of Vietnamese refugees to Manila. What am I going to do with all of them piled up in Manila at the time we're having the big fight in October? How am I going to provide food, shelter and medical care to those people?' It was clear President Marcos was ventilating his frustrations and difficulties to Admiral Taylor.

"Mr. President, the State Department has authorized me to take as many Vietnamese refugees as we can and spread them throughout your country anywhere, we have bases, or hospitals or necessary services throughout your country. We can take care of them for at least six months as the Vietnamese find permeant housing elsewhere in other global places. In that way they are not piling them up in Manila as you say. Your altruism will put you in a good light in the world-wide opinion of the Philippines." Admiral Taylor knew if he could massage President Marco's ego, he could get a lot done.

"One more thing admiral after the big fight in October I want these refugees out of the Philippines and settled elsewhere, am I clear? I also want your State Department to send me more money to take care of these refugees until all these people have left my country. That should give you at least about six months to work on it. The only reason I have let them come into my country, so that your military can solve my problems in Zamboanga." It was clear President Marcos was frightened of losing the southern region of the Philippines to the Malaysian Federation.

The next day most of the ships from Viet Nam were within two days sailing time of reaching Subic Bay. Admiral Taylor met with his naval commanders.

"Look, President Marcos has agreed to take care of these refugees for at least six months until after the "Thriller in Manila" but he doesn't want them all in Manila. He wants to look good on the world's press After you process each refugee begin transporting them to Vigan in the north or to Zamboanga in the south. Clark Air base in Cebu is also a particularly good choice to re locate refugees. Transport them to any base, or hospital or anywhere where they can receive housing, food and medical care. Spread them out so that they are not all in Manilla."

The USS Kirk rolled into Subic Bay, where processing had already begun for placement prior to dis-embarkment. Daily, Francine's mind wandered to how Jack was doing; there was no word from him. At times she was depressed once her future was bright and rosy; she was in love with Jack and was going to have his baby probably in July or August. Now she lived from day to day not knowing what was going to happen to her and their baby. Although she had received some medical care for her broken arm, she had lost a lot of blood she was not strong enough to undergo surgery. She was still very weak and uncomfortable from the throbbing pain in her right arm.

"Francine Chang" announced the young ensign as he came to visit her at her bedside. "Are you Francine Chang"?

"Oui" (yes) she replied.

"We are going to put you on a transport plane and evacuate you to Zamboanga. From there you will go to Camp Navarro. There are a group of nuns who have set up an infirmary attached to the Church of the Immaculate Conception. They can provide you with housing and medical care and take care of your baby. The infirmary is used by local people for their medical needs. It is very close to camp Navarro. Sister Catherine who runs the infirmary has been around for a long time. I think she is some kind of war hero but I'm not sure. They are willing to take care of you until at such time you can take care of yourself and have your baby safely. You will be medevacked on a flight from Subic to Zamboanga tomorrow morning."

It was the last thing she wanted to hear. How would she ever see Jack again? He had no way of knowing that she was now going to a place called Zamboanga wherever that was. "Where was Jack?" she wondered. Did he make it out of Saigon before the communists came?" Bohol seemed more distant than ever before.

"My dear Sister Catherine did you hear what will be happening to us?" said Sister Gertrude one of the three German nuns that had come to do their missionary work with Sister Catherine at the church of the Immaculate Conception. Colonel Cueva at Camp Navarro will give us some supplies and equipment to help take care of some of the refugees from Viet Nam that are coming to our small infirmary. There will be several hundred coming to Camp Navarro and twenty-five who need acute medical care to our infirmary." She said eagerly.

"We'll have a meeting with our other sisters, Ingrid and Gretel. We also will meet with Father Aquino at our Church of the Immaculate Conception. He will want to know if he can provide spiritual services to some of the catholic refugees who will be coming here for a short-term stay.

Francine's journey to the Infirmary of Church of the Immaculate Conception was long and arduous. She was slightly stronger now, but the pain in her shattered forearm was still very intense despite the pain pills the medics gave her on the USS Kirk.

"Good morning my dear," said Sister Catherine as she met Francine at their infirmary for the first time. "This is Sister Gertrude and Sisters Ingrid and Gretel they are from Germany. We are here to take care of you until you are well enough to travel on your own," she said in a soft and kind voice.

"My name is Francine Chang, my arm is broken, and I am pregnant. My baby will be due in August. I do not know what to do or where to go. I left my fiancé behind in Saigon he was evacuating American Personnel from the embassy," she said in a clear steady voice.

"Well first things first, we need to get your broken arm repaired by the doctor at Camp Navarro. It looks like you'll be strong enough for surgery soon without harming your baby," said Sister Gertrude in a clipped Germanic accent. "Parles-vous francais ?" (do you speak French) as she recognized Francine's accent.

"Oui et cinois", (yes and Chinese also) she said proudly

"Bon alors je pense que nou sommes de bons amis". (We will be good friends)

Sister Ingrid asked Francine if she was catholic, Francine replied that was raised as a Buddhist, but her mother was catholic. Francine explained that her mother was French and her father Chinese. She grew up in North Viet Nam and had to flee to the south to escape the communists. She had been shot by the communist troops while fleeing her plantation in the South.

"Well God has looked after you to send you here my dear, if you do not mind Father Aquino will pray for you and your baby," said Sister Gertrude trying to comfort Francine.

"Not at all," was Francine's reply.

"God damn it! I am tired of waiting for the government's response. They are willing to pay us only ten thousand pesos to release the mayor and the councilman and only if we release the mayor first. Who do they think we are?" Commander Razak was angry and was complaining to his small band of insurgents as to how slow negations were going with the Marcos Government. He had kidnapped two local political politicians thinking that holding them for ransom would be a quick and easy way to get the money he needed for equipment and supplies to carry out his own Islamic insurgency.

"If that bastard Taruc was able to do it then we should be able to get ransom money for us also, the way Taruc did it in Luzon," he said angrily.

He was fuming and frustrated that things had not progressed well. It had been over six weeks since he kidnapped these two hostages. He kept them on a river barge in bamboo cages and could move his river barge in and out of local inlets and estuaries without being seen from overhead aircraft. The estuaries meandered through dense tropical canopy that often completely covered the waterways. Searching by aircraft for their hideout became exceedingly difficult if not impossible. The Zamboangan Peninsula has a very lush tropical jungle with dense overgrown vegetation on both banks of each inlet. The overgrown vegetation helped conceal his craft while moving his river barge from place to place. It became exceedingly difficult for government soldiers to find his various hiding places. Commander Ali Razak proved to be a very elusive foe for the Marcos Government.

"Well, we will show them that we mean business. Abu! sharpen your bolo and get our Polaroid camera. Tomorrow after our morning prayers we will cut off their heads," he said defiantly.

Abu bin Jaafar was Ali Razak's next in command. Small and diminutive with evil looking pig eyes, a worm of a scraggly moustache and a narrow pointed forehead. He also believed passionately and fervently that Mindanao should be an Islamic state allied with other Muslim countries. He wanted Mindanao to secede from the Philippines by causing as much terror to the local population and share in the glory of seceding from the Philippines. Abu Jaafar was a known terrorist to the Philippine Government. It was Abu who would throw a grenade into a packed movie house filled with children, or detonate a car filled with explosives next to outdoor markets or public eating areas. His ruthless activities filled him with glee as he enjoyed the results of his violent escapades. All in the name of Allah. Abu Bin Jaafar as a member of the NPA defined the word terrorist he did indeed spread fear with the mere mention of his name. He had no soul. Next morning after prayers, the two hostages were led out of their bamboo cages; bound and blindfolded they were made to kneel in the direction of Mecca. Abu had sharpened his bolo to a razors edge.

"Abu do it slowly so that they can feel the last sensations of life draining out of them for as long as they can." Razak said with a sadistic smile on his face.

Without hesitation Abu Bin Jaafar began to slice through the throat of the mayor. Bound and blindfolded, the mayor screamed in terror and agony as he felt the first cut on his throat. In vain to he tried to get up and get away and wriggle off the boat like a fish that had been landed with the hook still in its mouth, but he was bound and held down by others in Commander Razak's group. The sharpened blade passed through the neck muscles, tendons, trachea, and jugular veins only at that time did the agonizing screaming stop. Blood came gurgling and streaming out of his nose and mouth. Gasses that had once filled his lungs for screaming hissed and bubbled as it made its way out through the flowing blood. His body became lifeless and limp as the blade passed through his spinal cord and neck bone. Abu's sharpened blade neatly and slowly decapitated the mayor's head. In no time at all both were decapitated. Their lifeless bodies thrown into the river and their heads remained as trophies for picture taking.

"Allah Akbar, God is great I have their pictures with my Polaroid Land Camera boasted Abu Bin Jaafar."

"Good I will send them to the Manila Standard so they can tell the world how the Marcos Government has not lived up to its word in meeting our demands. I know of a place where we will find better hostages that will give us more money and power," Razak said hopefully.

"That son of a bitch, did you see what that bastard Commander Razak is doing down there in Mindanao. He is cutting off heads of our local politicians and the newspapers are eating it up. The press and my own people are blaming me for not giving in to their ransom demands," said President Marcos while shouting at Morley Warbuton and Captain Winchester.

"Look, I let those refugees into my country only if you guys could solve the problems I have in Mindanao. My own army cannot do it, Hell! I can't still pay them right now. I am banking on the "Thriller in Manilla" to bring in millions of dollars for me and it is less than four months away. I am depending on you guys to help stop this insurgency around Zamboanga. I want my big fight with Muhammad and Joe to go off without a hitch. I do not want trouble from the press and also, I want to get these refugees out of my country that was my deal with your state department and your president.

"Yes sir Mr. President, we understand your predicament. The insurgents in Zamboanga are very elusive and evasive. It's been extremely difficult to find their basecamps. However, we have now set a up a specialized small elite team of five Green Berets that can strike quickly and efficiently. They are quartered at Camp Navaro in Zamboanga. All have had experience in jungle warfare in Viet Nam. We have a seasoned helicopter pilot who is not afraid of flying into dangerous covert missions. His name is Lieutenant Jackson Garron at our disposable." Morley said with experienced efficiency hoping he could get President Marcos off his back.

"Hmm Jack Garron, I know that name from somewhere, but I cannot remember from where, it must not be important," President Marcos said with a puzzled frown on his face. "Gentlemen get these insurgents off my back before the "Thriller in Manilla". I want to be the champion to my own people and to the world press. I want the press to paint a particularly good picture of me and the Philippines. It is up to you, do what you must do," he demanded.

After six weeks, Francine was the only refugee left in the small infirmary who needed medical care. Some of the refugees had already begun to transition away from Camp Navarro and were beginning to resettle in Canada the U.S or Australia. She did not visit Camp Navarro as she preferred not to stray too far from the infirmary. She helped the nuns as best as she could with her one working arm in taking care of the local population as they sought out free medical services with their own health issues. It had been almost two months since she had her surgery on her arm. Other than wearing a big heavy cast, she was feeling better for being six months pregnant.

"Where was Jack? It has been almost three months now? There was no way of knowing if he was still Alive or dead. How could there be no word from him?" She wondered to herself. She did not know that he was less than a few miles away at Camp Navarro.

At Camp Navarro, Jack was on a mobile elite strike team, he had to stay close and not wander off the base. He was the only helicopter pilot selected to fly the elite strike team to wherever the insurgents were hiding their hostages he had to be close by. All the team needed was a fixed location to find and free the captured hostages. His letters from his grandparents told him that Francine did not make it to Bohol. At this time there was no local telephone service to make phone calls to Loay, he could only rely on mail.

"Where was Francine?" He wondered, it weighed very heavily on his mind and each day it gave him a sinking feeling that she and their baby did not make it out alive.

"One bad move and I cut your throat," said Abu Bin Jaafar to Francine as he was holding his bolo to Francine's throat. Earlier she had gone to sleep along with the three nuns expecting not to be woken up until morning. Slowly Commander Razak and Abu Bin Jaafar stealthily; crept into the infirmary to kidnap the nuns and Francine.

"If you scream you are dead. Call those three nuns to your bed. Tell them that you need help," Abu said menacingly in English with a heavy Filipino accent.

Francine was bewildered she thought she was in a dream; but she felt the cold hard steel next to her throat and knew it was not a dream.

"Who was this thug, was she going to be raped"? she thought.

Obediently she called out, "Sister Catherine and Gertrude I need your help she shouted at the top of her shaky voice." They came running from their rooms along with Sisters Ingrid and Gretel in their bathrobes to Francine's room to see what was wrong.

"What is wrong Francine?" they asked, "Are you going to have your baby now?"

They saw Abu Bin Jaafar brandishing his knife to Francine's throat.

"Who are you and what do you want with us?" Sister Catherine shouted at Abu Bin Jaafar.

"Never mind that", said another voice coming from behind them. "I am Commander Ali Razak aiming a pistol at Sister Gertrude. "We will take three of you and leave one behind with a message. Get dressed we will leave now," he said in a threatening manner.

"We will certainly not," Sister Catherine said defiantly. "We will stay here; we demand to know what you want with us."

He did not answer with words; instead, he pulled the trigger and shot Sister Gertrude in the chest.

"Does that answer all your questions, now get dressed," he demanded "you have five minutes before I shoot the next one?" His words loomed large, heavy and powerful, and in stunned silence not believing their beloved and kind Sister Gertrude

110

had just been shot. They slowly dressing in disbelief. It was not until their feet and hands were bound and riding in the back of a covered Toyota truck did, they realize what was happening. Francine began to cry as she was afraid for her unborn baby. The other three nuns were bereft with grief with the sudden knowledge they had been kidnapped and one of their own had been brutally murdered. They all began to pray repeating "Hail Mary" repeatedly. It gave them comfort to repeat the prayer while holding on to their rosaries. They left poor Sister Gertrude in a puddle of blood. Before they left, Abu Bin Jaafar pinned a note to her dead body. When Father Aquino found out about Sister Gertrude and the others, he quickly notified Colonel Cueva the commanding officer at Camp Navarro about the murder of one of the sisters and the kidnapping of the others. The kidnappers had been gone for two days when Captain Winchester read a copy of the ransom note to Jack and his elite team of Green Berets at Camp Navarro.

"Gentleman we have an extreme urgent priority. President Marcos wants us to deal with this situation now. Top priority, do what you have to do to complete this mission."

He read the ransom note from Commander Razak:

".… To all infidels, Allah is great and Mohamed is the only true messenger of God

To the Catholic Church, the German Government and President Ferdinand Marcos. You have three weeks to get five hundred thousand pesos for each nun to come back to you with their heads still on their shoulders.

To the American Embassy, you have three weeks to get five hundred thousand pesos for us to release the pregnant refugee girl from South Viet Nam.

If not, we will behead all of them like we did with the pictures we sent you.

We will send our instructions for payment to the commanding officer at Camp Navarro.

Don't disappointment me like you did last time or all of their pictures with be in the Manila and world newspapers… "

"Holy shit sir," said a Sargent Holliday one of the green berets. "What are you going to do sir? He nervously asked Lieutenant Jackson Garron."

"We can't do anything for now until we get some intel as to where the hostages are being held in the meantime, we'll standby and wait, and hope we can get to them before they are all killed" Jack said quietly.

The news of the kidnapping of the three nuns was electrifying it went out on the worldwide press, much to the chagrin of President Marcos. It was the last thing President Marcos needed before his big day later in October. The American and German Governments were firm they were not going to pay for any ransom however the Catholic church was vacillating they had never been in a situation like this before. Archbishop Jaime Sin was now the Archbishop of Manila. Archbishop Sin was of Chinese descent and therefor had a Chinese sir name. He called Monsignor Silva into his office asking him for advice since he had known Sister Catherine during the war years.

"We must pay your eminence. It is our duty to protect innocent lives. I know Sister Catherine she is off the highest order in terms of her faith, her service to humanity and her duty to God, replied Monsignor Silva. "We must save her life," he implored his announcement to Cardinal Sin.

"But you see, Monsignor, if we pay for the release of the hostages, then surely there will be more hostages demanding more ransoms from us. We will be blackmailed forever. I cannot do it." Archbishop Sin sighed in a long, lonely breath. "The church cannot and must not pay ransom money." We will pray to God together and ask for divine deliverance."

Devine deliverance came from an unexpected source.

"Lieutenant Garron," said the bar keeper at the officer's club. "There's this Filipino guy waiting outside for you in the back of the club he said he is a friend of yours." Jack was having a cold soft drink trying to stay cool while waiting at any moment for the word to take off and fly out with his team.

"Did he give his name?" Jack said curiously.

"Nope, he just said he was a friend of yours."

"OK I'll go and see what he wants, probably wants a free ride somewhere," grumbled Jack.

Jack stepped out of the back door of the officer's club it was twilight and already getting dark he had taken no more the five steps. He didn't see the two men who grappled Jack from behind putting him in a bear hug while another man put a cloth sack over his head. Surprised and disorientated, he was held motionless from a strong bear hug. Jack could not do anything to protect himself as he was led away to a waiting car parked nearby. The man who was sitting in the back seat; put a knife to Jack's throat.

"Do you feel this? I will use it if I have to. Now sit still, and you will not be hurt. Keep the hood over your head, do not take it off. I know who you are and why you are here. A small Camp like Camp Navarro has many eyes and ears. Now listen very carefully. The man you are looking for is called Commander Ali

Razak. Once a month on the last Friday of the month he goes to the Taluksangay Mosque for noon prayers. It is not too far from here. He takes his river barge with hostages in bamboo cages to a small Island called Sacal, about two miles directly across from the mosque. He ties up in the small inlet close to a deserted place called Shirley's Fuel Storage. It is rumored that MacArthur stopped there to hide from Japanese patrol planes while on his way to Australia. You cannot see it from the air because the overgrowth has covered over the inlet like a giant green archway. After Razak ties up, he and his troops take a small boat to the Mosque for noon prayers, usually leaving one man behind to guard the hostages. About a hundred meters from his river barge there is a small open area where a skilled helicopter pilot could land a helicopter. You would also have to fly a kilometer under the canopy of trees and just above the waterline otherwise you will miss it. Do you understand me so far?" he said in a tone of finality.

Jack nodded his head in agreement.

"Who are you and why are you telling me this?" Jack asked in astonishment it was the break he and his team were waiting patiently.

"Commander Ali Razak has caused nothing but trouble for me. He has tried to take over my leadership of the NPA. He has just killed one German Nun and imprisoned three other nuns along with a pregnant Vietnamese girl thinking he will get paid handsomely for their release. This time he will not receive a single peso. Our movement is not against the German Government or the Catholic Church or even the US embassy. It is only the regime of President Marcos that we have a quarrel with. I don't need more enemies, nor do I need bad publicity. He has even decapitated and killed ordinary citizens which goes very badly against us. My name is Bernabe Buscayno,

I am also known as Commander Dante of the New People's Army. Now go do your job."

He reached over Jacks lap opened up the car door and pushed Jack out of the car. Sprawling on the ground Jack took off his hood, however the car was already speeding away.

A day later, "Captain Winchester I think we have the break we have been waiting for," said Jack excitedly using the camp's radio, after explaining the circumstances of his information to Captain Winchester. "We have less than a week to get ready." He proceeded to tell Captain Winchester what he had just experienced. Captain Winchester was in Subic Bay along with Morley trying to assuage President Marcos's feelings to keep the Vietnamese refugees longer than six months. One day later Captain Winchester's flight landed at Camp Navarro. Together with Jack and the strike team they worked out a plan to rescue the hostages and put an end to Razak's reign of terror. Double checking their maps everything Commander Dante said seemed to be accurate except there was no way of knowing which way the estuary meandered throughout Socal Island.

"This poor woman needs more water" said Sister Catherine, "Can't you see she is pregnant?" She pleaded in a Visayan dialect.

"That isn't my problem, and you only get limited food and water, don't ask for any more than what we give you or we will slap you around a little to behave," said Abu Bin Jaafar in a very unsympathetic voice.

It had been over a week since they were being held as hostages. The river barge was tied up to an abandoned dock next an old shack called Shirley's Fuel. The open aired bamboo cages were placed in the hold of a river barge, large enough to accommodate two large bamboo cages, tall enough for two humans to stand erect and stretch out on the floor. Each cage held two hostages, Sister Catherine and Francine in one and the other cage held Sisters Gretel and Ingrid. Every two hours they were let out for a half hour or so to stretch their legs or go to the bathroom and to eat and drink their meager rations. Being in open aired cages the hostages had to endure hot tropical heat as well as short soaking torrential downpours that occurred periodically throughout the day. In the tropics if you want the weather to change just wait fifteen minutes. Their captors were unsympathetic to the plight of the nuns and Francine. After all they were going to cut off their heads anyway with or without a ransom. Razak was no longer going to play games with anyone, including Commander Dante whom he despised as being weak and unwilling to take risks for the good of the NPA movement.

"Abu we are going to the Mosque for noon prayers you'll be the one to stay here with the captives, we should be back in three hours with fresh supplies. Don't kill them yet; we need them for ransom money. Do you understand?" Abu nodded his head in agreement and watched as Commander Razak and six of his entourage seated themselves into a small motorboat and proceeded out of sight down the estuary and across the channel to the Taluksangay Mosque to attend noon prayers. Abu was the only one left guarding the hostages.

"Please, give us more water can't you see this poor woman needs it," said Sister Catherine pleading passionately with Abu.

"Ok I will give her more water." He said defiantly

Grabbing a coconut shell and removing his pants he carefully removed a grenade that he kept in a bag that hung around his crotch. Earlier on in his life he had been wounded and lost a testicle in a knife fight from a close encounter with a government agent.

"What better place to hide a grenade?" he would say later to Ali Razak, "No one ever checks your crotch by the local military police while looking for hidden weapons."

In front of his hostages, he took the coconut shell and urinated into it and filled it to the brim. He flung his urine through the bamboo slats into Francine's face.

"OK I gave you water," he laughed out loud in a sadistic manner. "I told you not to ask for anything more than what we are prepared to give you," he laughed again as he was enjoying torturing his captives. He retired the bag with grenade still in it around his crotch again and kept it there for any emergency that may arise in the future.

"You were born "haram" forbidden by Allah, you are a rude and horrible man, you are worse than a dog and you do not follow the holy scriptures of the Quran" said Sister Catherine angered by his actions. "God will never forgive you for what you are doing to us. You use your religion for political gain and monetary gain not for the service of Allah. Islam is a beautiful religion, yet you use it for your own purposes to gain political advantage. You will die and go to hell you are not a true Muslim. You use the Holy Quran to get more money and power while pretending to justify your cause in the name of Allah and the holy Quran," she said angrily trying her best to insult him and most of all to let him listen to the truth.

Overhead a tropical thunderhead let go of a deluge of torrential rain instantly soaking everyone. It continued to pour heavily in a torrential downpour.

Abu was angered at Sister Catherine's remarks, he did not like being insulted by a non-Muslim especially by a woman. Insulting his mother and being called a dog was a great insult.

"I will show you what my true religion is," he said losing his temper as his violent and vicious passion began to boil inside of him while the rain continued to soak him. He went to the small cabin where the crew slept and came back with his sharpened bolo sword that he had used to cut off the heads of the mayor and the councilman two weeks earlier. He opened one of the cages and grabbed Sister Ingrid by the hair forcing her out of the cage. He made her kneel down on the wet deck by putting his knee to her back, grabbing her hair, forcing her head to tilt backwards exposing her vulnerable soft white neck. He turned her in the direction of Mecca Through the torrential rain the other captives began screaming and pleading with him to stop realizing what he was going to do to Sister Ingrid.

"All of you are infidels I will show you what the almighty power of Allah can do," he shouted at the hostages. "Allah Akbar, God is great now watch this."

Sister Ingrid closed her eyes and began praying. He put the blade across her throat and began his motion to slice her throat while all the time smiling cruelly at Sister Catherine. In his haste and his enraged passion, he left the cage door open. Sister Gretel ran out of the open cage and jumped on his back in an effort to stop the beheading. He easily threw her off his back. She landed supine as she fell to the soaked deck. Instead of cutting of Sister Ingrid's head he raised his bolo as high as he could and began to plunge his bolo through Sister Gretel's heart, only stopping inches from her heart as a rifle shot rang out from somewhere far away through the pounding rain exposing a gaping hole in his right chest. He went down immediately letting go of his bolo within an inch of her heart.

Sister Ingrid was bleeding from her neck but not seriously hurt, while Sister Gretel lay on her back stunned on the wet deck wondering why Abu was lying next to her staring at the sky with a gaping hole that was slowly oozing blood from his right chest. Abu was still Alive but seriously hurt.

Indeed, God's answer is always great.

"We are here to rescue you Ma'am," said a soaking wet American soldier. "Let' us get you out of these cages and off this barge as four more soldiers appeared out of driving rain.

"Are you Sister Catherine?" "My name is Sargent Holliday I have been sent to rescue all of you and get you back to safety" said Sargent Holliday. Corporal Palmer over here is our sniper specialist he almost lost the two of you because he didn't have a clear view of the both of you through the driving rain. Let's go to the deserted shack and get inside we still have some unfinished business to do before we can leave for Camp Navarro. Sargent Buck and Corporal Mar will stay with you and attend to all of your wounds and immediate needs," he said very calmly.

The rain stopped as quickly as it began, it does that in the tropics.

"What about the man who was shot and still lying on the boat" enquired an incredibly grateful Francine for being rescued?

Sargent Holiday looked at her intently. "He'll stay here miss; we don't have time for him right now we're not out of danger. If he is still alive when we get back, then we will take him with me and my squad in our chopper back to Camp Navarro for questioning. Our pilot is waiting for us there. "He is one Hell of a Goddamn pilot miss" if you excuse my French" as he replied to Francine's questions.

"Your French is excused Monsieur Sargent."

"How did you get that big heavy cast on your arm Miss?"

"I was shot by North Vietnamese Soldiers as I was fleeing South Viet Nam. The doctor at Camp Navarro Hospital did surgery on me to repair some of my broken bones. I still have another operation to go through. I have to wear this large heavy cast."

"How will we get back?" said Sister Gretel grateful she was still Alive and amazed that she had performed such a heroic deed in saving Sister Ingrid's life. She was a nun after all, she had never physically hurt anyone in her life.

"On our signal when it is safe, the Philippine Navy will be sending a launch to pick you up from here and get all of you back to safety. Sargent Buck and Corporal Mar will escort you back to Camp Navarro there will not be any more harm done to any of you. In the meantime, we still have some unfinished business that needs to be done first," said Sargent Holliday in a business-like fashion.

"What is the pilot's name?" Francine suddenly asked excitedly in a loud and eager voice.

Lieutenant Jack Garron, best pilot I ever flown with, why do you ask?" said Sargent Holliday.

"He is the father of my child; he is the one who flew us out of Viet Nam to the waiting American ships. We became separated, where he is, I need to see him?" she pleaded in excited desperation.

"Well, I'll be a son of a gun, he is waiting for us at his helicopter. Be patient, we will bring you to him when it is safe to do so. I promise you it will not take long" said Sargent Holliday.

" Garron, Garron," mused Sister Catherine. "I know that name from somewhere, but from where?"

As Jack had approached the inlet at Socal Island with his strike team he ran into a horrific thunderstorm. He barely was able to see clearly without crashing his helicopter into the river or smashing his rotors against the trees. Jack skillfully maneuvered his helicopter to follow the meandering estuary. His rotors just barely touched the bottom of the umbrella shaped trees that enveloped the estuary. He flew just a foot above the water line sometimes skimming it with his landing skids. Through blinding rain Jack spotted the small clearing about hundred fifty meters from the river barge just as Commander Dante had told him. He carefully and slowly set his helicopter down while his Green Beret Team exited the helicopter through the pouring rain. It was Corporal Palmer who took up his overlook position with his sniper rife and scope and had spotted Abu Bin Jaafar putting his sharpened bolo to Sister Ingrid's neck? He fired his sniper rifle the moment Abu was about to plunge his bolo into Sister Gretel's heart. It was a tough shot not because of distance but because of the blinding rain that prevented him from seeing his target clearly through his scope. His accuracy was amazing, he was the best at what he did.

"Look Sargent I want in on this, I did not come out here for nothing," complained Jack.

"Look Sir, you are our ticket outa here I cannot afford to lose you when we ambush the patrol. The plan was for you to wait by the helicopter and get us the hell out here double time if we should run into some trouble."

"Bulls shit Sargent, I want in on this and besides an extra M-16 might come in handy."

"OK sir, it is against my better judgment," as he acquiesced to Jack's request.

The team felt the best place to ambush the returning group of insurgents was just as they would be getting out of their small motor craft. At the entrance of the inlet was the best place to ambush the returning group of Muslim insurgents. Commander Razak's group probably would not suspect anything was out of place after returning from their noon prayers at the Taluksangay Mosque. Sargent Holliday placed Jack behind the roots of a large Banyan tree for better protection while the rest of his team lay quietly under the thick undergrowth of Pako Ferns. As Jack hid behind the large roots of the Banyan tree beads of sweat cascaded like rivulets into his eyes, eventually cascading down his face. For the sake of the ambush, he dared not move or fidget that may give away their advantage. There was plenty of cover for the fire team but not much cover at all for the returning insurgents. Razak's group would be the most vulnerable just as they would be exiting out of their small motor boat under cover of the lush overgrowth. Total surprise and firepower were the team's main element of a surprise ambush. As predicted Commander Ali Razak returned from noon prayers with his contingent of six followers. As he was tying up his small skiff at the mouth of the estuary, he sensed there was something wrong. The jungle was much too quiet. Not a living sound was made. What was it? Everything looked normal but his inner sense told him that there was something wrong.

"Get back! Get into the boat he screamed to his followers I think it's a trap." It was the last words he would say. It was too late, the well-trained veterans of many Viet Nam campaigns including Jack opened up on their quarry. For a few moments it sounded like thunder. The insurgents were easy targets sitting in a boat. Their flight from danger was a moot point. It was a turkey shoot. In no time at all it was finished. After the smoke had cleared the strike team could see the lifeless blood-spattered bodies where they had fallen. Sprawled and slumped in different directions not one of them moved or even twitched a muscle. It was done quickly, cleanly and dispatched professionally.

"Corporal Palmer take photos of their faces. Corporal Kimball take any IDs you can find and any other personal items you can find. We'll give it all to Intel when we get back to Camp Navarro. After you have everything you needed dump their bodies into the river,' said Sargent Holliday quickly.

"Good Job Lieutenant, do you want to join our team and become a grunt?" said Corporal Kimball in amusement.

"No thank you corporal, I have enough excitement in my life just flying a helicopter."

Sargent Holliday radioed Corporal Mar that the mission had been accomplished as planned with no casualties. They were to come back to Jack's waiting helicopter to pick up the rest of the squad. He was to go ahead and radio the Philippine Navy to come with their launch and return the hostages safely back to Camp Navarro along with the Green Berets. Jack would take the ambush team and fly them out and return to base with Lieutenant Garron. Corporal Mar acknowledged this on their two-way radio and also advised Sargent Holliday to bring a stretcher. He also had a surprise for Jack and would show him once they returned to Jack's awaiting helicopter. Abu still lay on the river barge he was conscious and still Alive. Twenty minutes later Corporal Kimball and Corporal Palmer returned for Francine still waiting at Shirley's food and fuel, along with a stretcher to carry Abu Bin Jaafar back to the waiting helicopter. Francine had been waiting a long time to see Jack. She thought to herself It was going to be a wonderful surprise.

Lifting Abu on to the stretcher they carried him back to the waiting helicopter followed closely by Francine. They were close and Francine could see Jack standing next to his helicopter along with the remaining Green Berets. Jack saw Francine, she was six months pregnant now and wearing a large white cast on her forearm. In disbelief he ran towards her in overpowering joy. He had not known she was one of the captives he had come to save. Abu was conscious but gravely injured as Corporal Kimball and Corporal Palmer put the stretcher on the ground close to Jack's helicopter. They walked over to where Sargent Holliday and Jack were standing next to the helicopter. Seeing Francine Jack ran past Corporal Kimball and Corporal Palmer so he could embrace Francine.

Abu realized he was being carried on a litter to the waiting helicopter that was just a few meters away. However, he believed he could still perform one more act of violent mayhem before he died and enter the gates of heaven as a martyr. As Jack began running to embrace Francine, Abu reached down into his pants, found the bag with the grenade still tied to his crotch. Pulling out the grenade and releasing the pin he set the live grenade on his abdomen. Francine saw what Abu had just done and threw herself on top of Abu moments before Jack could reach her. She did not have any second thoughts about saving Jacks life. He was the man she loved more than anyone despite scarifying herself and her baby. Francine and Jack started a lifetime of lives together almost a year and half ago at her plantation. She would do anything for him including giving up her life to save his. Jack, not understanding what was happening, he reached Francine within arm's length. She had quickly lain on top of Abu. With a horrendous sound the grenade exploded instantly killing Francine her baby and Abu. The force of the explosion and concussion threw her backwards in a violent spinning motion hitting Jack on the temple with her heavy cast. Abu fulfilled his self-proclaimed destiny but did not enter into the gates of heaven as he martyr non one knew of his death. Her cast made a sickening cracking sound to Jack's skull; he went down instantly in a lifeless lump just in front of his helicopter.

CHAPTER VII

Tripler Army Medical Center Honolulu August 1st 1975

"Hello son, said Ron Garron to Jack." Welcome back to us we thought you would never wake up. We are sorry to hear about Francine. Your letters to us told us you had wanted to marry her." Jack looked blankly at this father then at his mother Ligaya..

"Where am I?" he said weakly.

"You're back in Honolulu Jack," said his mother. "You have been here unconscious with a major concussion for a week. I have been taking care of you. The Army put you on a plane and medevacked you from Camp Navarro. You have been here at Tripler Army Hospital here in Honolulu for a little over a week."

Vague images of explosions cascaded though his mind. He slowly closed his eyes and went back to sleep.

His parents did explain that his sister was traveling to Beirut on a nursing assignment to work at the American Hospital there, that is why she is not here to see him she could not get back to see you right now. I hope you understand Jack.

"Yes, it is OK "he said weakly.

As Jack spent time recovering and receiving medical care at Tripler his memory began to come back to him but there were lots of missing pieces.

"Hello Lieutenant," said a group of cheery voices. It was the Green Berets coming by to say hi to Jack. "We heard you were here at Tripler so we thought we would swing by to see you before we head out to Fort Benning," said Sargent Holliday.

He was surprised to see them and shook their hands eagerly.

"Can you guys fill me in as to what happened, the last thing I remember? I was running over to embrace Francine, that is the last thing I can remember."

"We are sorry to hear about Francine and your baby sir, said Corporal Mar. We are deeply sorry, had I known she was your girl maybe I would have done a better job searching that son of a bitch for any hidden weapons he was hiding on his body," he said apologetically.

"Francine saved your life sir; she threw herself on top of that crazy son of a bitch in order to save your life, if you excuse my French sir. In my book she is a genuine hero, none of us will forget her," Sargent Holliday said as he smiled at Jack.

"Can you tell me what happened next? My mind is completely blank I don't even know how I got here."

"Well sir, he continued, "After the grenade went off you were knocked out cold. Francine's cast on her broken arm hit you fairly good alongside your head. You had a knot on you the size of a goose egg. Since you were our only pilot out of the situation and you were out cold, we had no way of returning, so we radioed the Navy again for another launch to take you,

Francine, and our team out of that god damn place. They got all of us out and brought us back to Camp Navarro."

"What happened to my helicopter?"

"We thought it best to blow it up, since there was no one better than you to fly it out. We did not want any sensitive items falling into insurgents' hands. The overall mission was a success sir. We were able to rescue the hostages, killed that terrorist Ali Razak and his men. We buried Francine in the grave yard next to the church thirteen gravesites from the front gate. Sister Catherine said she was a Buddhist, so we just put two crosses side by side one for your lost child and the other for Francine. On one cross just had a simple inscription on it:

"Francine Chang A Brave Woman Who was Casualty of War Died July 15th 1975 and the other cross read: The Child of A Brave Mother," Died July 15th 1975. We did not know what else to do sir."

Jack thought about their actions, there was no one to blame, they did what they could. He reasoned it was just another accumulation of circumstances a rendezvous of many incidents that come together all at the same time in a vicious moment of fate and time. And so, it was, that Abu had used that grenade on himself, killing Francine, and their baby. At that moment in time that Jack or anyone else for that matter had no control of the situation.

"Look guys we did a great job, there is no one to blame. By fate probably Francine should have died several times by now, perhaps it was her time. I am very grateful for the care and tenderness you showed Francine. And the hostages?"

"They are OK sir, from what I hear Sister Catherine puts flowers on Francine's grave almost every day, she plans to go back and retire in Ohio. The other German sisters have taken Sister Gertrude's body back to Germany. I don't think they are coming back to Zamboanga," said Corporal Mar quietly.

"Fort Benning, why are you guys going to Fort Benning, that's the home of the 101st Airborne?" said Jack inquisitively.

Corporal Kimball said, "Oh its Captain Winchester's idea he feels we should get some training jumping out of planes and helicopters with parachutes and using rope ladders, nighttime goggles and such things. I think he has something up his sleeve he has some special plans for us, but he hasn't told us."

"Well sir we had better get going we don't want to miss our flight to Fort Benning." Sargent Holliday said with sadness as though Jack was already a missing member of their elite team.

"You take care Green Berets," as he shook hands with all of them It was all that Jack could muster for a goodbye to a group of brave and good men. They are indeed America's best". he thought proudly.

It was October 2nd, 1975 Jack had watched the fight between Muhammad Ali and Joe Frazier. It lived up to its name; it really was a Thriller in Manila. He had been home with his parents for six weeks now on continued medical leave. There was a knock on their door of their two-story condominium that sat on the lagoon at Hawaii Kai. Jack's mother answered.

"Mrs. Garron, is Jack home?"

"Yes, who is calling?" she replied.

"Could you tell him it is Morley Warburton I have something urgent to talk to him about."

"Why yes of course, come in, Jack there is a Mr. Warbuton here to see you. Can you come down?" she shouted upstairs at Jack.

"Jack good to see you again as they shook hands," they both sat on the lanai overlooking the incoming tide of Hawaii Kai's lagoon. How are you feeling these days, we thought we had lost you forever with that concussion you received? Listen you did a great job for us in Zamboanga."

"I wound up losing three innocent people on that mission Morley", Jack said sharply.

"Ah yes, I am sorry to hear about Francine, and your baby. No one could have ever predicted what those crazy bastards would do, especially shooting that German Nun. That was a complete surprise to all of us," he said sympathetically. "However, Razak is gone; the insurgency has died down for the moment in Zamboanga. President Marcos is happy, he finally has the monkey off his back and is taking all the credit for quelling the insurgency in Zamboanga. And Mrs. Marcos is no longer interested In Muhammad Ali. At least Mindanao is still a part of the Philippines for now. Best of all he made more money than he expected from yesterday's fight. He has allowed the Vietnamese refugees to stay for a year in the Philippines until we can find placement for them elsewhere, probably in California, Texas, or Louisiana. It looks like most of them will be resettled without too much trouble. President Ford is anxious to put a good light on this. Not only that Jack, but that other Muslim guerrilla leader Commander Dante, we know of his whereabouts, soon it will be just a matter of time before President Marcos's troops will capture him, we did a good mission Jack."

"Morley, you did not come here to tell me what I already know, there is a problem, and it is pointing straight at me," he said to Morley accusingly.

"Jack, French intelligence is informing us that they are picking up local gossip that they may anticipate a problem in Beirut. Intelligence tells us Lebanon may break out in a civil war and that perhaps French and American civilians may be involved. A group of militant militia factions such as the PLO, Hezbollah, Arab Socialist Ba'ath Party and many other minor militia groups in Beirut are beginning to form a revolt against the Lebanese government. We think those boys might be plotting to fight against Christian militia and Lebanese government troops. We're not sure right now but we want you to get ready for Aviano Air Force Base in Italy. We have a special assignment for you there. Once again, you will not get any credit for this, how soon can you report to Captain Winchester at Aviano Air Base in Italy

"Oh, Shit not again Morley" sighed Jack

"Yes, Jack we have you for another four years or so and don't forget Leavenworth is still waiting for you if should decline", said Morley Warbuton with a degree of satisfaction in his voice and a wry smile on his face.

(n.b. Authors note Filipino forces did capture Commander Dante in 1976 and was sentenced to ten years in prison. Commander Dante survived an assassination attempt, he returned to a peaceful life of farming with three pieces of shrapnel still lodged in his back.)

PART iii

CHAPTER VIII

Durham City, England, 1955

Wilfred Mason was an eight-year-old sickly child who was born into poor working-class family in Durham City, England, not too far from the Northeast Coast.

Bitter winter gales blew with icy cold ferociousness emanating from the North Sea during late fall and winter and into early spring. Overall, during this period of time, was a period of darkness, cold, damp inclement weather. His parents were poor, his father worked in the collieries deep underground extracting coal to heat the coal burning firesides for warmth throughout those cold winter nights for northern England. Coal burning fireplaces was the main source of heat during those bitter cold winter months. Most of the heat went up chimneys and did not efficiently warm the homes of much needed warmth, However, it was the sulfur laden smoke, from the coal's particulate matter that gathered in the atmosphere in almost stagnant like fashion. The sulfur laden particulate matter turned the cold winter air into a heavy-laden blanket of pea green colored fog tinted with yellowish sulfur laden clouds. Between 1955 and 1958 the winter weather was especially egregious taking its toll on the English population with high morbidity and mortality tables with upper respiratory infections including pneumonia and bronchitis. However, it was coal that was needed to heat the homes for the thousands fire places in and around the Northeast of England. With the wet and damp winters along with the polluted air Wilfred would often come down with a case of bronchitis or chronic lung infections and would lay in bed in a feverish condition coughing up green colored mucous. He was not alone many of England's residents especially those living in large cities who were elderly or very young died from pneumonia of other upper respiratory infections from fireplace smoke. During the late 1950's England's Parliament realized what the health problems were and began slowly phasing out coal burning fireplaces to be replaced with natural gas heaters. Wilfred hated the dark, cold winter nights. For Wilfred, winter was miserable, he rejoiced when late spring arrived. Summer nights were once warm again and balmy. He enjoyed the sensation of warm days with evenings of languid summer sunlight.

Wilfred's mother worked as a maid at Pemberton Manor not too far from his home. On one cold winter's day his mother took the bus to Pemberton Manor. Wilfred accompanied her to her work as he was on school holiday and did not wish to stay at home by himself. As a small boy Wilfred did not know the meaning of class or have an understanding of his station in English society. However, on one occasion he had seen pictures in a magazine at his barber shop of various Hawaiian tropical fruits. In it, he saw a picture of a pineapple. Pineapples were very scarce in the grocery stores around Durham City, most people could not afford one. For working class people buying a pineapple was beyond their financial capability. But when Wilfred saw this picture of luscious looking pineapple, he thought to himself surely it must be the king of all fruits. Its golden colored skin covering its large, sweet, juice laden body donned with a beautiful array of green leaves like a crown topping the fruit gave the appearance of regality. Wilfred surmised it surely must be the best tasting fruit in the world if only he could taste it. He had always wanted to taste one but never had the opportunity. It just so happened as his mother took him to her work at Pemberton Manor that Lord Pemberton was having his birthday party that day. Lady Pemberton decided to give her husband as a birthday gift a large platter of fruit arranged in a form of a pyramid. There were bountiful tiered displays of apples, pears, grapes oranges tangerines, bananas but on the very top of the fruit pyramid was the crowning touch of a beautiful large luscious, golden pineapple with a corona of green leaves. Lady Pemberton made her rounds showing the wait and scullery staff the display of fruit before she gave it to Lord Pemberton for his birthday gift. To be kind to everyone, she approached Wilfred.

"Child would you like to taste any of the fruit on this fruit tray before I give it to Lord Pemberton for his birthday, we have enough fruit for everyone to sample." She expected Wilfred to choose a common apple as everyone else did from the bottom of the pyramid.

"I want the Pineapple please" he said eagerly as he saw his chance to finally eat the king of fruits.

"Young man" Lady Pemberton said in a sour tone. "This Pineapple is for Lord Pemberton, only he can have it. You are not allowed to have it nor shall you have it. You can have a green apple." Lady Pemberton gave his mother a disparaging look as she was about to be scolded in front of everyone.

"Mrs. Mason please explain the situation to your child that he should know his place."

"But you said I could have any fruit on the tray," blurted out Wilfred.

Looking crossly at Wilfred's mother "Mrs. Mason please take your child home; he and you are not to be seen today," she said firmly.

In tears, his mother left with Wilfred in tow and not a word was said. His mother just looked at him with tears in her eyes and immediately he felt the pain he had caused her. At that moment he shamefully knew his place in society and the meaning of class. He had brought reprehension and shame to his mother. How ignorant he had been but now he truly understood his station in life. From then on, he clearly understood that common working poor people were at the bottom of the societal pecking order. He could have had a small grape or an apple at the bottom of the fruit pyramid, but the pineapple was meant for only those with the appropriate class distinction. It left a burning impression in his mind that he would never forget that moment in time he felt the pain for his mother and for himself. His lot in life was set in stone it forever left a bitter taste in his mouth.

At twenty-four, Wilfred had become a young man. His stature was slight and pasty probably from a diet of fish and chips and boiled potatoes, meats and vegetables. Those long cold winter nights had taken its toll on his body with a lingering cough from being sickly with infections that lingered on during those hard winter nights. He knew that Durham City was not the place for him, but he had no place to go or elevate his status in society. He wanted to live a warm, sunny, healthy climate away from long dark cold winters and not to be reminded of the subtle social markers that existed in his dull life. After all, he and his family were members of the working class he was expected to stay that way for the rest of his life. Wilfred had limited opportunities for change and prosperity. He wished there was a place where more than anything he could elevate his station in life. It came unexpectedly.

He was working as a desk clerk at the Blue Star Hotel. The hotel was located close to Durham Castle which catered to mainly European tourists. By a random chance of fate as he was sitting at a bus stop waiting to go home, he casually picked up a newspaper that had been discarded on the bus seat. There in the newspaper's help wanted section he read an advertisement for employment:

"Wanted person to relocate to Beirut Lebanon for training to work at the Holiday.

Inn. Must be single, able to speak French, English and some German.

Experienced purveyor to the tourism industry, traveling expenses to be reimbursed after 6 months of continuous employment. Room and Board provided along with starting monthly salary to be determined based on experience.

Enquiries with vitae to be sent to 29 Wakenshore Road, Durham City, UK 00512"

Lebanon, where was Lebanon? He excitedly looked on the world map and found its location, Lebanon had a Mediterranean climate far away from the northern latitudes. He was able to meet the requirements of the advert. In school he had learned how to speak French as it was a requirement and a few phrases in German that he picked up at The Blue Star Hotel. He took a chance and responded to the advertisement for employment in Beirut.

Six months later in the Spring of 1972 he landed at Beirut International Airport and reported to management at the

Holiday Inn located in the hotel district of downtown Beirut. Wilfred had passed his oral interview with representatives from the Holiday Inn who told him he would make hundred fifty dollars a month, opportunities for growth and advancement to managerial staff, with a hotel room provided on the first floor and one meal a day. Wilfred accepted the offer and said his goodbyes to his family and friends and that he would send money home to his family. Taking a chance, he scraped up enough money to purchase a one-way plane ticket to Beirut. The journey was exhilarating he had never been on a plane before. However, the prospects of making a hundred fifty dollars a month seemed too low but room and board plus a daily meal and an opportunity for advancement seemed to outweigh his low salary. But above all he wanted to elevate his station in life to get away from his social reminders and elevate himself in his societal status. He began his training at the front desk and could exercise his language skills without too much difficulty to the many clients that came to the Holiday Inn. He loved Lebanon's climate it was perfect for him and with the variety of exotic foods, including pineapples was beyond his expectations. Nothing was boiled anymore, food was an eclectic array of numerous choices of European, African, Arabic and Asian dishes, He found that there did not seem to be a class structure, either you were Christian, or Muslim, French or English or a mixture of other friendly ethnic groups and at that time it did not matter too much who was who. Beirut with its lights, culture, charm and exotic life style was the Paris of The East. Other than his low salary and a failed promise of promotion or elevation in his status of employment, he was relatively happy. Unfortunately to his dismay, he did not have enough money to send home to his family. However, there he stayed; he felt this was his new home it was better than England with its dull and boring lifestyle. The people who came to Beirut spoke in French, English, Farsi, Asian and various types of Arabic dialects. Beirut is a charming and cultured city encompassing many cultures both East and West, so different from England, overall, he loved it. But life was static until one day in January of 1975 he met an interesting and usual man from Baghdad Iraq. Wilfred's life would never be the same.

CHAPTER IX

Honolulu Hawaii June 1974

"**C**ongratulations Tanya," said the dean of the Nursing Department at The University of Hawaii's school of nursing. "You have passed with a Bachelor of Science degree in Nursing he said proudly. Tanya shook his hand and took her diploma. Ron and Ligaya were very proud of Tanya as they attended her graduation ceremony. Her brother Jackson could not be there as he was still deployed somewhere in Asia

"Well, what now Tanya, what are your plans?" said Ron inquisitively as they walked to the reception area at UH.

"First I'll need nursing experience" she replied eagerly.

"Yes of course," Ligaya, said "but where? Without experience who would hire you so how do you get nursing experience"?

"Well, my class and I attended a recruitment conference at the East West Center here at UH. A recruiter from the American Hospital in Beirut Lebanon came to our campus to recruit new baccalaureate nurses for the School of Health Sciences in Beirut. It sounded very interesting and all I need is my bachelor's to work as a nurse in their hospital. It doesn't pay much but they'd reimburse my room and board. I'd get the much-needed experience I need right now and It's not too far from the American University. I think I'd like to go," she said proudly.

"When will you leave and how long do you plan to stay?" said Ron.

"I'd like to leave as soon as possible as soon as I am accepted and can make arrangements for lodging and transportation but what I want most of all is the nursing experience. I plan to stay for at least two years and then come back to Hawaii to sit for my state license."

"I guess it's a plan." as Ron realized that she had thought it through and seemed fine. He knew that without experience she would have a hard time finding work as a newly graduate nurse.

"Beirut isn't that the Paris of the East?" Ligaya asked. "Is it safe there Ron, it seems so far from Hawaii?

"As far as I know it's safe, it is in the middle of energetic economic business boom. It sounds like it should be on someone's vacations plans as a place to visit," Ron said reassuringly.

Tanya was twenty-three with dark hair, her mother's smooth skin, dark brown eyes her body was lithe from participating in high school and collegiate athletics. She featured her mother's looks and her father's keen intelligence. Currently her world was a pearl in an oyster shell.

By September that year she had been accepted as a nurse in the orthopedic department at the American Hospital in Beirut. They had even found a shared apartment for her with another nurse from U.H. She could take the ubiquitous taxi cabs to the hospital, so transportation was not too much of a problem Things were looking great and by Thanksgiving she had reported to the Director of Nursing at the Hospital and began her two-year tour in the orthopedic department.

CHAPTER X

Claremont-Ferrand France, February 1975

"**M**on dieu mon ami, Ah bon jour François quet plaisir de vous revoir." (My god hello François, we thought you were dead) said Marcel Bernard happily, Vice President at Michelin World Headquarters Paris France for Asian affairs. François walked into the world headquarters of Michelin Rubber Company unannounced to meet his old boss.

"Ici ausiege de Michelin nous pensions que tu etais mort." (Our staff thought you were dead.) We are so happy to see you that you are Alive. Mon dieu!" (my god)

"Yes, I was in Hong Kong when the communists took over our Michelin rubber plantation in Dau Tieng District in South Vietnam. From Hong Kong I slowly and eventually came to France. I don't know what happened to my sister Francine. I don't know if she is dead or Alive. I have come to find out where she is, perhaps you can help me si vous plais" (please)

François was tall like Europeans, thin with straight black hair, light brown skin, his eyes were almond shaped and probably gave him away as having mixed Asian blood.

"She might have been murdered by the communist troops or made it out Alive with the other refugees. I just don't know:

142

he said emphatically. "I am sorry my sister and I lost the rubber plantation in Vietnam Marcel." he said with a deep sigh.

"It was not your fault François. Who can ever understand how the fates of war work or have a good or happy conclusion eh? We just do not know how points in time and space interreact each other. It was out of yours and mine control my friend. I am deeply sorry about Francine," said Marcel sympathetically. "However, it is good to see you again. What can I do for you my good friend"?

"I do not know what to do right now, do you have a position in Michelin somewhere for me?"

Lighting an American cigarette, Marcel took a long draw and then exhaled through his nose.

"My friend François, times are difficult right now. With the loss of rubber sap from Vietnam and other parts of South East Asia I am not sure how I can use you. You are skilled in many languages François, but we are scaling back our worldwide production quotas, our rubber sap supply is down right now. At this moment in time, I deeply regret there is no room for you at Michelin for a man of your many abilities. Perhaps a year or two from now the world quota for rubber sap supply will pick up and production can increase again, and then you come see me."

"It is ok Marcel, I thought I would ask you, but I'm not sure what I can do right now or where I can go."

Marcel paused for a moment took a long look at François's intelligent face, and then reached into his drawer and pulled out his check book.

"François, I am going to write you a check for twenty thousand French Francs to help you right now. However pretty soon we will be on the Euro. I suggest cash it while you can. I am also going to give you a letter of introduction of the name and address of a special friend of mine who works for French Intelligence in Paris. His name is Monsieur Renee Montrose. There perhaps they could use your special language skills and also help you find Francine. That is the best I can do for you at this time my friend."

François gratefully took his check for twenty thousand French Francs and his letter of introduction to Monsieur Renee Montrose, Chief Intelligence Officer for the Middle East division. Hugging Marcel, he recognized the generosity of Marcel's kind spirit and perhaps Renee Montrose could help him find his sister. Several days later François reported to the Directorate General for External Security at 141 Boulevard Mortier in Paris. He had a 4pm appointment with Renee Montrose.

"Ah monsieur Chang your letter of introduction is very impressive. Marcel and I are old friends we go back a long way to the Algerian Campaign. We fought side by side against the Algerian uprising. Mon dieu! (my god) that was so long ago, and we lost Algeria. And now we have too many Algerians with their fanatic Muslim friends calling France their home and the troubles it brings to France. Also, Africans from our former colonies want to come to France. Now they bring their problems to us as well. My God It is the sign of the times for the price we paid. However, either you are French or not all. What can I do for you?"

"Monsieur Montrose" Francois started nervously. "Monsieur Bernard felt you might be able to help me find my sister. I lost track of her with the fall of South Vietnam I do not know if she is dead or Alive?"

"Yes, I know, Marcel called me and told me about you regarding your many business travels to the middle east and your fluency in several languages. He asked me if we could find any information regarding your sister Francine, is that correct?

François nodded yes.

"I have some interesting information for you, but first, I want to make a deal with you. We need a man like you to work for us in Lebanon. We are hearing that there might be trouble there soon. Your knowledge of the middle east because of your business travels to Lebanon, Iraq, Syria and Jordan are invaluable to us. We are getting information that there might be civil war soon in Lebanon, but we need someone to keep an eye on things at the ground level so to speak and provide us with intelligence as you see it. The French Government, let's say, has many assets in Lebanon that we do not want them to fall into wrong hands. You have no history or connection with French Intelligence. You would be quite safe; it is not dangerous work. We will provide you with living expenses and from time to time we want you to report to the French Embassy in Beirut as to what you see and hear at the local level. Ask for Monsieur Durand. I will provide you with his contact number and a letter of introduction if you decide to go. Qid Pro Quo Monsieur Chang what do you say? You will be doing the French Government a huge service"

"And If I decide not to take your offer what news can you tell me about my sister? "

"Well Monsieur Chang then there is nothing I can do for you," he said with finality with the authority of an autocrat.

Realizing he was trapped, Francoise acquiesced to his new assignment. At least he would have some income until he could land on his feet. And besides, he had been to Beirut it was a lovely and beautiful city situated next to the Mediterranean Sea. It was another city of lights

"Can I get out if I decide it is too dangerous?"

"Oui (yes) any time. But at least try give us twelve months of your time OK?"

François agreed and began listening to Monsieur Montrose regarding the story about Francine's whereabouts.

"As best as we know from American and Vietnamese sources, your sister left the Michelin rubber plantation on an American Helicopter just a few days before the fall of Saigon. The helicopter landed on an American ship called the USS Kirk for destination to Manila. She left Vietnam Alive."

François could not believe it. It was the words he had been waiting to hear. Francine was Alive! Now It was up to him to see what he could learn what was happening in Beirut and find Francine, probably in a refugee camp in the Philippines.

Chapter XI

Beirut January 1975

Lebanon's location was an ideal Mediterranean climate. Mild winters with a cool but not too cold rainy season, and sunny warm days during spring, moderated by a cooling ocean breezes during the summer. Managed by the French under a mandate by the United Nations from 1923 to 1946 which eventually allowed Lebanon to become its own independent country.

Although Arabic is the national language many citizens still prefer to speak French. The French found Its location and numerous business opportunities morphed into a beautiful vacation resort. Beirut was modeled similar to Paris. A city of Lights. Beirut prospered immensely and up until the mid-seventies, Beirut's development as a world class city was enhanced by a building boom with elegant hotels, business, cabarets, regal restaurants, apartments, homes and beautiful government buildings. Often there was not enough available labor in Beirut to fill the required specialized employment vacancies. Lebanon would import hired labor from other countries.

Wilfred Mason was getting impatient. He loved his assignment at the Holiday Inn in Beirut, but his salary was still the same, and his expectation of a promotion from desk clerk to manager had still not come to fruition. He had been working as a desk clerk since 1972 and still at the bottom of the hotel's hierarchy. Surely management could see how well he was doing at his job and he deserved an elevation in status, but he was still at the bottom of the pecking order, His health had improved significantly in the warm sunny climate of Beirut, but why was he still a desk clerk? Feeling dashed about not being promoted to management and disappointed about not sending money home to his mother and father he sat down at the bar at the Holiday Inn to have a beer at the conclusion of his shift.

"Hello there old chap" in the style of an Englishman, but the accent of someone from the middle east.

"Yes, who are you, how do I know you?" asked Wilfred.

"I saw you drinking alone, could I join you? I also like to drink a schooner of beer and I thought you might like some company as I am by myself."

"Are you a guest of the hotel? I don't remember checking you in," asked Wilfred. curiously."

"Oh no, I am staying next door at the Hotel Phoenicia, Although I think they have better beer here at the Holiday Inn, at least it's cold."

Wilfred studied him closely. He was well dressed in a dark suite, white shirt and a black tie unusual though for people who live in a warm climate. He was, youngish looking, he was tall with a dark thick moustache with dark piercing eyes. His wavy black hair gave him the appearance of someone with authority.

"My name is Saddam; I'm from Baghdad. In my country I have had to deal with many Englishman. I work for my government in the tourism business. I've learned that Englishmen enjoy a pint of bitters late in the afternoon or even at teatime. I enjoy it as well. Would you like a cigar old chap?"

"No thanks mate my lungs are not so healthy, but they are getting better in this warn climate."

Wilfred was impressed with this man's charm and friendly manner and enjoyed his company and his knowledge of English customs and language. Wilfred told Saddam his history of how he was able to arrive and work in Lebanon. Saddam told Wilfred what life was like in Iraq. They made agreements to have a cold beer together once a week and just to sit down and chat. Always Saddam paid for the beer.

By late March they were quite friendly, trading home addresses of each other 's home and that one day they should come visit each other's country.

On one special day Saddam talked earnestly with Wilfred. "Old chap, I need a favor from you," said Saddam very seriously while looking at Wilfred straight into his eyes.

"What is it mate?" Wilfred asked curiously.

"How would you like to earn a thousand dollars for doing nothing old boy."

"A thousand dollars American for doing nothing, bloody hell what is it mate what do I have to do?" he asked inquisitively.

"Since you are the desk clerk here the Holiday Inn could you please tell me when a chap by the name of Colonel Antoine Barakat checks in and how long he will be staying at the Holiday Inn. I'm expecting him any day now. He is an old family friend of mine and we have lost touch with each other. His family told me that he will be checking in at the Holiday Inn sometime very soon, and that I could reach him here."

"A thousand American dollars for a name, only a name, what possible harm could it do? Really what possible charm could it do? With a thousand dollars he could send it to his family. He would be very proud of himself to do such a wonderful deed to send money back home," he thought to himself. But a thousand dollars and converting it to British Pounds that was huge and enticing. He thought about it, after all, it was only for a name what harm could a name do?

"OK Saddam old boy I will do it for you since we are good mates now. How do I tell you that this bloke, Colonel Antoine Barakat has checked in?"

"I will give you the number at the Phoenicia where you can leave me a message at the front desk. Just tell me when he checked in and for how long he will be staying that is all I want to know. After all I want to spend some time with him, we have lost many years between us."

He reached inside his jacket and pulled out an envelope containing ten one-hundred-dollar bills. Believing that he had done the right thing Wilfred accepted the envelope with a telephone number written on it.

"Call me please at this number on the envelope when he checks in, do you understand?"

"Yes Saddam, thanks mate" Wilfred said gratefully and wound up buying the beers for he and Saddam. Saddam must be a very wealthy businessman to afford a simple and large accommodation of such a simple request such as this, thought Wilfred.

April 1st Colonel Antoine Barakat checked into the Holliday Inn his room was on the second floor. Dutifully Wilfred called Saddam at the Phoenicia and left a message at the front desk. Indeed, Colonel Barakat had checked in and would be staying for ten days in room 204. Wilfred was relieved that he had done his duty and was pleased with himself that he had sent his money home to his family.

April 1st Colonel Saddam Hussein called his president, Ahmed Hassan in Baghdad Iraq.

"Insallah Colonel Hussein, good news God is great and wonderful, you have found out when and where that bastard Colonel Barakat could be found. I want that son of a bitch out of my life. He has fought me tooth and nail to keep me and our Syrian friends out of Lebanon for a very long time. He sides with the government army and those Christian militias. We have never been able to get a foot hold in Lebanon. Our Ba'ath party needs more control in Lebanon to expand our conservative Muslim cause. I hate him. I want him dead. Even our friends in Syria, President Hafez al -Assad is in agreement with me. However, I do not trust that Ayatollah Ruhollah Khomeini in Iran even though they kicked that Shah out of Iran. I do not trust him. He is a deceitful son of a bitch as well. However, I am glad the Shah is no longer there. The Shah was nothing more but a stupid puppet of the West."

"It is a pleasure to serve you my President. Our sources in our own Socialist Ba'ath Party in Lebanon, the PLO and the Fatah Movement all had local intelligence on Colonel Barakat. The underground intelligence network gleamed that Colonel Barakat would be checking into the Holiday Inn but we did not know when and for how long."

"Yes, kill that son of a bitch Colonel Barakat who has been a pain in my side. Now he is siding with the Jews, Christians and holding fast with the Army of Free Lebanon, preventing us from turning Lebanon into a true Islamic state."

"I have found a willing informant who is not too bright, he has helped me locate the date and time when Colonel Barakat will check in at the Holiday Inn. It'll will be done, Allah wills it. It is a pleasure to serve you my President Hassan. I hope I can still serve you for as long as you are our president." In his mind Saddam was already plotting to become the next president of Iraq.

"Saddam, how will you dispose of him?"

"The PLO are good at planting car bombs even on busses, they have used this technique in Israel quite effectively. I have a man who is willing to drive a car to the front of the Holiday Inn packed full of explosives. The driver will park the car close to the front lobby and set the timer. The driver has five minutes to get out of the car and run for his life in order to get out of the blast zone. The explosion will be so strong that we expect the damage will be extensive. Colonel Barakat staying on the second floor will have cursed his last words against us. We will hear from him no more."

"And so, it is written Saddam, it's up to you and your followers may Allah bless you and always be with you. I'll tell our friends in Syria what our intentions are."

On an early April morning a tiny four-seater French Peugeot drove up to the Holiday Inn. The car was packed full of explosives and parked only a few meters away from the front lobby. After setting the timer to the explosives the driver casually got of his car, looked at his watch and then ran for his life. He had five minutes to clear the blast zone before the timer ignited the deadly explosive charge.

The explosion from the car bomb was horrific, it could be heard all over Beirut as many buildings wabbled and twisted on their foundations. The driver who had a five-minute running start even then was knocked down from the powerful concussion wave. Wilfred had just reported to work and was standing by the lobby's front desk. In a moment, a blinding flash seared his eyes. The concussion alone shattered his ear drums and ruptured the blood vessels in his eyes and ears. Instantly chards of glass from the front door and windows flew at him like miniature missiles, severing his arm above the elbow and knocking him down as blood gushed from every orifice of his body as every glass chard ripped through his body. Seconds later a five-ton block of concrete pancaked onto him from the second floor. Wilfred died almost immediately if not from the concussion and the flying glass then surely the concrete slab did its work as well as for Colonel Barakat and the one thousand other hotel guests who died that day at the Holiday Inn.

Saddam had never checked in at the Phoenicia as he knew it would be impacted from the bomb blast, instead, he stayed far away from the blast zone. The news made international headlines around the world. It was the beginning of the Lebanese Civil War which started as the "Hotel Wars". Hotels in the downtown district were quite useful because of their height and strong structures. Hotels were often used as look outposts for sniper positions to enable sneak attacks between government, and Muslim factions. During the civil war many of Beirut's beautiful hotels in the business district were damaged or destroyed. Lebanon's civil war lasted into the 90's. In its wake the civil war killed and injured the lives of thousands of Lebanese civilians as well as horrific property destruction that had blossomed during the building boom. As the months wore on many other hotels were bombed and ruined as the various factions used hotels to gain an advantage or a foothold over the other. Eventually Beirut was separated by a green line. Muslim control on one side, and Christian or governmental control on the other. It was instant death if you crossed the green line if you did not belong or have the right documentation for the correct side.

Saddam called President Hassan that afternoon and told him how and what happened. He also acknowledged that this was the beginning of the Lebanese civil war and that he, Ba'ath Party, and our Syrian friends would have an opening now to move into Lebanon. The civil war would start in earnest as a major conflict later that year.

"The Holiday Inn was a good choice; it was a symbol of American greed and power in consort with their criminal friends the Israelis." President Hassan told Saddam.

"Was it totally destroyed?"

"Yes Mr. President, the Americans and no one else will never be able to use it again."

"Then God is with us Colonel Saddam, go in peace. We we'll talk later to our brothers in Lebanon and Syria to see what the next target will be. Come back to Baghdad Saddam, I have more work for you to do for our Ba'ath party. The Americans and Israelis must be taught more lessons. Those damned criminal Israelis , imagine expanding their imperialist empire in the ill-gotten gains of the Golan Heights, it is insufferable Saddam. The Golan Heights must be returned as it was. Those Israeli pigs must get out of the Golan Heights and go back to Israel one way or the other."

154

"Yes Mr. President, I'll return to Baghdad as soon as possible." His mind was working feverishly how he will assume the presidency of Iraq. It did not take long as President Hassan died of illness in 1976 and Colonel Saddam Hussein who was the most powerful man in Iraq at the time assumed the presidency of Iraq immediately after the death of President Hassan.

Several months after the explosion François Chang telephoned Monsieur Durand at the French Embassy. He had been in country for almost nine months and was making his way around the Muslim quarters in Baghdad trying to gleam pieces of gossip and news. He had stopped at a café in the Muslim quarter for a morning coffee and catching up on the latest news from yesterday's newspaper he had overheard a private conversation from two middle eastern men sitting at a table next to his.

"When will we go after the American University Sheik Waleed?" one man said in loud French with a strong Arabic accent,

"Shut your mouth you fool! Talk in Farsi don't talk in French anymore you idiot, someone might overhear you. It is being planned right now be patient, Allah will tell us when the time is right." They sipped their coffees slowly observing several people in the café, nothing seemed out of order. François kept reading his newspaper and sipping his coffee he did not move a muscle, blink an eye or squirm in his seat.

"It will be soon I promise you" said Sheikh Waleed. as he continued to talk in Farsi. Sheikh Waleed had been greatly influenced by the clerics in Iraq, Iran and Saudi Arabia who wanted to drive Israel out of the Golan Heights and introduce Lebanon into a more fundamental and conservative Islamic state. Being tall and very skinny, his teeth were stained a dark brown from smoking too many unfiltered cigarettes. With his Arab headgear, full length tunic and a narrow face gave him the appearance of a long skinny rat. However, he was an excellent orator and could whip his conservative followers into a frenzy and was given the assignment to create havoc and mayhem at the American University.

The two men stopped talking as François casually got up from his table, while paying for his coffee on the way out of the café. He acted in a calm and natural manner folded his newspaper and tucked it under his arm and casually left the cafe. The two men observed François intently looking for any telltale signs that he had overheard their conversation and if he had suspected. anything. He looked like a foreigner, perhaps a tourist from Asia somewhere, and seemed to be of no threat to them he did not have the appearance of a Western spy.

"Monsieur Durand did you understand my message?" as François reported everything he heard and saw.

"Oui (yes) good job François, Bon chance. I will report it to the ministry." And with that François hung up the phone and wondered what was going to happen at the American University?

CHAPTER XII

Aviano Air Force Base, Italy

September 1975

Jackson Garron complained to Morley, "Well, now that you have flown me halfway around the world to Aviano Air Base Morley, what 's up that you need me so badly?"

"You'll see Jack, but right now Jack I can't tell you what this special operation is about until we get more definitive intel."

They walked together to a large hanger to take a look at two oddly designed helicopters or were they planes? Jack could not decide what he was looking at.

"What the hell is that Morley?"

"Captain Winchester had it transported from Area 51 in Nevada. It is a top-secret experimental craft. We have never used before in actual field operations. We have two of them" said Morley.

"It's a what again? Morley I am used to Hueys or Cobras but nothing like a bastardized looking helicopter or is it a plane?"

Morley explained that this experimental aircraft had been redesigned to look like an irregular shaped kite so it could not be detected by radar. Its skin is totally made out of an irregular shaped light weight Kevlar so it would be protecting the craft from light arms fire.

"The funny thing is Jack', Morley continued, "there are civilians who saw this thing flying at night in area 51. We had to fly it at night to keep its secrecy at a maximum. The public was convinced that our experimental crafts were UFOs. We wanted to keep it top secret, so we flew them at night to conceal their actual design and identity. Many complaints came into the sheriff's office that they had seen UFOs flying at night, can you imagine that Jack, crazy huh?"

"Instead of one large rotor above the pilot's deck there was two smaller rotors on either side of the craft close to the cockpit and extending out from the tip of two short stubby horizontal wings like a fixed wing aircraft. What makes this craft weird looking," smiled Morley, "that each rotor can turn by rotating it ninety degrees changing the craft from a helicopter to a fixed wing plane with a two fully functioning turbo prop. engines. Each propeller or rotor is attached to a turbo prop engine for maximum speed and power. The blades are made from special top-secret titanium alloy, so thin and the pitch of the blades are so precise that air noise is reduced by seventy five percent said Morley proudly. "There is no rear rotor Jack, just two tails for horizontal stability and to help keep the nose pointed in a straight line. It is still experimental Jack, and it has not proven itself under combat conditions. You will have to fly by the seat of your pants. Here is the kicker Jack, when you rotate both propellers to vertically again 90 degrees you can take off, land, maneuver and hover like a helicopter. You will be able to land on a dime. Once airborne, your rotors can rotate from vertical to horizontal again and fly it like a fixed wing aircraft. It makes your craft fly faster than a helicopter. Best of all it has night vision cameras and thermal imaging for nighttime operations. We never had that before in Viet Nam that's why we could not do nighttime operations. It has been stripped down; you have no armament on it except for the Kevlar skin to help you keep fuel consumption at a minimum and for your safety as well. For now, it will be only used for transportation to keep the weight down to help you with you maintain minimal fuel consumption, which will be considerable Jack. We hope the Kevlar can sufficiently protect you from enemy ground fire as there is no metal armor. Its skin, speed, and stealth are the only protection you have right now. Oh, Hell Jack! In the future the Pentagon may even try it on some of our fighter jets who knows."

"Holy Shit!" said Jack. "What is the hell is that large boom sticking out from the nose and close to the propellors. Do I spear the enemy with it? I tried that once before in in Vietnam it didn't work too well."

"That Jack, is a fuel boom so you can refill in mid-air from an airborne tanker, a flying gas station if you wish. You can refuel in midair even at night without having to land."

"You expect me to fly that thing and refuel in midair at night? So why don't you get some of those air force jockeys to do that?"

"Jack, we know you have fixed wing experience since you had your pilot's license at age sixteen. We tried pilots but, they had difficulty learning the flight dynamics of a helicopter in the short time we have. They could not master hovering and slow speed flying a few feet above the deck within the short time frame we have to work with. That is why we picked you Jack; we need a hot shot pilot."

"How much time do we have and where am I going?

"I can't tell you that just right now, you might have three weeks or maybe or three days, or three hours" said Morley. "In essence you have very little time to learn how to fly this thing, especially how-to re-fuel in midair at night. We have two craft like this, each one is to be used in a single special tactical operation that we'll explain later to you in a briefing to you and the rest of your team. Cam Hayes will be your co-pilot and Joe Kibbler and Fred Dean will be the pilots in the second craft and also, Joe has more air time on this craft and will be your trainer. He can fill you in on the nuances of handling such a strange craft and instruct you how to re-fuel in midair. Each craft besides the pilot and copilot can hold up to eight passengers with a range of seven hundred kilometers and a top speed of two hundred eighty knots.

Beirut

Mena Delacruz had also graduated as a nurse from the University of Hawaii, Mena shared Tanya's apartment as part of their nursing agreement with American Hospital. She was also working at the American Hospital in the Trauma Care Center as an

Emergency Room Nurse. Mena was born in Hawaii. Her family had emigrated from the Philippines to Hawaii and encouraged her to become a registered nurse. She was petite, slender and beautiful, with long black hair that sometimes got in her way unless she tied her hair in a ponytail. She had an easy-going personality; she and Tanya had become fast friends and shared most interests in and around Beirut.

"Tanya!" she shouted. "Look at this flyer I found," as Tanya was drying her hair in the bathroom. "American University is holding a book fair tomorrow on Arabic culture and history at the library and will be featuring a guest speaker about Egyptian

History. Both of us have the day off tomorrow, let us go and attend what do you say?"

"Sure" Tanya said, "it sounds interesting. I've always been interested in Egypt and I still want to know how in the hell they built those incredible pyramids. Perhaps the guest speaker can shed some light on how the pyramids were built. It sounds like a plan."

Mena was not the only one to see the flyer, only a week earlier Sheik Waleed and his followers saw the same flyer as well.

"But Tanya" as she mused, "do you think it is safe? What about those hotel bombings?

"I don't know, I think it's safe, that was down town in the business section far away from us. No one has ever bothered us here at the hospital or university. I don't think anyone will bother us. The bombings were probably a spat between two different groups I think we're ok."

At a small village on the outskirts of Beirut Sheik Waleed was meeting with his small group of Ba'th Party and PLO insurgents.

"Ah! At last." With a long sigh of satisfaction, "this moment is perfect for us," said Sheik Waleed. "We know the library will be full, hopefully with American and perhaps Israeli students. We can now strike and make our demands known and chase the infidels out of Lebanon and Palestine." His dozen followers cheered him as they fired their Uzis wildly into the air in unified celebration. "We have Iraqi Grenades, and Uzis, Syrian explosives and Rocket Propelled Grenades. They are gifts from our brothers in, Syria and Iraq. There is nothing that can stop us now Insallah!" He shouted. Allah Akbar! They all chorused loudly and rejoiced with him.

When François Chang checked in with Monsieur Durand at the French Embassy. Monsieur Durand advised François that the American and French Embassies had also been receiving some additional ground intelligence for over the past month, that something might be happening soon at the American University. Now based on François's informant tip that perhaps tomorrow, there may be a chance that something might be happening at the American University. However, it could not be confirmed, nor did they know what it might be. Could he go to American University and check it out and then report back? It may be something or perhaps nothing.

"Oui, no problem Monsieur Durand I will go there tomorrow walk around to see what I can observe and report back to you."

"Bon, au revoir," (good, good bye) Monsieur Durand replied.

"Look over there Tanya," said Mena "the lecture is over there in the west corner of the library by the podium and the slide projector screen. Let's get some seats by the door in case we have to leave because the lecture might be boring."

Mena sat down first, closest to the door. A few feet away from Mena, Tanya took her seat which was next to a handsome looking Asian or European man he was quiet but not sure where he might be from.

Noticing how attractive Tanya appeared François began to strike up a conversation with Tanya.

"Bonjour mademoiselle" (hello miss) in a soft French accent that caught Tanya's interest. "My name is François Chang" he said in a hushed voice, "are you interested in Egyptian History?"

"Yes" answered Tanya she was not shy about talking to handsome strangers. "I'm very interested and curious about how those pyramids were built. I still don't know how they were built. I am from Hawaii and working at the American Hospital along with my roommate Mena sitting next to me."

"Ah yes,' said François, "and I am from Vietnam, my mother is French, and my father is Vietnamese," guessing she was of mixed blood. "I am very pleased to meet you Tanya."

"Thank you so much François, my mother is Filipino, and my father is American. Well then, we have something in common François."

Professor Abu Lela started his lecture regarding Egyptian civilization. On that day twenty guests attended the lecture in the library at American University, they were mostly American Students with a smattering of French students. The audience did not appear to have any Muslim guests in attendance. However, François was not interested in the lecture he was alert looking for something unusual or irregular to occur.

Sharifa Binti Abdulla Hussein led the attack at the library of American University. Sheikh Waleed picked her because he wanted a martyr for his cause. Sharifa was an unmarried seventeen-year-old young woman and was born and raised in Medina, Saudi Arabia. At age seventeen she moved from Medina to Beirut, Lebanon to stay with relatives in order to find better work so she dutifully could send money to her impovished family in Medina. Beirut's economy was booming, and it was not uncommon to see Muslims, Jews, Turks, Seiks, French and Christians working side by side in various occupations. The mainstream of society had found ways to get along with each other and usually appreciated and respected each other's culture without too much difficulty. However, as in all religions it was usually the ultra-conservative extremists who took great liberties with the Quran or even the Bible and the Torah for that matter, who fanatically produced problems for mainstream society. Her brother and uncle accompanied her to Beirut as Saudi women were not allowed to travel by themselves. Before leaving Medina, she had listened to charismatic young, intelligent tall, handsome firebrand cleric by the name of Osama. His family was in the construction business and seemed to be quite wealthy so, Obama was free to travel and preach without having to work. His rhetoric and reputation were spreading throughout Saudi Arabia and to other parts of the middle eastern world. He was passionate about death to Americans and Jews. Osama preached that Israel stole Palestine from the Palestinian homeland and has not allowed Jerusalem to be the capital for the Palestinians. He wanted Muslims everywhere to start a revolt or antifade to recapture the Palestinian homeland. She was greatly influenced by this charismatic young man and took his message to heart. His message affected her greatly and wanted to find a way to carry out his message. "I hate the Jews" she said to herself, but deep in her heart she did not know really why she hated Jews, she never even met one. It was always what she had been told by the men in her life. Once in Beirut, she was an easy recruit for Sheikh Waleed and his PLO and Fateh insurgents. They had been looking for someone like Sharifa to join his group he wanted a martyr badly to rally his idealism and sympathy for his cause. Having a woman martyr enabled him to carry out his plans with greater public sympathy support and resources. Having Sharifa as part of his group enabled him to have her go first and martyr herself so he would not have to lead the assault. Waleed was smart enough not to put himself in front or in initial danger so he would not have to lead the attack.

Before the attack Sharifa and Sheikh Waleed met just outside the city limits.

"Here, take these two grenades and run your necklace through the holes in the pins and hide the grenades around your neck, let them dangle between your breasts under your tunic. When you get your grenades out, just pull the pins. With the first grenade throw it into the center of the seated audience. With the second grenade just pull the pin and hold it so you can kill the people closest to you, don' t let go. No one will ever see you carry the grenades. Wear your full-length tunic and don't carry a purse in case you're stopped and searched. Afterall, who would ever search an Arabic looking woman wearing a tunic and a hijab, it is usually forbidden to search a woman. It is OK to expose your face as most women in this town do. Your hair will be covered that is normal and natural. Take a taxi to the American University and we will meet you there at the appointed hour."

"But I am used to wearing my burka, I feel naked exposing my face in public. The Holy Quran has taught me to cover my nakedness," complained Sharifa.

"If you wear your full burka it might draw too much suspicion, after all there are eight of us. Entering an American campus, the way we are dressed, our appearance would not look right and might give us away. We will come from different directions and meet you at the library at the appointed hour. And besides, once you pull the pin you will be a martyr in heaven to be blessed by the Holy Messenger of God. You will be blessed and seated next to Allah as a holy martyr. You will be remembered in stories and songs and probably you will not feel a thing it will all be over in less than a second. It does not matter if you expose your face in public this one last time. You're a brave and devout Muslim woman, you are beyond suspicion or reproach, do not be afraid of dying for a worthy and just cause, your family will be honored as they will be rewarded as Islam takes care of their own."

"Women are so easily deceived they are weak and stupid that is why we have and always will have control over them, they believe everything we tell them. They fear. retribution and punishment from us. We can use the Holy Quran for our own purposes and needs". Sheikh Waleed had once said in private to his male followers. They unanimously agreed with him in a rousing loud cheer.

In early August seventeen year old Sharifa Binti Abdulla Hussein walked into the library at American University and stopped just short of the doorway as Professor Abu Lela was five minutes into his presentation.She reached under her tunic, pulling out her two grenades, with one in each hand she stood in the doorway frozen with fear. She could not pull the pins, shaking and sweating her hands trembling she dropped both grenades in abject fear.

François noticed Sharifa at the door way and her unusual behavior, there was something wrong. He saw the grenades that Sharifa had dropped on the floor and quickly realized what they were and shouted for Tanya to get on the floor. Once she was on the floor, he dove on top of her to cover her from harm.

"Bitch! Bitch! You're a coward dog of a whore. I told you what you must do, you coward". Sheikh Waleed shrieked in Farsi at Sharifa. He was angry that he lost his opportunity to have a martyr especially a lowly common female for his cause. He and his followers entered the library and stood directly behind Sharifa. In anger Sheikh Waleed pulled out his pistol from under his jacket and shot Sharifa in the head with multiple rounds. Blood and brains splattered over Mena and some of the members of the audience who were sitting closest to the door. He had no more use for her. The room came alive with screaming and chaos as other members of Sheikh Waleed's insurgents began shooting wildly their automatic weapons at random. Professor. Abu Lela was hit and killed immediately, as were several others closest to him. The insurgents were not trained to shoot automatic weapons, as they pulled the triggers of their Uzi's. The guns kicked upwards mostly hitting the ceiling and walls and missing the majority of the audience who were panicked and trying to escape in any way imaginable. Professional soldiers know to put their automatic weapons on semi-automatic. when engaged in a fire fight for better accuracy and control. The room was filled with smoke and loud hysterical screams, Mena was still seated screaming and holding her ears as the loud retorts from the Uzi's muzzles hurt her ears.

Tanya was still under François's prone body, confused and screaming at the terrible turn of events, However, they were not hit. When the shooting was over Sheikh Waleed shouted at the top of his voice.

"Stand up! you put hands behind heads now!" he shouted in broken English, again firing a burst at the ceiling with his Uzi to get their attention. "Live you follow my instructions."

The group stood up, crying, shaking and screaming at the mayhem and horror they saw around them There were five dead bodies including Pressor Abu Lela. Several were wounded but were able to stand and walk very weakly.

Tanya saw Mena's face and shoulders her upper torso was covered in Sharifa's brains and blood. She screamed at Mena thinking she was badly hurt. "I'm not sure but I think I'm OK" Mena said shaking from head to foot as she was still stunned.

She was sobbing uncontrollably. François was also confused; he did not understand or anticipate what had just happened, but he did notice Sharifa's two grenades lying on the floor. During the confusion of noise and smoke and terrifying screams he crawled over Tana's shaking body and put one of the grenades into his pocket. Sheikh Waleed's followers rounded up the remaining hostages, three were wounded but could walk bleeding steadily. Nine were Americans. five were French and one Vietnamese however there were no Israelis. Perhaps they knew something that others did not. The insurgents herded them into a group, bewildered and confused and acting like statues, they did as they were told.

In a heavy Farsi accent, he spoke in broken English. "From now on you be my hostages, I hold you I I get what I want. Obey orders all be safe. Disobey, then I shoot you like this coward on the floor," as he pointed his weapon at Sharifa's dead and lifeless body half of her head was missing in a bloody mess. As the example he wanted to impress onto his hostages already terrified minds. They got the message.

"Where are you taking us?" said François in French, as he was regaining some of his composure. All the while hiding the grenade he had found, deep into his pants pocket

"You'll find out soon enough," he said in a thick Farsi accent. "Move quickly, follow my soldiers of God. Try something foolish we shoot you on sight."

For his purposes right now, Sheikh Walled needed them alive. Later on, he planned on shooting each hostage one by one at the top of each hour. With automatic weapons and having rocket propelled grenades to be used against the security forces. He pointed at the hostages as they were poked and prodded like a herd of cattle. Sheikh Waleed knew he had to move quickly as the police and armed security were probably on the way right now to American University. He did not want an immediate fire fight with them here in the library or on the grounds of American University. Later he wanted a fire fight with the Lebanese Security Forces, but not now. With hands behind their heads Sheikh Waleed's group was transported by taxi's that had been commandeered by the extremists, to the Mosque Mohammed-Al-Amin that was not too far from American university. The mosque was an ideal place to defend. It was the place Sheikh Waleed knew he could keep his hostages safely from outside attackers It was a fortress that could not easily be penetrated by government assault troops unless they destroy the entire mosque. The Mosque Mohammed-Al-Amin was a beautiful large mosque. Laid out in a rectangle with sandstone-colored walls. It had a huge central sky-blue tiled dome with four smaller blue tiled domes offsetting each of the four sides of the building. Throughout the mosque on each wall richly designed Arabic motifs adorned this most beautiful mosque enhancing the character of this house of God. At each corner there are four minarets with two balconies on each minaret. The lower balcony was used for the cantor to call to prayers as he faced Mecca five times a day. The only entrance was a heavy steeled door under a parapet of arches located at the top of a flight of steps. As a place of worship, as with all mosques it was a beautifully designed building for worshiping of God. Most mosques in the Islamic world are extremely elegant and magnificent and represent the spirituality in their design that man feels for God.

"Who cares if I shoot up and destroy this mosque for my purposes it's ideal. It's probably a Sunni Mosque anyway, I hate those Sunnis and their own sect of Islam as much as I hate Americans. So, who cares" Sheikh Waleed said to himself.

The Iman of the mosque shouted at Sheikh Waleed.

"What are you doing here, with these people and your weapons?" "This is a house of God. Get out! Get out! He screamed. "I do not want your kind here. You are not welcome here. This is a holy place, a place of peace and worship to Allah. Go back to your Shia brothers, this is a Suni mosque you motherless dog," as he screamed at Sheikh Waleed.

Seeing that Sheikh Walled was not going to get cooperation he needed from the Iman, he pulled out his pistol and shot him once between the eyes and two bullets to his chest. "He was probably Sunni anyway," he told his startled followers, "I hate the Sunnis as much as I hate these western infidels we have for our captives," he said to his followers in a dry humorless voice. "Take his body to the back of the mosque and cover him up so no one will see him. We'll all be dead anyway by the time his body begins to rot."

Huddled in a corner of the mosque, Tanya hugged and kissed François for protecting her. He thanked her as well for being brave and not panicking. As with all mosques, the foyer has a fountain which was used for cleansing before prayers. Tanya helped Mena clean the mess from her face and body.

"Come Mena let's help the wounded with what we know what to do." With pieces of clothing Mena comforted and helped the wounded who were going into shock from loss of blood. Tanya looked for items in the mosque that could be used for first aid.

"What are you doing you pig of a motherless whore" asked Sheikh Waleed.as he was deliberately provoking Tanya. The thought of raping Tanya and Mena had crossed his mind as they were going to die anyway, but for now it was only a fantasy.

"I am trying to help the wounded," Tanya explained,

"Sit down or I shoot you I did not ask you to do that," he shouted at Tanya.

Dutifully she did as she was told.

"What do you think they will do to us asked Mena to Tanya and François?" Both shook their heads in unknowing gestures.

"They'll probably hold us for ransom until they get what they want, after that I don't know." François replied to the two American nurses.

For Muslims who wanted to attend daily prayers, Sheik Waleed would turn them away telling them that the Iman was very sick maybe from a highly contagious disease and could they try come back next week. They could go to another mosque not too far away. Without questioning, they believed him. Sheikh Waleed was able to keep the mosque for himself, his followers and his hostages away from outsiders.

It did not take long for security forces to find out where the hostages were located. Captain Samir of the Free Lebanese Army used his bullhorn and spoke loudly in French as they surrounded the mosque.

"You there! In the mosque, release those hostages and no one will be hurt. We have you surrounded you have no way out. What is it that you want?" as Captain Samir used a bullhorn to speak to the insurgents.

Realizing he could not open the front door without being shot; Sheikh Waleed climbed the stairs of one of the front facing minarets. On the front facing minaret Sheikh Waleed surveyed the situation. It was as he predicted; snipers already had him in their cross hairs, but they did not dare shoot. It did not bother him.

Sheikh Waleed shouted to Captain Samir below him in fluent French he read his demands from a piece of paper to Captain Samir:

"Allah is great, and Mohammad is his messenger"

"First, Israel must leave the Golan Heights immediately. .

"Secondly, return the Western Bank back to the Palestinians as part of the

Homeland that belongs to the Palestinians."

"Thirdly, Jerusalem must be the capital of the Palestinian Homeland."

"I will give you five days to agree to my terms and then I will let the hostages go. If not then I will kill each hostage on the hour beginning at twelve noon, and finally we want safe passage to Syria. if you agree to my terms even in principle and we know that the Israeli Army is pulling out of the Golan Heights, then I will let the hostages go." He had no way of verifying that any of these events were going to happen anyway. It did not matter to him he had no intention of letting the hostages go. He also knew that he and his followers would die in a blood bath alongside the hostages. He continued, "We have nine Americans, five French and one Vietnamese, they are all Alive, three are wounded. he knew they would not give into his demands, but at least he had a public platform for the world to hear. Killing the hostages gave him the podium for a worldwide audience. It was the political platform for a referendum he needed to express the concerns for the PLO, Hezbollah, and any other group who sympathized with the Palestinian cause. For his purposes the UN was absolutely useless. The Palestinian cause fell on deaf ears.

"I will give you five days till noon, and then I will start killing them one by one."

"That's impossible," shouted Captain Samir, at the minaret where Sheik Waleed was standing, "Your demands are much too difficult to achieve in five days!" shouted Captain Samir. "Give us fourteen days at the most, I promise you we will have answers for you by then."

"Non, five days at the most, it is in your hands now" answered Sheikh Walled as he disappeared back inside the minaret.

Sheikh Waleed knew that somehow, he had seen François Chang somewhere before, but where? Had he recalled the account in the café a few weeks ago he would have remembered François and would have shot him immediately, but for now his mind was more focused on other things, for the greater glory of Allah and his political objectives.

"Where are you from, you are not a westerner? I have seen you somewhere before, who are you?" he said to François in fluent French.

"Perhaps around Beirut you might have seen me" François answered calmly as he already anticipated that he might be identified as the man sitting in the café at the table next to Sheikh Walled and his follower. "I work for the Michelin Tire Company in Paris. I often travel quite frequently to Lebanon making deals for Latex rubber".

"Where is your ID I want to see it" Sheikh Waleed shouted as he did not believe François.

"I left it at the hotel", François replied.

Pulling out his pistol, Sheikh Waleed answered angrily. "I do not believe you; I know I have seen you somewhere, are you a spy for those government dogs?"

Approaching François, he pressed the barrel of his pistol onto François's temple.

"Tell me or I blow your brains out now," he screamed at François. Sheikh Waleed's followers watched in mild amusement as François's knees began shaking but remained silent; this was perhaps his last moment on Earth.

"Hello Bernard" said John Blake as arrived on the scene from the American Embassy. Surveying everything, "I see Captain Samir and his security forces have the mosque surrounded with snipers in every direction and every one of your troops are wearing body armor." He said gravely. "What's going on Bernard?"

Bernard came from the French Embassy as quickly as he received the news.

"Ah, John mon ami, (my friend) we have a political and civilian mess on our hands" and so Bernard brought John up to speed on the details that had just happened previously.

."I think we have an inside man as one of the captives his name is François Chang, he is working for us gathering local intelligence I sent him to the University to see if he could gather some news for us. We were suspicious that something might happen there but we had no confirmation only rumors from the locals. I sent him there to see if he could assess the situation, I did not realize he was going to be in the thick of it."

"Holy mackerel Bernard if they find out who he is they'll kill him for sure. Can we get in and perform a rescue?"

"Non! There is only one entrance which is sealed by a heavy metal door, if we blow the door there will be a massacre on our hands for sure before we could free the hostages."

"Do you think Israel will agree to withdraw their army from the Golan Heights?" asked John hopefully as he already knew that was impossible.

"It will freeze in hell first," Bernard said bitterly.

"I need to report back to my State Department," as he recognized that the standoff was not going to have a positive outcome as John left Bernard standing at the scene. Bernard was unsure of what will happen next or how he and perhaps Captain Samir and his forces or John Blake for that matter had and any chance at all of engineering a plan to rescue the hostages without people getting hurt. How were they going to solve the problem and rescue these hostages alive with minimal risk of life? It was obvious Israel would never acquiesce to those demands. Or even provide help for that matter, so why even ask them for assistance or compliance with their demands.

For Captain Samir and the Free Lebanese Army, they had five days to find a solution. At this moment in time, they did not have a workable plan to get the hostages out alive.

"I hate these political radicals," Bernard said to himself," they never listen to reason and surely will kill everyone including themselves. They eventually they die for nothing for a meaningless political causes and are not held accountable to the problems and social mess they have created."

"I'll ask you once more, who are you?" François replied in a soft shaken voice.

"I told you, I work for the Michelin Rubber Company."

As Sheikh Walled cocked the hammer and began squeezing the trigger. Seeing what was going to happen to François, Mena impulsively threw her shoe at him hitting Sheikh Waleed hard on his temple causing Sheikh Waleed to misfire his weapon. François's life was spared by a flying shoe as the bullet just missed François's forehead and shattered into the blue mosaic tile decorating the mosque. Enraged he took his pistol and fired one round at François 's head, but all Sheikh Waleed heard was just a click from an empty magazine. He had used up his magazine's capacity on Sharifah, the Iman, and during the raid at the library and his last round on François. He had not kept track of his bullets and therefore did not reload his pistol again.

With only powder burns on his forehead and an intense ringing in his ears, François was relatively OK.

"If you kill me now, the security police will surely have heard the shots and will storm the mosque," François said heatedly as he discovered he was still alive without being seriously wounded. "Already they have heard your shot and perhaps assembling a mass assault right now. I'm sure we will all be killed and your demands will never be broadcast to the outside world. " Votre escapade n'aura ete pour rien", (your escapade will be for nothing) as loudly as he could in French so that everyone could here. Stunned at the current turn of events Sheikh Waleed realized that François was right. Quickly Sheikh Waleed climbed the stairs of the minaret. Entering the balcony, he scanned at the encircled attackers, he was relieved that there was no evidence that anyone was beginning to storm the mosque. It was still a standoff. Returning to the hostages,

"You are lucky," he said to François, while pointing a finger, no one is charging our mosque, but soon I will take great pleasure in killing you first and she second when the time is right." he said menacingly to François and Mena.

"Yusof, go the minaret and keep a lookout for us. Begin firing if you see anyone rushing towards our mosque." Yusof did so and positioned himself on the balcony of the front facing minaret.

Aviano Air Force Base, Italy

"Lieutenant Garron, Lieutenant Garron" the night orderly shouted at Jack in the officer's sleeping quarters. "Get up sir you are needed in the situation room immediately."

"Jesus! What time is it?" Jack said grumpily,

"It's three in the morning sir, you are wanted immediately."

"Three in the morning, oh my God, it seems like I just got to sleep. OK, I'll be there, let me get dressed and cleaned up. I feel like I just got run over by a steam roller."

Thirty minutes later, Jack presented himself at the situation room.

"Well good morning Jack, it's so nice to see you again, there is coffee over there, black and strong you'll need it", said a cheerful Captain Winchester.

"Captain don't you ever sleep?" said Jack irritated at Captain Winchester's cheerfulness.

"No time today Jack, we have important business to take care off, Captain Winchester said in a more sober tone.

Jack sat down next to his co-pilot Cam Hayes, next to him was Joe Kibbler and Fred Dean, pilots of the second experimental craft.

"Gentlemen we've got a hot situation in Beirut, therefore we brought you here in the first place. For the past few months

French intelligence has shared with our state department that there might be trouble brewing at the American University in Beirut. However, there was never any conclusive proof and therefore there was no reason to sound the alarm perhaps it was just rumor mongering until now. Four days ago, a band of terrorists and their crazy fanatical leader named Sheikh Waleed took over the library at American University four days ago, killing several people and taking fifteen hostages, nine Americans five French and one Vietnamese. They are now hold up at a mosque called the Mosque Mohammed-Al-Amin. He has promised to shoot each hostage one by one by noon tomorrow. We have reason to believe that the one Vietnamese hostage is an agent working for the French Embassy. The mosque is well suited for holding hostages, it is almost impenetrable with one front door made out of heavy steel and no windows.

"So how do we fit in?" said Joe Kibbler, "you need ground troops with heavy assault weapons not helicopter pilots.

"Ah! That's where you are wrong Joe." Said Captain Winchester. "Look carefully at the diagram of the mosque that he had pinned on the blackboard, carefully look gentlemen. The mosque has four minarets one on each corner, each minaret has two balconies. If you can fly at night to Beirut, then we believe that is the only way possible to rescue those hostages, it would be up to you and Jack to hover your crafts as close as possible to the minarets. In doing so a heavily armed assault personnel can lower themselves using rope ladders and night vision goggles onto the highest balcony. Jack, you will hover over to two minarets of the front facing minarets then lower two members of your assault team onto the top balcony of the minarets. Joe will hover your craft over the two rear facing minarets. Joe you will lower the other members of your team on to those balconies. Jack, Joe you need to synchronize as close as possible your assault after all it will be about three O'clock in the morning. and you might not be able to see each other, Use your night vision technology to help you. I don't want you guys crashing into each other All in all, there will be eight heavily armed soldiers working their way down the stairs of the four minarets into the main chamber.

"What about the Lebanese security forces surrounding the mosque?" asked Cam Hayes, "Won't they get in the way>"

"Yes, they will," said Captain Winchester. "We have asked the Lebanese government to tell their hostage Captain Samir to quietly pull their security forces away from the mosque. The Lebanese Government has agreed with the plan as it is the only way possible to rescue the hostages. They will not be seen or heard of once we undertake this operation, we hope with the lull, the insurgents will have developed a false sense of hope that the security forces might have given up. The four teams," continued Captain Winchester, "will converge onto the central part of the mosque. which is where we believe the hostages are kept. Coming from four different directions we think each two-man team can surprise, overpower and confuse the insurgents and dispatch them quickly, we aren't interested in prisoners. Take control of the hostages as fast as you can without them being harmed. Your team will use flash grenades for surprise and affect, then kill any insurgent you see. Yes, the hostages will be terrified and scared but unharmed. We think they will be unharmed if your team announces who we are and have them lay flat on the floor That is why you have been training on how to fly these top-secret modified crafts for the past several weeks. Jack and Joe, once the two men team has landed on those four balconies then take off and land both air crafts on the strip of land outside the front of the mosque. Be careful not to accidently turn on the microphone on one of the minarets. We don't want you broadcasting to the local insurgents what is going on. Wait for the hostage team to bring out the hostages through the front door. And Jack! Don't engage the enemy as you did in the Zamboanga. Once inside the mosque let the Green Berets do their job Jack. We need you guys to ferry those crafts full of hostages back to the US embassy, because no one else can. Jack and Joe will fly the hostages back to the American Embassy for medical care, and debriefing. The eight-man team will work their way back to the American embassy by overland, we'll have two heavily armed personnel carriers with dual 50 caliber machine guns mounted on each one The APCs will then work their way back to the embassy with the Green Berets on board. How are you on re-fueling in midair Jack?"

"Not good sir, I am not use to it, I find it very difficult especially during nighttime operations when the wind kicks up it is downright hard, almost impossible."

"You will have to do your best Jack, the mission depends on it," said Captain Winchester sternly.

"It is downright crazy Captain", Jack said. "And even if I could refuel in midair at night, hover my craft over those damned Minarets with as little training as I have had, and drop two soldiers onto a narrow balcony, and be able fly at night with instruments that I am not comfortable or familiar with, just how do you expect us to have a successful mission? And besides Captain! Worst of all, what crazy bunch of idiots would be fool hardy enough or mad enough to volunteer and undertake such a dangerous mission with fifty percent odds that they could not get the hostages out safely nor themselves for that matter?" Jack objected bitterly.

In a loud voice from the back of the room, "We have volunteered, and to a man we can do it sir."

Jack turned around to look at the back of the room to see who in the hell said such an outlandish brazen remark.

"Well, I'll be damned" said Jack to Joe. It was Sargent Holiday's rescue team.

"Good to see you again sir, said Sargent Holiday. "It looks like we'll be flying with you once more sir. There are eight of us and to a man, each of us has volunteered for this hell of a God dammed mission, if you excuse my French sir. No one can stop us we want to do it. We have been training for this mission at Fort Benning since we left you at the hospital in Hawaii."

"Well, I'll be damned." It was all Jack could say to Joe in total surprise. It has been a while since he participated in the ambush of Ali Razak and his band of insurgents. The ambush reminded him of his participation in Zamboanga and the loss of Francine and his baby causing him a twinge of anxiousness.

"The State Department got wind of abducting hostages and asked us if we could prepare for the eventuality of getting hostages out safely? I just could not tell you Jack until we're absolutely sure that all the pieces came together." said Captain Winchester. "I believe the moment is now that all the pieces have now come together. We want you to fly these especially equipped experimental air craft that you and Joe will manage. Sargent Holiday's Green Berets are all assembled for the right combination of equipment and trained men to do the job. It's our only way that we could pull this mission off successfully with at least a fifty percent chance we could get the hostages out safely. Besides, that crazy son of a bitch Sheikh Waleed plans on shooting them one by one tomorrow at noon anyway. By that time, it will be too late anyway gentleman". His words rang true, there were no further arguments.

"Take off will be at 1800 hours tonight so get plenty of rest gentlemen. It is about fourteen hundred kilometers or so from our base in Italy to Beirut if you fly about two hundred fifty knots an hour you should be there in seven or eight hours, you'll be there about three in the morning. Joe you will take four members and Jack take the other four members of Sargent Holiday's team. You will refuel at the rendezvous point which will be the North East corner over Cypress at the location on your flight instructions. Do it cleanly with one attempt, try not to waste fuel by trying to redock with the fuel boom. If you should miss the boom from the tanker then retry as quickly as you can. However, you have no other choice to make or you will be out of gas. You should have enough in reserves to get you there. You only need to connect once and lock in to fill up your craft. Fuel consumption is critical for the both of you. Both of you will have barely enough for a safe one-way trip. Once at the American embassy you will leave your craft at the compound. We will take care of them from there. Hopefully we will get you back home soon. Memorize your orders, your flight plan, radio frequencies as well as your headings, Jack will follow Joe, have your co-pilots help you if you with navigation. Joe is the team leader since he has had more experience in his craft than Jack. God willing, we will see all of you at the American Embassy along with your freed hostages. Good Luck Gentleman. May God go with you."

"I remember most of your squad, Corporals Palmer, and Kimball and Corporal Buck," said Jack "but are you missing someone?" as he spoke to Sargent Holiday carefully as they exited the door into the cold night air.

"Yes" said Sargent Holiday, 'It was corporal Mar he was killed in a training accident not too long ago at Fort Benning while preparing for this mission," Sargent Holiday said softly. It was corporal Mar who felt guilty about Francine's; death because he had not searched Abu Bin Jaafar thoroughly enough for his hidden grenade that eventually led to the death of Francine and her unborn baby. Jack felt badly for the loss of corporal Mar.

"He must have taken his guilt with him to his death without alleviating his shame," Jack said to Sargent Holiday "Corporal Mar must have felt awful that he might have caused Francine's death. No one is to blame Sargent Holiday. It was just a combination of fate of war and a culmination of circumstances."

"Now here he was again, on a mission that seemed impossible" Jack thought to himself Jack's mind wandered from Vietnam to the Philippines and now he was involved in another conflict with intersecting fates and consequences all at the same time in a world hot spot, He had put himself in danger too many times by now he thought to himself. "I want out" he wished.

CHAPTER XIII

The Mediterranean

At 1800 hours both craft lifted off vertically together loaded with equipment, two pilots and four members each of the assault team and as much aviation fuel as possible. Joe's craft was in the lead followed closely by Jack. Once at one thousand meters both craft changed the angle of the two rotors to horizontal and flew off as fixed wing aircraft at two hundred fifty knots per hour Sargent Holiday rode in Jack's craft. Joe radioed Jack that the estimated rendezvous time with the refueler will be in about four hours and to stay in tight formation. Fred Dean will navigate us there to the correct time and coordinates. Our destination point will be to meet the tanker over the north eastern tip of Cypress at 2200 hours. We will fill up there for fuel Jack".

"Roger that Joe" Jack said into his headset.

The four-hour flight was uneventful other than flying against unforeseen strong head wind which caused both air craft to use more fuel than what was anticipated.In order to reach the rendezvous, point with the tanker at the correct time, both craft had to make up lost time.

"I'm glad Joe is leading us in." said Cam. "I would hate to do this by myself. We have been fighting against a strong head wind skipper since we took off, it slowed us down. We had not planned for this, the weather report forecasted a pleasant evening for flying," he said to Jack. Jack was amazed at all the incredible things his craft could do. "Imagine refueling at night in an air craft. Incredible," he thought. "Roger that Cam" acknowledge Jack.

"We see the tanker's flying lights about five kilometers out," radioed Joe. "I'll turn on my flying lights so we can approach and be able to see the fuel boom, identify myself as the mark and let's get hooked up and get refueled as quickly as possible so we don't run out of gas."

"Cam and I don't want to push this thing to the nearest gas station if the tank is empty,'. Jack said sardonically to Joe Kibbler,

"I want you to go first, that way I can talk you through it I have more experience than you Jack. Refueling at night is tricky business."

"Yeah, I know Joe, I have tried five times at night and only had two successful attempts. In doing so, I used a huge amount of fuel to dock with the drogue chute and that was when were close to base. not over the ocean seven hundred kilometers from nowhere.OK thanks Joe, I appreciate the support, just guide me in carefully Joe."

"Slow and easy, smooth and gentle, Jack, it's like making love to a beautiful woman take your time and when you are inside that parachute drogue, then slam it in hard Jack."

"Roger that Joe," as Jack thought about what Joe had just said in his metaphor, he longed for the tender moments he once had with Francine.

Approaching the land mass of the North East Coast of Cypress, the KC-130 tanker plane began deploying its lengthy flexible boom with a small drogue chute at the distal portion of its fuel boom. The boom operator on the KC-130 could maneuver the boom to some extent and control the flow of aviation fuel to the receiving aircraft, but really it was up to the pilots to maneuver their crafts to dock with the drogue and then snap it in and lock for refueling. The drogue looked like a huge white shuttlecock instead of a rubber ball there was an opening for the pilot to guide his fuel boom into the drogue chute. Wafting in the wind, the drogue chute wafted from side to side and up and down. Its fuel port was about a meter wide and required precision flying to engage the tanker's fuel tank. Jack turned on his powerful lights maneuvered his craft closer and closer to the drogue.

"Roger" to receive incoming craft, said the pilot of the KC-130 over Jack's head set, "ready when you are."

"Copy that," said Jack returning the KC-130's request.

Hot land masses often develop violent rising hot air called thermals that linger even after sunset, rising as much as thirty thousand feet they cause even the largest of planes to pitch and drop violently and unexpectantly. Other than an unexpected head wind the air had been relatively stable but as they approached the land mass over Cypress Jack began to experience turbulence and buffeting, he had trouble holding his craft steady for refueling.

"Steady, steady, Jack, nose up a little, throttle back slightly, decrease your angle," came Joe's reassuring voice. Jack missed on his first attempt. Pulling back on his collector Jack lined up again all the while the air turbulence was buffeting him up and down and sideways as well as the drogue shoot. The alarm began to sound regarding his reserve fuel tank. His reserve tank showed he had about fifteen minutes of flying time left. Joe's craft had the same warning lights flashing on his instrument panel as well. Joe was dangerously low on fuel. Jack had to refuel and get out as quickly as possible so that Joe could fuel up in less than ten minutes. Jack missed on his second attempt as the thermals continued buffeting his craft, as well as the KC-130's drogue boom.

"Easy, easy" said Cam, "third time is the charm nice and steady skipper.'

It was not easy but Jack was able line up his boom with the drogue, like a hummingbird sipping out nectar from its favorite flower. Slowly and carefully he connected with the tanker's fuel boom the third time around. Putting his boom into the drogue, the tankers fuel boom operator pumped as much aviation fuel as quickly as possible into Jacks craft. It took less than five minutes he had enough fuel now to get to Beirut. Jack knew he had to pull out quickly for Joe to have time to refuel he also knew that Joe would have difficulty as well from the unpredictable winds.

"Ok Joe it's your turn, how's you fuel consumption?"

"I think I have about five to ten minutes of reserve fuel. My fuel is critical right now, enough for two or maybe three trials at the most. before I run out."

"Show me how it's done buddy, you are the old pro at this sort of thing. Remember it's like making love to a beautiful woman, slow and easy and get the right angle to slam it in hard," encouraged Jack.

As Jack predicted, Joe had difficulty from the wild oscillating thermals that buffeted his craft, making lining up his approach almost insanely impossible. On his first pass Joe was able to line up with the tankers fuel boom. With slow, precision flying, he was able to Inch up closer and closer to the point of contact with the drogue. Joe's ship was just a meter way before docking. Unexpectantly, a strong thermal hit Joe's craft causing him to slip violently sideways. In doing so, his starboard propeller clipped the drogue's gas line cutting the fuel line completely in two. It happened in less than a second, Joe could not react in time, nor could the tanker's boom operator retract his boom quickly enough. The tanker's boom operator watched in horror and astonishment as fuel spewed out in all directions until he cut the power to the fuel pump.

"Son of a bitch," was the last words that Jack heard on his headset. Two minutes later Joes' craft, Fred Dean and the assault team plummeted towards the Mediterranean Sea. They had run out of fuel.

"Skipper, Skipper shouted Cam in excitement, "Joe's going down, he's going down," as Cam cried out in disbelief.

Jack sat in silence in his pilot's seat as he put his craft on auto pilot. "Now what? "he thought.

Looking at Cam "Do I turn around, and abort the mission or continue and botch up the mission even more Cam? I can't do this without Joe," he said desperately over Cam's headset.

Sargent Holiday came to the cockpit, put his head set on and talked to Jack.

"I heard what you just said to Lieutenant Hayes. Look sir, we have come this far, the four of us want to continue, instead of two of us going down each minaret there will be only of one.

We believe the outcome will be the same. The only difference is you will have to fly each of us to each of the four minarets. We get paid to do a job sir; it is what we do best. I have lost four of my team today, but we want to go on and save those hostages sir. Without us they surely are dead, otherwise losing Joe and my team is a moot point now isn't it? What do you say sir?"

Flying to two minarets was hard and dangerous enough in his experimental craft, flying to all four surely could mean certain disaster. Looking at his instruments and fuel consumption he was beyond the point of no return, he had no choice but to continue. Jack radioed back to the air base in Italy and reported to Captain Winchester of Joe's approximate position and the events that had just happened. He was going on to Beirut despite Captain Winchester's stern objections to abort the mission, but it made sense to continue Jack was beyond the point of no return.

"Sheikh Waleed, the security forces have all pulled out," shouted Yusof, "what does that mean?"

Sheikh Waleed thought for a moment, "Ah, they will charge us tomorrow at noon, they have withdrawn hoping that we will let down our guard and weaken our defensive position. for tomorrows assault. All of you get some sleep tonight." he said to his followers tomorrow at noon will be terribly busy and long day for us.

02:30 hours found Jack's aircraft over Beirut; Cam navigated the craft towards the Mosque Mohammed-Al-Amin it was well lit up by floodlights. There in the flood lights against the dark night were the four minarets, Jack chose the closest one and began hovering his craft looking at the narrow balcony he hoped Sargent Holiday's team could descend onto it using their rope ladders and be able to transfer onto the balcony safely with all their equipment. The flight gods were with him tonight, there was no wind, the air was still and calm, it was a perfect night for hovering in one place for a short period of time. The down draft and noise were minimal so the soldiers could descend without swaying too much in the violent downdraft. Confidently using his craft's night vision cameras and aided by Cam to steady the rope ladder, Jack hovered as close as he could to the first minaret. Hovering thirty meters from the top of balcony, Sargent Holiday was able to avoid swaying on the rope ladder from Jack's downdraft. Deftly, despite a heavy back packs Sargent Holiday and Corporal Buck lowered themselves step by step with their tactical gear down the rope ladder onto the balcony without too much difficulty.

"They made it they're on skipper, they made it OK," said Cam.

The stealthiness of Jack's craft kept it almost invisible and quiet. If there were any curious bystanders on the ground who might have looked up and alerted the local authorities. Perhaps thinking, that it might be a UFO, what else could it be?

Jack repeated the same maneuver successfully and skillfully three more times for each minaret. Slowly and precisely taking as much time as he needed, he transferred each Green Beret using their rope ladders safely and carefully to their respective minarets. In doing so, Jack used copious amounts of fuel that had not been anticipated at his preflight tactical briefing but at least they were on the mosque. He had done his part of the job; it was now up to the Green Berets. Cam reported, "They're all on, they're on their own now until they come out the front door." Jack set his craft down on the strip of land that was close to the mosque Captain Winchester had told him about. How was he going to get fifteen hostages to the American Embassy in a craft that holds eight people beside the two pilots.? He would have to fly twice in order to shuttle back and forth without running out of fuel. His operational plans had not taken this predicament into consideration as well.

He waited for the assault to begin and hopefully hostages and the Green Berets would be charging out of the mosque exiting from the door for evacuation to safety soon.

Sargent Holiday flashed his flash light three times at the other minarets it was the signal to go.

François became more acquainted with Tanya. He also thanked Mena for saving his life by throwing her shoe at Sheikh Waleed the moment he was about to pull the trigger. Being held hostage together brought him closer to Tanya. In time he found out that Tanya's brother flew helicopters in Vietnam. François also told Tanya his life story about fleeing from North Vietnam and the rubber plantation that he and Francine operated in South Vietnam. He told Tanya about his travels to Asia and the Middle East setting up shipping contracts for latex rubber from his plantation. However, he did not tell Tanya about working for French intelligence he thought it was not safe to do so. He told Tanya about his sister leaving South Vietnam however he did not know of her whereabouts, other than when she left Vietnam, she was alive. It was his goal to find her after leaving Beirut. His plan was to go to the Philippines and start there. Tanya mentioned she had grandparents living on the Island of Bohol and that if she got out safely, she would write to them to see if they could help François find a way to begin his search. The four days in captivity brought them closer together. They promised each other if they got out alive from this mess that they would continue see each other.Both Mena and Tanya continued to take care of the wounded hostages as best as they could.The hostages were stable but very weak from the loss of blood and in dire pain from their wounds. Sheikh Waleed provided no comfort to the hostages he was going to kill them anyway so why should he help the wounded? He allowed Mena and Tanya to dress their wounds with anything that would work but that was all. Luckily, there was a fountain or a font in the foyer of the mosque for bathing and cleanliness before ritual prayersIt provided. a constant flow of water for washing, dressing wounds and drinking. There was no need to provide food after all they were all going to die soon anyway.

As predicted by Captain Winchester the hostages were huddled and camped under the beautiful blue tiled central dome of the mosque with sleeping armed guards on the perimeter floor of the encampment. No one was expecting trouble, the security forces were gone until tomorrow so how could the civilian police ever get in unless the front door would be opened by a violent explosion. By that time, the hostages would be dead. Violently the minaret doors burst open from each of the four stair cases leading from the minarets, and four heavily armed soldiers burst into the room, each throwing flash grenades creating a deafening loud thunderous noise, brilliant blinding light and a thick cloud of smoke that quickly dispersed throughout the mosque. For a moment, the scene was confusing.

"Get down! Get down! We are Americans coming to rescue you! Get down on the floor, get down now!" The rescue team shouted over and over again as loud as they could. The hostages were just as surprised as the insurgents. Automatically they laid flat on the floor. Sheikh Waleed could not recover in time to grab his weapons, so he hid behind one of the wounded hostages. Wearing night vision goggles to help see through the darkness and through the smoke the Green Berets carefully opened fire with their M-16's assault rifles. It was easy to recognize the combatants, as they were standing looking for their weapons and the hostages were lying prone on the floor covering their ears and screaming loudly in fear. Overwhelmed with the confusion from the flash grenades and the noise from the assault team they laid still hoping not to get hurt. With precision accuracy the Green Berets quickly identified the insurgents with their night vision goggles. Each insurgent was professionally and quickly rendered dead by the four-man veteran team. The noise was deafening, smoke was everywhere as Sheikh Waleed continued to hide behind one of the wounded hostages. Through the chaos, Sargent Holiday began giving orders.

"Corporal Buck find the front door and look for Jack's helicopter. Corporal Palmer and Corporal Kimball begin to look for identification papers, take their photographs and fingerprints. We will give it to intel later. The rest of us will begin leading the hostages out the door to Jack's waiting helicopter. We don't have too much time so let's hustle, get the hostages out now, hustle, hustle," he shouted to his squad over the receding noise and commotion.

"Excuse me Sargent," said a very frightened voice. "My name is Mena Delacruz my roommate and I are trained nurses do you have any first aid equipment on you such as bandages, morphine or any sulfur?"

"We sure do Mena, go see Corporal Palmer outside and he will give you what you need."

Once the hostages were outside and close to Jack's craft a lone figure armed with a rocket propelled grenade launcher in one hand and a rocket grenade in the other silhouetted himself against the doorway at the top of the steps shouting "God is great! God is great!" he screamed as, he began a motion of loading and aiming his grenade launcher at Jack's craft.But before he could load the RPG with a rocket and pull the trigger, François had already reached into his pocket pulled the safety pin from the grenade.François threw the grenade at Sheikh Waleed it was the grenade he had found next to Sharifa's dead body at the American University. The grenade blew Sheikh Waleed's body back into the mosque in a bloody mess. He was never to quote God's name in vain again. In time Sheikh Waleed became a martyr to his followers and enhanced the excitement level whenever his named was mentioned at rally's or meetings. He fulfilled his own destiny.

"Son of a bitch? You were god damned brave if you excuse my French mister." Sargent Holiday said incredulously.

"Your French is excused monsieur Sargent," François replied calmly.

"That was close mister how did you get that grenade?" asked Sargent Holiday.

"It is a long story monsieur Sargent I'll tell you all about it later, in the meantime let's get out of here, before we're overrun with local radicals" said François emphatically.

"Here's the problem Sargent, we've fifteen hostages and one craft. I can carry eight. I think I have enough fuel to make one trip for sure perhaps two trips if I am incredibly lucky. However, I'm not sure I can make it. I would not hold your breath or bet on that to happen if I was you. Put the two nurses and the wounded in first, then four more hostages, that is. all I can take for the first trip. If I don't make it back in forty five minutes, try for the American Embassy. After that, your team and the hostages are on their own do the best as you canI am afraid the locals will be here soon to see what is going on and they will be really pissed once they see what we have done to their mosque."

194

"We'll do the best we can sir, my team and I will stay here and protect the hostages. The two APC's should have been here any moment. if it doesn't come within forty-five minutes then we'll have to hoof it. It's not the first time we have had to do this." said Sargent Holiday.

"Have the remaining hostages hide here with your team for protection. I will be back with help within forty-five minutes.

"Cam! can you plot us a course to the American Embassy?" Jack shouted.

"You bet skipper, let's get ready to lift off and wind this craft up."

As the wounded hostages were loaded in first, Tanya recognized Jack.

"Jack is it you? Is it really you?" She ran to him and put her arms around his neck with tears of joy running down her cheeks. Her own brother had rescued her.

"Tanya how did you get here?' he said in amazement he could not believe his own sister was one of the hostages.

"You have a lot to catch up on Jack" she said happily while hugging his neck.

"Tanya, we have to get out of here now we can talk later before we're overrun by those damned Muslim militants, I'm sure they know we're here by now. They won't be too happy for shooting up their mosque," he said hurriedly. "Get into my aircraft and I will ferry us to the US Embassy." She did as Jack told her and mounted into Jacks craft.

"Hello, my name is Cam Hayes, I'm Jack's copilot. "Are you and Jack engaged or something? I saw you two hugging each other."

"Oh no. thanks for rescuing us I thought for sure we were going to die today. My name is Tanya Garron, I'm Jack's sister."

Cam stared at her in disbelief Jack never mentioned about having a beautiful sister nor did Jack know that would be rescuing his own sister. With a full load Jack took off for the American Embassy. François volunteered tostay behind with the other hostages. and the four Green Berets. The armed personnel carrier did not arrive as promised by Captain Winchester to ferry the Green Berets to a safe destination.

"I should be back within forty-five minutes at the latest," he shouted at Sargent Holiday. "I'll be back to pick to up the remaining group". Again, he realized he would be using more precious fuel.

John Blake and a medical team met the hostages in the parking lot of the American Embassy as Jack landed his craft very carefully. They had become aware of the assault at the Mosque Mohammed-Al-Amin

"Sir, I have to get back to the mosque quickly as possible to pick up the remaining hostages and relieve those GI's protecting them." Jack said hurriedly.

John Blake replied, "We knew one craft went down in the Mediterranean the news from Aviano Air Base was confusing. Our intel became garbledWe cancelled the armed personnel carrier because we thought the mission had been aborted. Luckily, we kept our radio channel open just in case one of you might have made it here. Later we heard on our open communication system that the rescue mission still had the green light for the rescue at the mosque. But until you arrived here, we did not know for sure"

"There are four brave GI's still waiting for a lift home Mr. Blake, where in the hell is those two APC's that was promised? I suggest you get on the horn and get those APCs back to the mosque ASAP," he said emphatically. "I have more passengers to pick up and I need to leave now, and those soldiers need to leave as well before they are overrun by Muslim militants."

"Jack, I want to go with you in case of any injuries. Corporal Palmer gave me his first aid bag; I can be of use," said Mena Delacruz firmly.

"Miss Delacruz, I do not have room for you I can fit only the remaining hostages."

"Jack, she can take my place," said Cam "she can sit in the copilot's seat. I think you can find your way back to the mosque without my assistance, besides it's almost daylight, and at this moment in time, Miss Delacruz will be of more use to you than I can." said Cam in quiet resignation.

"OK, let's go! We're running out of time." It was 0445 when they lifted off from the embassy back to the mosque. Daylight was just beginning to break on a crimsoncloudless sky the blazing sun would be rising soon above the morning horizon. It would be a hot day. Navigating his way back to the direction of the mosque he was able to see the four minarets silhouetted against the morning sky, the sun had not quite cleared the morning horizon. Approaching the Mosque Mohammed-Al-Amin he could see it clearly now but there seemed to be something wrong. What was it?

Syed Haji-al- Noor had just woken from his sleep. He was late getting started for his morning routine. He dressed and bathed quietly. but he did not eat so as not to disturb his family. Finding his bicycle, he peddled as quickly as he could to the mosque for the announcement of morning prayers of "Fair".

"I must get to the mosque before sunrise," he thought to himself. "I don't want to be late for "Fajr." I must make my morning call to prayers before sunrise. If the Iman is well enough, he would go to the minaret turn on his microphone and begin his call to prayers." he thought. Syed was motivated to pray five times a day because of his love for God and devotion to Islam. Arriving at the top of the front steps of his beloved mosque he could not believe his eyes. The door was wide open, his holy mosque, his beautiful and holy house of God was in shambles. Standing aghast, he saw the carnage of the dead militants, the blood-soaked tunic of Sheikh Waleed, the damage to the interior from François's grenade and the numerous shattered blue mosaic tiles shattered and stained with blood that adorned the wall from automatic weapons fire from the Green Beret's team. Analyzing what might have happed, he came across the body of the Iman at the rear of the mosque. He was covered in a cloth shroud, with dried blood covering his chest and face. One eye dangled from his eye socket, his mouth was agape in a silent scream. What could have happened? Looking at the grotesquely shaped dead bodies strewn around the interior of the mosque he was able to find brass bullet casings from the Green Berets M-16s. He was not unfamiliar with weapons or munitions of war as he was a veteran of the 1948 Arab Israeli conflict and the 1967 6-day war with Israel. There on the floor he saw copious amounts of 7.62mm bullet casings scattered thorough out the mosque.

"Many NATO countries use this type of ammunition. The murderers of my people in my mosque surely must be French, or Americans or perhaps Russians. Russians bastards have no interest in Lebanon right now, the French respect our mosques but the Americans do not respect holy sites. No one else but Americans have an interest here at this time. No one else other than Americans would be so foolish to come here and initiate such carnage and sacrilege to a holy place. This is a house of God, a holy place, a sanctuary for us to pray, and commune with God., We always give thanks to Allah for our blessings in this holy place. It is a mess an unforgivable catastrophic denigration of a house of God. Americans must die for destroying our ancient, beautiful and sacred mosque. Israelis don't use these caliber bullets, I must warn my people what happened," he thought to himself. He was still unaware of the hostage situation that Sheikh Waleed had created. Climbing the minaret that was facing Mecca, he reached the balcony where the microphone was placed. Allowing the loud speakers to warm up, he surveyed the landscape around him. There, hiding prone in a small and narrow concrete drainage ditch were seven looking westerners and four American soldiers kneeling down with their rifles guarding the freed hostages, not more than seventy five meters from the front door of the mosque. Why were they there? Perhaps their escape plan did not work and now they were trapped like judas goats before being slaughtered.

"Americans have destroyed our mosque! Americans have destroyed our mosque! The announcement came out repeatedly loud and strong. "They are hiding here in the drainage ditch, get your weapons, they're trapped," he said loudly over and over again.

François guessed what was being broadcast over the loud speaker system.

"Monsieur Sargent, I think we've been spotted get your or men ready, an attack is about to happen very soon.

"Damn! Where are those APCs?" "We don't have enough ammunition to last for more than ten minutes then we're out, and we don't have enough men to hold off a crazed band of fanatic insurgents. Men, take cover as best as you can pick your targets carefully and conserve ammunition. The hostages laid prone on the bottom, flat against the small concrete wall of the canal. Do not raise your heads we will provide covering fire for you, as he shouted his commands to his men and hostages." It was too late now to take off on foot and head for the American Embassy. That would be an impossibility as it became clear they would soon be outnumbered and outgunned and exposed out in the open with little cover.

Syed began yelling and pointing, "They're over there hiding in the drainage ditch kill them," as a group of angry armed civilian Muslims looked at the carnage of the mosque and then realized what these strangers had caused the damage to their beautiful holy mosque. Blindly, the first wave of Muslims charged the Green Berets shooting wildly on the run with their AK 47's. The Green Berets reacted with professionalism, as disciplined soldiers of many Vietnam Era campaigns, they knew how to defend their defensive perimeter with precise marksmanship with minimal use of ammunition. The attackers were quickly killed before they could even get within twenty meters. Enraged, another wave of Muslims charged the hostages and the Green Berets, their anger and hostility were vented towards the hostages. Enraged in blind and wild anger they charged in random intervals. With AK 47's shooting on automatic the group wildly missed their marks. The angry insurgents were dispatched with the same results as the previous attackers.

From his aircraft Jack could see the firefight in front of the mosque littered with bodies. He knew he could land his craft on the space he had done so before, however; the hostages would have to make a twenty-meter run for their lives from the ditch to board his waiting craft.

Syed shouted to his followers "Get up into the minarets we can shoot down onto them instead of charging them we have the high ground advantage." During the brief lull, the attackers climbed the steps of the closest minarets with their AK 47 assault weapons. Having a better advantage point they were better able to aim and shoot at the soldiers and hostages that were hiding in a defensive position in the drainage ditch.

It was at this time Jack landed his craft as close as dared to the hostages without putting himself and his craft in harm's way.

During the brief interlude Sargent Holiday led his team to Jacks' waiting craft.

"Let's go! Let's go! now, now! now! Hustle let's go,." shouted Sargent Holiday at the top of his lungs as they were about to leave and run for safety to Jack's waiting aircraft. Immediately gunfire from the minarets rained down on the defenders hitting Corporal Palmer in the chest causing a sucking chest wound before he could take five steps. He went down in a crumpled heap. Sargent Holiday received wounds to his arm and below the knee as he scampered over the concrete drainage ditch but fell backwards on top of the hostages as they were following him to the safety of Jacks craft. Corporal Buck received a neck wound that burned like fire, but he could still breathe despite the heavy loss of blood. François Chang was the only hostage that was wounded, he was hit in the upper arm. He did not panic, instead with one arm he helped Corporal Buck back into their exceedingly small defensive position of the drainage canal. The rest of Sargent Holiday's team were unharmed.

"Get back! Go back to the drainage ditch for cover," he yelled at the top of his voice. "We'll never make it alive to Jacks copter," shouted Sargent Holiday. Those were the last words he could say before he passed out going into severe shock.

While providing suppression fire the rest of the team eventually depleted their ammunition. Jack's air craft was being hit with small arms fire but pinged off the tough Kevlar coated skin without causing real damage. Without telling Jack, Mena opened the door and alighted to the ground.With her first aid bag draped over her shoulder she ran as fast she could in a zig zag fashion through a storm of bullets from the attackers. Bullets kicked up dust and dirt within centimeters of her feet and legs. Corporal Palmer was down and could not move. He was alive but gasping for air, as air, blood and saliva bubbled out of his sucking chest wound, mouth, and nose. He was unconscious but slowly drowning in his own blood.Reaching Corporal Palmer, she kneeled down and opened up the first aid kit that Corporal Palmer gave her earlier while they were still in the mosque. Pushing hard she is inserting numerous 4X4 bandages into his open chest wound, she stopped the air leaking from his chest and gave him an immediate dose of morphine. She found a plastic IV tube in her kit and deftly inserted it down into his trachea to assist in breathing. She triaged him he would survive if he could get to a hospital in time. She held her ground as bullets continued to zing within centimeters of her head and dance around her body in a continuous spray of dirt and dust. Undeterred she continued to apply first aid to Corporal Palmer as best as she could. Without a moment's hesitation she ran for the drainage ditch diving for cover. Crawling on hands and knees she made her way to Sargent Holiday whose lower leg had been shattered and loosing copious amounts of blood from his arm and leg. She found her tourniquet kit and tied off his leg above the knee and his arm just below the shoulder with as much pressure as she could muster. His bleeding stopped but he was too weak and in shock to move or give commands. She treated François's wounded arm with a bandage to stop the bleeding. He would survive if he could get to a hospital for emergency first aid. Meanwhile, in the safety of the minaret, Syed slowly and deliberately sighted his AK-47 at Mena's head who was beginning to attend to Corporal Bucks neck wound. He had her clearly in his front and rear sights and prayed to Allah to blow her head off with a spectacular head shot. She was an easy target.

"She will die without knowing what hit her. This infidel is destined for Hell as with all the other infidels. May they all go to Hell as their punishment, no one should ever destroy a house of God," as he shouted out loud to his fellow attackers.

As he was about to blow off Mena's head there came loud crack and multiple loud retorts from somewhere in the distance. A crescendo of, loud rapid fire came lightning fast. Multiple sounds of two 50-caliber machine guns sprayed the minarets. Syed was killed instantly before he could pull the trigger to shoot Mena. his body toppled to the ground. In a quick moment, the minarets were being raked by heavy arms fire. The Minarets were being quickly splintered and fractured into small pieces. The attackers deserted their stronghold from their minarets as they were defenseless against heavy armaments. The civilian militia ran for cover as they could not out duel powerful 50-caliber machine guns.

Jack was startled "What in hell was that?" Jack said to himself. "Where did that noise come from?" he asked himself while still sitting in his craft. He had no firepower of his own other than his service pistol which was useless at a time like this. He did not wish to abandon his craft. If he should get hit, then there would be no one who could fly his craft out of here. He had no choice but to sit tight in the safety of his aircraft. It provided him with a measure of safety, however, he could not leave, he felt that he needed to stay and assist the hostages if they could make it to his craft. Looking at the situation he realized it was futile to stay. It looked as if his team was lost and his rescue mission a total disaster. Reluctantlyhe began to wind up his twin turbo props. He had decided to abandon what was left of his rescue team and the hostages. "Perhaps I can find some help somewhere, perhaps at the embassy, he said to himself." For a moment he lost hope. He was ready to punch out and take off to prevent his craft from falling into enemy hands. But what was that miraculous sound? In disbelief, there they came the sweet sounds of clanking treads and diesel powered "battle taxis" as they were sometimes called.There came, two APCs, perhaps 50 meters away charging at full speed to the mosque spewing black smoke from their exhaust like battle flags. Each one mounted with two 50-caliber machine gun. The barrage was lethal, raking the minarets and at the fleeing attackers as they abandoned their positions.John Blake at the American Embassy had been able to contact the commander of the APCs and ordered them to get to the mosque as quickly as possible. It was not a moment too soon.

The timing of the arrival of the APCs was a miracle of sorts. When all seemed dark and lost, divine providence often steps in to make changes for everlasting life altering events. Our God surely is great and a wonderful God no matter whose God he or she belongs to. The hand of God is always there for everyone and for all religious persuasions. It guides us mortals in mysterious ways that we will never understand.

Ron Garron realized this while floating in Leyte Gulf so many years ago. Ron's interaction with Jackson the Zebra Eel at Molokini Reef made him feel that everything in his life would work out for the good. He was not afraid because of his predicament as he floated in Leyte Gulf. Strangely fate seemed to step in at the right time rescued by of all things a Filipino fishing boat. Ron's impact on world events were very miniscule, but yet the consequences of his actions caused major life changing events affecting the future history of others in other parts of the world His ripple effect was small and miniscule based on the world stage, but were incredulous and gigantic to those who came in contact with him.And now the divine hand of God has stepped in again, to save Ron's son Jackson in a similar set of circumstances. Without knowing it Jackson Garron had already impacted and changed the lives of those around him. Jackson's life would continue to impact the lives of others as well and would continue to careen into others like a billiard ball on a pool table, through time ad infinitum. History can never be undone or repeat itself. Only a similar set of circumstances, characters and situations may replicate itself.

Still sitting in his pilot's seat, he quietly said, "Thank you God for saving my ass and my mission."

"Hello, my name is Captain Faysal of the 11th Armored Cav, I heard your team needed some help over here so I thought I would bring my two APCs over and see what we could do for you guys," as he approached Jack.

Jack shook hands with Captain Faysal.

"Am I glad to see you, are you from Lebanon?" recognizing his Arabic name asked Jack. "You saved our asses captain, but I would not hang around here too much longer before we are under a full-scale assault and I was about ready to punch out."

"I agree lieutenant, the quicker we make tracks outa here the safer everyone will be. By the way, my parents emigrated from Egypt. I was born in Detroit, received a football scholarship to Michigan State but instead I decided to attend and graduate from West Point so I can enlist in the service of my country. I get this from everyone," was his curt reply. "What can we do for you Lieutenant Garron?"

"Can you get the wounded to the nearest hospital and the remaining hostages to the American Embassy as quickly as you can? Also, I have got this crazy nurse who thinks she is superwoman and somehow, she thinks she is impervious to bullets. I need her to go with you guys to continue caring for the wounded."

"Sure, thing lieutenant, no problem, my APC's can carry everyone."

"Mena are you crazy or what? Do you know how close you came to getting killed, I don't know how you're still alive?" as Jack hugged her all of her 5-foot 95lb frame and kissed her on the mouth in unbridled passion. He was astonished at her display of unmitigated bravery.

"She probably saved the lives of François, Sargent Holiday and Corporals Palmer and Buck. Had she been in the military she might have been nominated for The Silver Star or something like that," thought Jack.

"Don't scold me Jack, I don't know why, but I did what I had to do. We must get the injured as quickly as possible to a hospital," she said firmly. "Corporal Palmer is critical and Sargent Holiday is quite serious, they are alive for now, but I don't know for how much longer they can survive. François's arm is broken and probably needs immediate surgery and Corporal buck needs stiches to close up his wounded neck. I need to go Jack."

"Mena, you are the bravest person I have ever met Mena; can I see you later at the Embassy," I think you are one of the most amazing persons I have ever known?"

"Yes of course Jack, but we have to go now goodbye," she said quickly with atone of finality in her voice.

All hostages and wounded along with Tanya and Mena were loaded into the two APCs and headed for immediate medical care. Captain Faysal spear headed his convoy with the wounded without further incident.

Jack's biggest problem was how to get his craft back to the Embassy. His fuel was critical, but he could not allow this experimental craft to fall into alien hands. He fired up his twin rotors in the vertical position and lifted off to head back to the Embassy. Five minutes after liftoff at twenty-five hundred meters, his fuel reserves gave out. There were decisions to be made. He was a kilometer from the Mediterranean but several kilometers from the American embassy. In his mind if worse comes to worse he would rather crash into the sea than in the middle of Beirut. He did not want to kill civilians or cause major structural damage to the buildings in Beirut not he could not allow his craft to fall in ill-gotten hands. With all the ability he could muster he feathered his craft out to seaward while he continued to radio his position. As a skilled pilot he knew how to fly his craft to get every inch of elevation and distance he could manage to in order to glide into the Mediterranean Sea. Five kilometers out, he crashed his craft into the Med. but at least it was not downtown Beirut that might have killed scores of civilians. Because of its lightweight frame his craft broke up into several large pieces. and began sinking almost immediately. Jack had already unbuckled his seat belt as he did not wish to be inside a sinking craft. His impact with the water caused him to be ejected out of his pilot's seat into the cold Mediterranean Sea. The sudden impact injured his ribs preventing him from swimming to safety. All he could do was to grab a floating piece of debris and hang on for dear life hoping someone might have picked up his distress signals. Fighting through the pain in his rib cage he floated for hours trying not to pass out from exhaustion. He closed his eyes one more time, the distant lights of Beirut began to fade quickly. Jackson was swept out to seaward on the outgoing tide.

Jack woke up confused, bright lights shone in his face he was in a hospital bed, there were strangers in uniform standing next to him but where was he?

"Well, the last time we met lieutenant, you brought me a pregnant Vietnamese woman in a helicopter full of bullet holes, now you're swimming around in the Mediterranean Sea. We have got to stop meeting like this lieutenant," said the XO of the Naval vessel USS Kirk.

Confused, Jack thought for a moment he was back in Vietnam.

"Where am I? The last I remember I crashed into the sea. I think I hurt my ribs; they hurt like hell."

"Well lieutenant you are back on the USS Kirk. We heard your distress call; it took a several hours, but we found you. Your craft was nowhere to be found we think it sunk. We had just finished sailing out of Haifa. President Ford ordered us to stay close to Beirut and be prepared to evacuate any Americans who might be caught up in the civil war in Lebanon," the XO said.

"I'll be god damned, back on the Kirk, holy smokes, thanks for rescuing me. My mission started out at Aviano Air Base to rescue hostages in Beirut. We started out with two experimental aircraft. We lost the crew on one over Cypress they went down in the Med. Now I've lost the other air craft and got several people seriously hurt if they are not already dead by now. My craft ran out of fuel as I was heading back to the embassy. So, I thought it best to ditch into the Med rather than crash in downtown Beirut. I think I messed up my mission big time," Jack said dejectedly.

"Yup, you probably did lieutenant" said the XO in a southern drawl. "In the meantime, you'll get rest and care on the Kirk, our doctors will help you with your injured ribs. Sometime soon we'll probably fly you back to Aviano Air Base when you're ready to travel. Get some rest, and when your well enough let's go have a beer instead of meeting under such dramatic circumstances. I'm beginning to wonder if you are a secret agent from the Pentagon sending you here just to evaluate our sea worthiness and effectiveness lieutenant. I have my suspicions about you" he said mockingly

The past twenty-four hours raced through his mind. "How did I get involved in such a mess?" he thought. Jack closed his eyes and slept for thirty-six hours.

Tanya marveled at Mena's bravery when she heard the news from François what she did helping the trapped wounded soldiers at the mosque.

"How could you do such an incredible thing.? You have never had any military training. Why did you do what you just did?" Tanya asked incredulously after she found out what Mena did.

"I don't know what came over me, I just knew, at that moment when we under heavy fire from the mosque and those soldiers were getting hurt. François had been shot in the arm and three other soldiers were seriously hurt, I just knew I had to do something. I guess at that moment in time, the bell tolled for me.she had once recently read "For Whom The Bells Tolls" by Hemingway" She struggled with the books title and could not grasp Hemingway's meaning. She realized now what it meant and understood what Hemmingway was trying to say. "It was just fate that I was there at that moment in time.I guess the bell tolled for me. I had to do what needed to be done. How are the wounded and the other hostages?" continued Mena? "I haven't had time to follow up to see how they are doing since the debriefing at the embassy.

"Corporal Buck will survive although he lost a lot of blood from his neck injury. I am afraid Sargent Holiday lost his leg below the knee; the surgeons could not save it. François will have a heavy cast on his upper arm he will need surgery to repair his broken bones. I'm afraid Corporal Palmer did not make it, he died in the ER at American Hospital," she said sadly. The remaining hostages have all returned to their homes to face news reporters and TV journalists to give interviews on what had happened."

Mena asked, "Now what do we do?"

"Let's go home Mena," was Tanya's answer. "I believe John Blake will provide us with a military aircraft back to Honolulu as a result of our kidnapping ordeal."

"François, what are your plans?" asked Tanya. "You can ride back to Honolulu with us." Tanya said hopefully.

"Mon Cherie, merci beaucoup. (my sweetheart, thank you very much) However, I must go to the French Embassy and report my experience to French Intelligence.I have done enough here. Once in Paris I will make travel plans to the French Embassy in Manila to see if the French authorities can help me find my sister Francine. Perhaps she is still in a refugee camp somewhere the Philippines. I also need to have my broken arm repaired and healed before I can travel."

"Will I ever see you again?" she said.

"Of course, mon Cherie, (sweetheart) a beautiful and brave mademoiselle like you is not easily forgotten. If you give me your address, then one day we will meet in Honolulu after my arm is healed and I am finished looking for my sister. Until we meet again." he said tenderly while passionately kissing her. "Bon chance was the last thing he said to TanyaJohn Blake arrived on the scene to tell Mena and Tanya to go back to their apartment, pack their things, a flight to Honolulu has been arranged on a military helicopter to a waiting ship just off the coast. From there a naval military transport plane will ferry them to Honolulu.

"John, Tanya" she blurted out, "I'm staying here for as long as I can. I believe I can be of value here in Beirut. I have decided to make the military my career as an Army Nurse I don't want to go back to Honolulu right now. I know I can enlist as an officer and serve my country for those who need me," Mena said emphatically. Mena looked at Tanya with a fixed gaze to let Tanya know she meant what she said. There would be no turning back, Mena wanted to stay and fulfill her desire as an Army Medic. She spent one more month in Beirut before enlisting as Lieutenant in the Army Medical Corp.

"Ok miss, there she is, the USS Kirk, we'll land on the ship and from there they'll fly you to the nearest air base to get you home on a military transport plane," said the helicopter pilot as he spoke into his headset. Before they took off for the USS Kirk John Blake told Tanya that they just received word that Jack was safely on board the Kirk recovering from several fractured ribs. He was alive and safe. Tanya could not believe her ears; she had wondered what had happened to Jack but no one seemed to know of his location other than he might have crashed into the Med. She was ecstatic to see him again she thought he was lost at sea for sure. Slowly with time on their hands they brought each other up to date as to how they arrived in Lebanon. He told Tanya about fleeing from Vietnam and landing on the same ship as the one they are now. With sadness and resignation, he told Tanya the story how Francine and their unborn child were killed while on a rescue mission similar to the one he completed now in Beirut and how Francine had saved Jack's life by sacrificing her own.

"I know who her brother is," she yelled excitedly at Jack. "It's François, the hostage you saved at the mosque. He has been looking for her since the fall of South Vietnam, he is going to go the French Embassy in Manila to find out what might have happened to Francine. Jack, we have to find him." she said urgently. François does not know who you are and what happened to Francine. You guys never met at the rubber plantation in South Vietnam because François was away on business in Hong Kong at the time you and Francine were at the plantation.

"Well, I'll be damned; he could have been my brother-in-law and my baby's uncle. I had planned to marry Francine as soon as I could. I never met him; I did not know who he was until now at this very moment."

After everything sunk into Jacks' mind, he asked Tanya, what happened to Miss Mena Delacruz? "She had to be the bravest person I ever met," he said in wonderment. "She decided to stay Jack, she's not coming back with us. She wants to make a career in the Military as an Army Nurse."

"I wish her luck," said jack quietly. He had hoped to become more acquainted with her.

"However," Tanya said "If I have something to say about it, François might still become your brother-in-law, He promised me he would come to Honolulu after his journey to the Philippines. How do we find him Jack?" Tanya said anxiously.

"I don't know, but I might be able to ask some people who could find out for us", said Jack hopefully.

"Well, well, well," said Morley Warburton after flying in to see Jack on the Kirk. "It seems like visiting you in the hospital is becoming an old habit."

"Morley I'm sorry, I think I screwed up the mission, both aircraft are gone. My sister told me that we lost Corporal Palmer, Sargent Holiday lost his leg and is still seriously wounded. Corporal buck and François Chang are still recovering from their wounds. Worst of all," he said to Morley, "we lost Joe's craft and his crew somewhere in the Med. I think close to Cypress and we shot up a mosque and I know those Muslims will hate us forever and somehow will retaliate against us wanting revenge, and we will probably retaliate against their tactics and they against us. It will never stop" he said with finality to Morley.

"Well let me bring you up to speed Jack, Joe and his crew were rescued by Greek Fishing boat they're back at Aviano Air Base. They are banged up quite a bit but they are all alive. You rescued all of the hostages, they came back alive and as we told you in the briefing that there was a fifty percent chance of success. Sargent Holiday and his men, without question knew that going into the mission it was indeed very dangerous and the chances of being wounded or killed were very high. Jack you brought out all the hostages safely. However, because this was a covert mission you will not get credit for ditching your craft into the Med and nor for your acts of heroism while saving innocent lives. Shooting up the mosque could not be helped; it was an act of war and had to be done. We will see what the consequences will be and we will probably retaliate if it is against us. Who knows where it will end? Once again Jack you did a great job for us."

Morley asked Jack to evaluate the experimental craft.

"Joe lost his craft while refueling because the propellers were too close to the nose. Modify the wings so that the propellers are further back on the fuselage away from the nose, so that cutting the fuel line from accidental wind gusts are minimalized. Also provide some armament for basic protection. I sat there like a sitting duck helpless taking on pot shots Luckily that Kevlar skin kept damage to a minimal, but it needs a thicker outer skin.I had no way to interdict and assist those hostages and those Green BeretsI had no armaments to rely on to supply suppression fire. I had no other choice I almost left them behind."

"What happened to Sargent Holiday and the rest of his team are they OK?"

"We had to reassign his team to different Green Beret units. Sargent Holiday will have an artificial leg and then he will receive a medical discharge. Sargent Holiday and the rest of the rescue team will receive the purple heart for those who were wounded as well as a distinguished service medal, Corporal Palmer's family will receive his medal posthumously."

"America could not ask for any braver men than these guys to serve our country", Jack said with reverence in his voice. "They did a hell of a job protecting those hostages under enemy fire."

"Yes, indeed Jack, they were exceptional, those soldiers were willing to sacrifice themselves while performing their mission in the line of duty. OK! now Jack we'll go back to area 51 and see what we can do to modify those recommendations you suggested."

Before Morley left, in desperation, Jack said, "Morley, I want out of my contract that I have with you guys. I have had enough. I'm willing to take my punishment for the crimes I've committed in Vietnam. I'll go to Leavenworth if I have to Morley. Please release me from your contract," pleaded Jack

Morley looked at Jack sympathetically he was realizing the Jack was going through the early stages post traumatic shock syndrome.

A week later, Morely met with Jack "OK Jack, here is the deal I'm going to offer you. We have one more assignment for you. Complete it and then you're finished with us."

"What is it?" Jack asked cautiously.

"The government of Malaysia has heard about our covert assault team going into hot spots for covert live action using our special designed tactical helicopters in close quarters to get in and out of hot spots. They have asked our State Department if we could assist them with a covert operation about putting down a Chinese Communist uprising headquarteredclose to the Thai border. Of course, this is another unofficial covert operation, and you will not get any credit for it Jack,"

"What do I have to do in order to get out of this contract I have with you guys?" Jack asked inquisitively.

"Their government wants us to fly several of those experimental aircraft you just flown with an elite squad of Malaysian Rangers to ferret out Chinese Communists who are hiding in Southern Thailand," said Morley. "All you have to do is fly close to the jungle canopy to prevent the communists from seeing you so you don't get shot down and then drop those Rangers off at their landing zone. Once the rangers have done their job, you'll return to the LZ and return to base. It requires a skilled pilot Jack, because of tree top level flying, in hot humid tropical weather with often unpredictable severe rainy weather and lightning strikes, similar to what you experienced in the Philippines. What do you say Jack?"

"Malaysia isn't that a Muslim country?" Jack enquired Morley.

"Yes, however, they are openly pro west, a former British Colony, they speak English and Malay and Chinese and some Indian dialects They have to keep a low profile so they don't incite retribution or reprisals from King Faizal of Saudi Arabia and other extreme conservative Muslim countries if they should lean too far to the west. That is why they will not acknowledge your presence and our equipment but will gratefully accept it but they want this communist insurgency to be eliminated from their political landscape. However, it will be kept under cover so to speak, you will not get any recognition for your actions and we will deny your presence and not send in anyone to help you if you should get shot down."

Jack took a few moments to think about this new assignment.

Looking at Morley sternly, "Ok Morley here's the deal. First, I want my sister to know where I am at all times, in case my family needs to retrieve my body if I get shot down. Secondly, I want this in writing that our contract is terminated once I complete and finish this mission in Malaysia. Thirdly, I want you to contact the French Embassy in Manila and leave a message there for Monsieur François Chang to contact my sister Tanya in Honolulu, regarding the whereabout of François's sister Francine. Fourth, I want Cam Hayes to go with me and be my co-pilot if he wishes to go and volunteer for the assignment. Also, I want my record expunged regarding my crimes in South Vietnam. I want nothing hanging over meLastly, I also want recognition to be entered into my service record for all the special assignments I have done for you. I want my family to be proud of me and not ashamed of my service record if I should die on one of your covert assignments. Morley you can no longer black mail me for your dangerous assignments. Otherwise send me to Leavenworth I think I have had enough excitement for one lifetime."

Without a moment's hesitation, "Done!" Morley was anxious and eager to get Jacks cooperation. "I promise I will fulfill our bargain."

"When do I leave?".

"How about we give you six months rest and recuperation at your home in Honolulu in order to get things ready and give you some rest."

An hour or so later Jack met up with Tanya at the Kirk's Mess Hall.

"Well Tanya, I have your answer about notifying François at the French Embassy in Manila.My people have direct connections with our State Department they promised me that they will notify the French Embassy in Manila to have François contact you so that you can convey to him what happened to Francine while she was in the Philippines, if you should wish to do so Tanya."

"Yes, of course, no problem, Jack I need to help François resolve his family issues so that he can go on with his life, Jack let's go home to mom and dad,"

"We should be there in a week or so Tanya; I have six months leave coming to me." He sighed happily.

Paris

"Ah, François is it good to see you again," said Renee Montrose. "The embassy in Beirut has advised us that you did a stellar job. You went above and beyond the call of your duty to us. You put your life on the line, all we wanted was the need for basic intelligence gathering and now you come back to us with a bullet wound to your arm."

"My arm is feeling fine as long as I keep it in my sling but I need several more operations and some recovery time, probably in about six or seven months or so my arm will be healed enough for me to travel. The surgeons at the American Hospital did a great job in repairing parts of my arm about a month ago I believe. But now, I need to go to French hospitals to complete the process."

"Marveilleuxqv", (marvelous) François, I have some more interesting news regarding your sister Francine. It seems that Francine was transported on an American ship the USS Kirk. Once the Kirk docked in Manila Bay your sister was airlifted to a small clinic close to an army base called Camp Navarro close to a city called Zamboanga in the Southern Philippines. We know she received medical care at the clinic serviced by several nuns. However, other than that, our intelligence staff could no longer retrieve any additional intelligence. The key people who were there have all moved on to other places. However, there is a Colonel Cueva who is still there, he is the commandant of Camp Navarro. He may be able to give you more news regarding Francine. We have sent him a letter introducing you. Perhaps he can help you."

"Is she still alive? Blurted our François.

"We are not sure, but we believe she has been receiving medical care and therefor she must still be alive."

"Louange dieu" (praise god) said a relieved François. "I'll fly to Manila immediately, and then I will go to this Camp Navarro" he said hastily.

"Not so fast, not so fast, I have more good news for you mon ami.(my friend)Our government has provided you an airline ticket to the Philippines. You'll have a connection in Manila Airport so you can change planes with no more than a two-hour layover so you can go directly to the province of Mindanao then to Zamboanga City. And as I mentioned, we've arranged for you to meet with Colonel Cueva. I think he can fill you in on some of the details that you've been seeking., Let's say it is a small gratuity from our government for your courage and endangering your life in the line of duty so to speak when it was not so necessary. But first François before you travel, you must give your wounded arm time to heal, be patient mon ami. (my friend) Give it time François please, be patient.When you're ready to travel, we'll have all your documents ready as well as some travelling money for you. Your ticket will take you straight to Zamboanga you do not need to go to our embassy. All of your travel papers will be in good order.In the meantime, you can stay at the Hotel Regina on us, not too far from the Louvre and so you can get well and enjoy the night life of Pari. Bon Chance mon ami." (good luck my friend)

François's arm needed one more surgical procedure in order for him to get well enough for him to travel to the Philippines. Almost seven months had gone by as François arrived at Manila Airport on August 15th1976 almost twenty two hours later from the time he departed. He was stiff and tired from his long flight his arm still ached but glad to be in the Philippines. However, now he was eager to get to Camp Navarro. Despite Tanya's request he had no thoughts or desire to check in with the French Embassy to get his messages. He did catch his connecting flight after a two-hour layover and landed in Zamboanga International Airport several hours later. Checking in at the Lavina Hotel which was close to the airport, it was there he decided he would make his base.He had phoned Colonel Cueva and requested an appointment. Taxi cabs were abundant and so it was fairly easy to get Camp Navarro. On the morning of the 15th, François arrived at Camp Navarro to keep his appointment.He was greeted by a Filipino Armed Forces Sargent who escorted François to Colonel Cueva's office.

"Colonel Cueva" as he spoke in English. Good morning my name is François Chang, my government and I have requested an appointment with you."

"Yes, I have been expecting you Mr. Chang regarding your sister is it not? Before we begin would you like some coffee or Filipino cake, or perhaps a cigarette.,

"No thank you, I am quite comfortable," as he was eager to hear Colonel Cueva's latest news.

"Do you mind if I smoke?"

"Not at all,' replied François.

Colonel Cueva reached for a pack of Marlboros, lit his cigarette and took a long drag while exhaling smoke through his nostrils.

"Colonel, I have been searching for my sister since she left South Vietnam almost two years ago. The latest news that I have received so far from my government was that she was sent by the Americans to a clinic somewhere here in Zamboanga to receive some sort of medical care, after that I don't know what happened to her. My government is unable to tell me anything else."

"Yes Mr. Chang, I had some of my people make some recent enquiries for you. However, I have bad news for you. I sadly and unfortunately must inform I you, that she was killed by a fanatical terrorist. She died in a heroic fashion. Eventually was buried in a graveyard next to the Church of the Immaculate Conception here in Zamboanga City. Did you know she might have been pregnant? The father was an American helicopter pilot, but we do not know for sure."

François was stunned with the news and sat silently in disbelief. Dead! Perhaps pregnant! How could he not know this?

"Mr. Chang, I have the address of the Church of the Immaculate Conception I'm sure you would like to see the graveyard, it is the thirteenth gravestone from the front gate" said Colonel Cueva in consolatory voice, "Right next to the church wall. I'm sorry you have had to come all this way for such bad news, but I prefer to tell you face to face and answer all of your questions one at a time rather than write you letters."

François recognized that Colonel Cueva had gone out of his way to retrieve the last bit of information that François needed to know what had happened to his sister. Pulling himself together he thanked Colonel Cueva for his due diligence.

"Thank you for your efforts and giving me the address of the Church and the gravesite where she is buried. I'll I probably go there tomorrow afternoon and see the grave site. You mentioned she died in a heroic fashion; how did she die Colonel Cueva?"

"The story is, she threw herself on a live grenade to protect the father of her unborn baby and also the soldiers who came to rescue her. Evidently, she and other Catholic Nuns had been held hostage by a fanatical group of Muslim terrorists for ransom. Francine evidently had her arm in a heavy cast to repair her broken arm as she was shot leaving South Vietnam. Our doctors here at Camp Navarro were treating her broken arm.The helicopter pilot was also injured from the grenade and had to be medevacked to an American Army hospital in Honolulu. There were also an American special forces operations team involved designed to root out insurgents and rescue hostages. They escaped unharmed. Overall, the operation was a success other than your sister and her baby. Another German nun was a fatality in the operation. Your sister seemed to be a very brave woman Mr. Chang."

"I'm wondering Colonel, did you find out the name of the helicopter pilot who might have been the father of her baby"? François said curiously.

"Yes, I believe his name was Lieutenant Jackson Garron, he and the Green Beret's rescue team were all stationed here for a short time at Camp Navarro. The Special Forces team were led by a soldier named Sargent Holiday."

"Why do you ask? Do you know them?" Colonel Cueva asked inquisitively as he saw the excitement in François's face?

"Yes, that's incredible, they rescued me less than a year ago in Beirut from a similar hostage situation. I know them, they saved my life. I took a round from a terrorist injuring my arm it took me almost seven months to the point where I can travel and use my arm." François shouted excitedly at Colonel Cueva." Once again, the news was electrifying, such a remarkable coincidence, another fate of war and yet he had not known anything about it until now.

Back in his hotel room François rummaged through his mind the final chapter of Francine's life and the past events that bought him here to the Southern part of the Philippines. How extraordinary that extreme life changing events were born from grandiose pollical ideas and schemes in faraway lands. Those grand ideas were implemented in order to change the world. Now those historical events trickled down to he and his family. Those life changing events and could never be undone. His family fled from North Vietnam to South Vietnam eventually working at the Michelin rubber tree plantation. And then once again, fate stepped in sending him to Lebanon and eventually here in Zamboanga. All this time it was Jack Garron who had rescued him in Beirut, and now he found out he was the father of his sister's baby. Even more incredible, it was Jack's sister, Tanya, whom he had fallen in love with and wanted to marry her. All this time neither of them knew the identity of the other. How extraordinary life had become.

"I have no one now, my family is gone. Tomorrow, I think I'll go and find Francine's gravesite and put some flowers on her grave and say goodbye. At least I'll know where she is buried" he thought to himself. "After that, perhaps I can start a new life with Tanya if she will have me, maybe even start a family of my own one day, I'll reach out to her tomorrow after I visit Francine's grave. God willing perhaps we can meet in Honolulu in the coming days," as he continued making his plans and reorganizing his life.

And so, on August 16thin the year of our Lord 1976, a little after 4pm, François stepped into the flower shop to buy flowers to place them on Francine's grave. The flower shop was located in a quiet three-story tenement row housing one block long with various small shops and restaurants built of hollow block bricks on either side of the flower shop. Above the shops on the top two floors were apartments and living quarters.The small flower shop was perhaps only fifty meters away from Francine's gravesite which was adjacent to the Church of the Immaculate Conception. François bought a dozen white Lilies and a dozen Gardenias to place on the Francine's grave. His quest to find out what had happened to Francine had come to its conclusion. Paying for his flowers in Filipino pesos, he began to turn away from the counter carrying his flowers, happily thinking about what he going to say to Tanya. At that precise moment in time and space François lost his life.

Circling the globe running up and down the east coast of Asia and the West Coast of North and South America sits the Pacific Ring of Fire. A huge rift, in the Earth's crust, an enormous and gigantic tear that has waxed new land from its interior and waned old land back again into the earth's interior. This geological process has been going on for. millions of years long before man ever evolved from the sea. The movement of land along the Pacific Ring of Fire will probably continue do so for millions of years yet to come. The Earth continuously renews itself and revitalizes itself in ongoing episodic natural events. The Philippine Islands closely straddle or in some parts sit directly on top of Pacific Ring of Fire. As François was about to leave the flower shop at 4:16 in the afternoon, a huge 8.0 earthquake on the Richter Scale hit Zamboanga City. An earthquake of 8 on the Richter Scale is a very violent and malefic earthquake. A reading of a one-point jump on the scale is not just an increase of one magnitude but an increase of one hundred-fold in intensity and violence. Almost instantly, eighty thousand people were killed in Mindanao when the earthquake's epicenter located in the Sulu Sea about seven hundred kilometers away from the mainland of Mindanao. It struck with such ferocity that it demolished the town of Zamboanga City almost instantly. François lost his life at that precise moment from the collapsing three story rowhouse that housed the flower shop. Moments thereafter as a result of the earth's crust slipping violently and abruptly along the fault zone, an eight-meter-tall Tsunami wave, traveling approximately at five hundred kilometers per hour washed ashore destroying buildings and flooding surrounding low-lying areas. François was never seen again; his body as well was probably thousands of others were swept out to sea. In a few moments it was all over, a hundred thousand people were homeless thousands were injured. The Catholic Church blamed the earthquake as God's punishment to the people of Mindanao because of sins caused by homosexual activity and promiscuity both inside and outside the bonds of marriage. Of course, the consequences of one have nothing to do with the other.

"Jack it's been almost six weeks since I have heard from François, I know there is something wrong. He was supposed to have been here in Honolulu by now. My last letter from him is that he was going to find his sister's grave siteHe should have been here by now. As far as I know, he didn't even check into the French Embassy as I had asked him, he seemed to refuse to go. I think he was in such a hurry to get to Zamboanga City. Do you think he was hurt in that big earthquake six weeks ago?"

"I don't know," mused Jack, as he was thinking about a day's sailing as the wind was mild and the sea was fairly calm.

"Jack this is important," protested Tanya. "Can you find out for me please; can you call your friends who have access to this kind of information and find out what we need to know? François was our friend and perhaps saved our lives," as she pleaded to Jacks sense of duty to François's heroics in Beirut.

"Ok!" Jack said sighing deeply. "Probably the weather will change anyway which would make sailing difficult," he thought to himself. "I'll go later on to the American Embassy.". he said to himself.

A week later Jack was able to retrieve some news from Morley Warbuton's friends in the CIA about François's whereabouts.

Tanya was sitting on the Lanai watching the outgoing tide as a lone Barracuda was circling the surface looking for shrimp.

"Tanya!" he shouted as he sat down next to her "I have some difficult news to tell you. Six weeks ago, François left Paris for the Philippines, evidently François never checked into the French Embassy he was in a hurry and went straight to Zamboanga to see Colonel Cueva at Camp Navarro. Colonel Cueva explained that François and he did talk about his missing sister and where she was buried. The very next day when François went to see his sister's gravesite is when that big earthquake hit the southern Philippines.Colonel Cueva sent out a search party in the area of the damaged church and cemetery in order to find survivors as well as looking for François's body but he was never found. Colonel Cueva believes that François and the other gravesites in the cemetery were scoured out and swept out to sea with the receding Tsunami. The Cemetery had been scoured clean of all human remains. He was in the worst part of Zamboanga when the earthquake and Tsunami devastated Mindanao Providence."

Tanya could not believe her ears, but everything seemed to make sense, otherwise she would have heard from him by now. Sniffling through her tears she opened up a letter that was sitting on the lanai table. It was from Kaiser Permanente Hospital she had been accepted as a RN in the Orthopedic Department. She had just passed her nursing exam a week earlier.

Jack sat down in sadness from learning about the truth of François's circumstances. Sitting quietly and sipping a cold beer, he watched the lone Barracuda continuing circling the surface; looking for its prey but unable to catch it on the outgoing tide of Hawaii Kai's Lagoon. He began to think about his new assignment in Malaysia. He did not like the idea of going to Malaysia, but it was his final commitment to the agreement he made with Captain Winchester and Morley Warburton. After this last assignment he would be free to do whatever he wished.

Ironically, Jack never knew how close he was to knowing about François's background and Jack's relationship with François's sister Francine. François life was briefly intertwined with Jack's life. Each one had no idea of the circumstances that brought them together. Jack and François were so close and yet so far away as it was with Francine. They never knew of each other's past. The fates and fortunes of war can be very fickle indeed.

"Malaysia, where in the hell is Malaysia?" Cam asked Jack learning about his new assignment, "and we'll be flying at tree top level to get Malaysian Rangers to their landing zone so they can an assault a Chinese Communist Camp? Holy smokes what a mission. Well, I guess I had better find out where Malaysia is on the world map."

"Yup, you better do that Cam, but we still have a few months of leave before we report for duty. Let's make the most of it."

"Jack, being assigned.to you as your co-pilot is becoming an adventure in itself. Shit, I better get used to it. I'll see you after I recover from drinking a case of beer and that's all at one time. I think I'll need it. See you in Malaysia Jack.

"Cam before you go," said Jack quietly, "this will be my last mission, once I've completed my assignment, I'm done with Captain Winchester and Morley Warburton forever. I've had enough excitement for one lifetime I don't think I can take this anymore. I want out Cam" he said earnestly. "How much more time do you have Cam?"

"I have one more year to go Jack, either I will re-enlist for another four years or I will resign my officer's commission and return to civilian life. I'm not sure what I'll do" Cam said while pondering his fate..

PART IV

CHAPTER XIV

Kuala Lumpur Malaysia, July 1976

The meeting at the Hotel Sentosa, which was located in the seedier and darker part of Kuala Lumpur did not go well between Ah Hing, Botak Chin, Abdallah Bin Laden and his nephew Osama.

"Look", Abdallah said in English, "we know you Chinese Communists want to dislodge the current government of Malaysia. We want to supply you with arms and equipment. so that you can continue your insurgency against the current government but at a price of course."

"Why?" said Botak Chin who was a notorious bank robber. "Why do we need your help?"

"We're concerned that perhaps the southern portion of the Philippines may secede from its current government and join the Malaysian Federation. We're afraid if that should happen that we in Saudi Arabia may lose religious and political persuasion in Mindanao. Malaysia is much too progressive and allows too much religious freedom and leans too far to the west." Abdallah said in protest. "If we would lose influence in Mindanao then it would go against our strict Sharia laws and our sphere of influence would diminish considerably. Then perhaps Indonesia will be next to follow suit, Indonesia is the biggest Muslim country in the world. There are those of us in Saudi Arabia who don't want Malaysia to annex Mindanao with Malaysian Federation. We need to return to a more conservative religious control. We don't like Malaysia's Islamic form of democratic government it is much too open and reflects the values of the West, even their flag looks like the United States' flag there is nothing that symbolizes Islam.

"It's true that we want to overthrow the current government and turn Malaysia into a communist state." said Ah Hing However, we don't care about your religion. Our Communist brothers in the North can supply us with all the weapons we need without extracting a heavy price from us," said Ah Hing defiantly. "There are many of our Chinese citizens here in Malaysia who are angry at the government and would give us their support if we could change the current state of affairs. I am sorry, but we do not need your support." Ah Hing said with finality.

"Why are you angry and so determined to refuse our help" asked Osama curiously.

"After the war we gained our independence from England in 1949 we Malaysian Chinese became angry and upset because the newly formed Malaysian government began forcing us out of our land and business holdings and forced us to give them to the ethnic Malays. It's we Chinese who built the business growth in Malaysia, not the Malays. The government wants the Malays to have equal footing in commerce and business at the same level as to what we Chinese have accomplished over the past years. The only pay us fifteen percent of what our holdings are worth. Worst of all governmental policies are always in favor of those Malays we Chinese get left out concerning our future and social issues. It's our Chinese foundations who built this country not the Malays and now we are second class citizens. Yes, we're terribly angry."

"How will you get money to provide you with the necessary equipment to feed your insurgency?" said Osama.

"My brother in arms here," said Ah Hing "robs banks for us. He only robs banks that are owned by foreigners, Malay or Indian owned, he never robs Chinese banks. He provides us with a steady stream of income for our cause. The Malaysian government is too slow, dim witted and too stupid to catch him" said Ah Hing. Also, our Chinese secret societies supply us with secret donations to keep our cause going strong."

"I am so fast on my Suzuki motorcycle that the Malaysian police and security forces can never catch me with their slow lumbering British personnel carriers. They don't even have helicopters to track me or ferry troops to ambush me," Botak Chin bragged with pride.

"The British left the Malaysian Government with left over world war two surplus and outdated. equipment," Botak Chin continued. "I simply outrun them and then disappear into the jungle or caves where their equipment can't go or find me. With my fast Suzuki motorcycle, I lose them every time," he said proudly.

"Mister Abdallah, I don't think we want your help to overthrow our government at this time. My communist brothers and us can do it for ourselves. In time we'll be able to turn Malaysia into a communist state."

"Is that your final answer?" asked Osama.

"Yes, we'll keep you in mind if we need your help to buy equipment and arms, but at his time we can do it on our own," Ah Hing said with finality.

"And so, it must have been written Osama" said Abdallah with disappointment in his voice. "So, if this is how it is going to be then King Faisal and our religious council will not be happy with us. May peace be with you mister Ah Hing and mister Botak Chin. Now then, can you show us where those famous Malay women are? I have heard that their passion is unbridled and unequaled anywhere in South East Asia. Osama and I would like to go home well satisfied, so to speak." Abdallah said eagerly.

"Yes of course. but at a small price it is only fair," smiled Botak Chin.

"Botak, the next time we meet it must be at another place a public place so that we blend into the crowd. I don't want agents from the Malaysian security Forces spying on us," he said in Cantonese.

"OK, then I will meet you at the end of July during the August Moon Festival in Kuantan on the East Coast. There is a dim sum shop there called Fook Yu. Meet me there after the sun goes down. There will be lots of our Chinese people milling around celebrating the Moon Festival so we will blend in with the crowd without being too suspicious."

"Where do you plan your next bank robbery, we are running low on cash?"

The town of Ipoh on the West Coast has the Bumiputra Bank of Malaysia. I will use my homemade pistol I made it in my bike shop. Even the guards do not carry weapons.

"Be careful my friend you know it is a capital crime if you get caught with a weapon. You know by law It is forbidden to carry firearms. One of our fighters got caught carrying a pistol. He received twenty lashes of the rotan, a splinted bamboo cane dipped in horse urine and then sentenced to hang sometime next year. In the meantime, he is in agony from the infections he received from that dirty rotan. That bastard Lee Kuan Yu started that policy in Singapore to end the violence caused by criminals who carry firearms. And now Malaysia has adopted the same policy."

"Never mind my friend, my Suzuki can take me away as fast as the wind. I can "makan angin" (eat the air) Botak Chin said in Malay. "The security forces will never catch me," he boasted once more.

"Well, Jack, I did what I promised to do," as they met at a Chinese restaurant and bar called the Coliseum in the heart of Kuala Lumpur. The Coliseum catered to Australians, Europeans and Americans because of their pork entrees and alcoholic drinks.

"I looked up Malaysia, because I didn't know where in the hell it was," said Cam Hayes. I found this in a cyclopedia. He described Malaysia to Jack."It's a peninsula that seems to be similar to in both shape and size of Florida. It sits almost on the equator where it is sandwiched between Thailand to the north and Singapore to the south. Malaysia is a Muslim country, but it used to be a British Colony they can mostly speak English besides their own national language of Bahasa Malaysia but now it is an independent country. Can you imagine that Jack?" English speaking in the middle of South East Asia, I didn't think that was possible."

"Yup they're kinda in a bind right now they're Muslims who provide religious freedom to their Indian and Chinese citizens but receive tremendous pressure from those ultra conservative Muslim countries who want Malaysia to give up their western ways. In addition to that Cam, there is a communist uprising here, trying to overthrow the government and turn Malaysia into a communist state. President Ford has agreed to send us here on a covert mission to see if we can help the Malaysian Security Forces stamp out the communists by striking at their bases somewhere in Northern Malaysia or Southern Thailand. Tomorrow we'll go to Butterworth Airbase in Penang to pick up our crafts and fly them to the Royal Malaysian airbase at Sultan Haji Ahmad Shah in Kuantan located somewhere on the East Coast. That'll be our base of operations. We'll meet Morley Warburton and Captain Winchester there at the base. Captain Winchester told me that those modified crafts we flew in Lebanon will be ready for this mission, Let's hope we don't have to refuel in midair again Cam."

"That's a roger Jack" said Cam hopefully.

"Colonel Hussein I want you to meet Lieutenants Jackson Garron and Cam Hays they will be at your disposal Colonel," said Captain Winchester with Morely Warbuton. We will leave you in the capable hands of Colonel Hussein, he is in charge of an elite unit of Malaysian Army Rangers. He will be your CO."

"Apa Khaber?," (how are you) It is an honor to meet the both of you. Don't worry about the language it is our Muslim custom to greet people with an open heart with that he warmly shook their hands and touched his heart. Welcome to Malaysia. I hear that both of you are veterans of the war in Lebanon and you Lieutenant Garron also a veteran of a clandestine campaign in Mindanao region in the Philippines. We have a lot to talk about later. We gratefully need your skills and experience. This will be your headquarters and training base it is the Royal Malaysian Airforce Base here at Sultan Haji Ahmad Shah in Kuantan. You will find we have a strange mixture of Kings, Sultans and democratically elected prime minister and parliament who govern our country. Malaysia is an unusual combination of an eclectic array of cultures and customs both East and West Christian and Muslim.

"Thank you, Colonel, both Jack and I will do our best for you and your country," said Cam eagerly without hesitation.

"Thank you, gentleman, in the meantime, Captain Winchester will show you where you can bivouac. Tomorrow we'll meet and I'll welcome you to Malaysia. I want you to get to know us first. We will meet tomorrow morning in the officer's mess 0800 and I will bring you up to speed so we can start training as a team."

"Say Captain," Jack said, after they had finished the meeting, "don't you and Morley ever get tired jumping into the world's hot spots?" said Jack. As they headed for the officers Quonset Hut to bed down for the night.

"Not at all, we serve at the pleasure of the White House as long as we feel that President Ford needs us, then we will do our best. It is what we have chosen to do until President Ford decides otherwise or is no longer president of the United States. It is as simple as that Jack; also, you guys are lucky" said Captain Winchester.

"How's that Captain?" said Jack.

"Your quarters have air conditioning. A rarity in these parts." Replied Captain Winchester.

"Ok Captain, you're a real war horse, show us the way where we can bed down and eat at the chow hall and thank god for air conditioning it's downright hot and humid over here in this part of the world. See you later gentleman" he said with finality in his voice.

At 0800 Jack and Cam met Colonel Hussein and their ten-man team of Malaysian Army Rangers. The team of two officers, and eight NCO's. The rangers were a mixture of ethnic Malays, Chinese and Indian cadre. All spoke English well as well as their own individual distinct dialects.

"How were your breakfasts gentlemen?" as he was speaking to Jack and Cam after breakfast the next morning.

"It was unusual," Cam said eagerly, we had a plate of rice, with curry, sprinkled with some sort of dried little fish, chili peppers and two boiled eggs on top. We had to use our hands, it was very spicy, but tasty, it was not bad, as Jack looked at him in amazement as Cam's enthusiasm bubbled out of him. "Ah yes gentleman "addressing Cam and Jack, "you will not find Kellogg's cereal, bacon or ham and eggs here in Malaysia nor will you find any beer on our base. We are a Muslim country alcohol is forbidden. However, if you desire to quench your thirst you can easily find it in downtown Kuantan in some of the Indian and Chinese bars. As for your breakfast dish we Malays call it Nasi Lamak, a staple in my country."

Addressing the assault team, Colonel Hussein introduced himself. "Anyway, my name is Colonel Hussein, I will be in charge of this special assault group. I grew up close by here in a place called Kampong Sungai Karang. I speak the kings English as well as our Bahasa Malaysia and also Cantonese. However, I am still struggling with Indian dialects I can't seem to wobble my head as fast as our Tamil cadre are able to do," drawing a small round of laughter. "I grew up here on the East Coast and was educated in public schoolsMy government sent me to Stanford to get my BA in History, and then Sandhurst Military College in the UK for my masters in guerilla warfare tactics in the Philippines during World War Two. Since I owed the government my education, I chose the Army as a good place to serve my six-year obligation. And so here I am. Our team will consist of two very experienced American helicopter pilots Lieutenants Garron and Hays, as well as a uniquely trained enlisted men of our Army Ranger team. We have also two of our own pilots, on our team who will be our co-pilots, Captain Sivasambo and Captain Leel must make this perfectly clear these two American Officers and their crafts are here in a clandestine fashion, their role will be top secret, their role as pilots is not to be given out to any public forum. Our mission is to destroy Chinese Communists bases that hold caches of supplies and arms somewhere in Southern Thailand." Addressing Cam and Jack, "In time gentleman, you will get to know our ten-man team you will find their names very unusual so don't worry if you cannot remember them at first, and they will get to know you as well. We'll train in all sorts of weather, day and night flying no more than ten meters over the jungle canopy as well as skimming over the ocean. Once we have confirmation of the locations of their base camps then we'll launch our surprise attack. Rangers, if you do not have any questions then you're dismissed. Lieutenants Garron and Hays please see me. Since we have a little time can you tell me about you strange looking air craft, I have never seen anything like it."

"Well sir" Jack said, "it is an experimental craft we have used it once in Lebanon with mixed success. At night, people think it was some sort of alien flying machine. because of its unusual shape with moveable rotors on each wing that turns this craft into either a helicopter or then it can turn into a fixed wing aircraft. That long pole sticking out the nose is our refueling capability for midair refueling. The skin is made out of some sort of synthetic composite materials called Kevlar, we found it prevented small arms fire from penetrating the craft. It also has night vision cameras so both pilot and copilot can fly at night for nighttime operations. I see we now have a new nine-millimeter machine gun installed under the nose and also, we have new thermal imaging cameras. We never had those before in Lebanon."

"Cam also added, Sir, it also has a range of about seven hundred fifty kilometers and get us up to a to a top speed of two hundred fifty knots per hour. But one of the most unusual things about our craft is its noise reduction almost by seventy five percent compared to similar rotary craft. "he said with pride and enthusiasm.

"American technology is utterly amazing; Malaysia has long way to go before we can develop or purchase such craft. The British, when they gave us our independence in 1948, left us with junk, old vintage munitions and arms, transport vehicles, tanks, personnel carriers and planes that breakdown frequently and often we can't find replacement parts. They are basically useless in a country that is ninety percent jungle, we need modern technology to fight the warfare we're' facing now such as these amazing aircrafts. We have this Chinese chap called Botak Chin, he is running us ragged, he robs our banks with open disregard to our security forces. we simply cannot catch him with the equipment we have on hand."

"What does he do with the money he takes?" asked Cam.

"We believe he is giving the money to the Chinese Communists to buy arms for their insurgency against our government. That's one of the reasons why you are here. In time I will tell you more. It was our Secretary of Defense Abdul

Taib Mahmud who heard about your exploits in Lebanon who recommended to our prime minister to contact your State Dept to bring you here. Our Defense Minister will eventually come to our base to meet you and provide us with critical information for the eventual attack on the communist bases. Tomorrow, however, I will bring you two guys to my house in Sungai Karang so we can eat and talk after evening prayers. My family already knows you have been invited for supper. So tomorrow we will meet and I will introduce you to Malaysian culture while we still have a little time."

Kampong Sungai Karang or Coral River as it translates from Bahasa Malaysia, borders the South China Sea, about twelve kilometers north of Kuantan. Following the coast road to Colonel Hussein's home, both Jack and Cam noticed how beautiful and pristine the landscape became. Miles and miles of long languid beaches of white sand, coconut trees arching out over the beaches reaching out to gently breaking sky-blue waves. A soft wind blowing on shore keeping the temperature pleasant. Not a cloud was in the brilliant blue sky It was not unlike Hawaii, Cam thought to himself.

On the way riding in the colonel's jeep Colonel Hussein pointed out a fishing village called Kampong Beserah

"Jack, I bet you don't know what this place is famous for?"

"Why no not at all, is this a trivia question, I've never heard of it, have you Cam?"

"Nope" was his short answer.

"It was here in world war two, that the British surrendered to Japan, realizing that Singapore and Malaya would quickly fall. Somewhere around here you can still find a plaque commemorating that piece of forgotten history, but I think the jungle has reclaimed it now. I want to show you something interesting why we lost so quickly to Japan."

Pulling off the coast road, Colonel Hussein drove his jeep a few meters down a dirt road stopping directly in front of what appeared to be a complex of many large concrete bunkers facing the ocean. Most of the bunkers had been reclaimed by the jungle but some could still be seen if you looked hard enough.

"What do you guys see?" asked Colonel Hussein inquisitively.

Cam said," they look like bunkers of some kind, at least ten or so."

"You are right Cam, they're British artillery emplacements designed to repel Japanese attacks from the sea. The British thought the conquest of Malaya would eventually emanate from seaward. So, the artillery pieces were fixed pointing only in one direction, they were always facing the sea. A British general thought the eventual attack and conquest of Malaya and Singapore would come as a naval landing engagement. Instead, the Japanese landed their army troops in the north in open areas just south of the border of Thailand. They were able to march their troops and vehicles southward striking swiftly into the heart of Malaya and then attack us from the West. The artillery pieces in those concrete bunkers were useless, they could not rotate 180 degrees to repel the Japanese assault from the West. Malaya and Singapore were lost in no time at all, because of a huge tactical mistake. Anyway, it is a historical fact that is now long forgotten, but I still find it quite fascinating," Colonel Hussein said quietly.

"Amazing" said Cam as he realized the huge military blunder. "What British General must have come up with that bonehead idea. Not much has been learned from World War One," he thought for to himself

"Let's go we have steamed rice, fried fish, chicken curry, Roti Chanai it is a kind of rice pancake to be dipped into curry, exotic fruits of Durian and Jackfruit waiting for us. My wife and daughter will be impatient with us if we are late," said Colonel Hussein to his two American guests.

Colonel Hussein stopped at his mosque or masjid for his evening prayers. The small village of Sungai Karang had been carved out of the jungle away from mainstream life., However of about two hundred and fifty individuals it had enough of a population to a government run primary school and a masjid for prayers. Colonel Hussein did not take long and proceeded to his waiting family along with Jack and Cam.

"First, you must take off your shoes it is how we keep our house clean, change your clothes, wear your shirts. I have two sarongs waiting for you. Tie them as tight as you can so they don't fall down. You will find them much more comfortable than trousers when we sit on the floor to eat." Colonel Hussein's house was very familiar to Jack's grandparents in Bohol. Due to occasional typhoons and heavy rains the house was made of wood and raised on stilts to avoid the high floods that bad weather brought with it. Being raised on stilts it allowed for goats, chickens, and ducks to live underneath to avoid the heat of the day and also eat the scraps of food that were pushed through the gaps of the wooden floorboards. It was also covered with a corrugated rusty tin roof that occasionally leaked when it rained. As he introduced his family to Cam and Jack, it was his daughter Amrah that caught Cam's attention. It was a momentary fleeting glance when each made eye contact with the other. Cam would go on to say it was like a bolt of electricity going through his body when he first saw

Amrah for the first time. Amrah had finished high school and was preparing to take her exams for entrance to the University of Malaya in Kuala Lumpur. She was interested in business administration and felt she could do well so that she could catch up with what the Chinese already knew. Covering her hair with her Hijab as respect for Islam she only momentarily glanced at Cam. Her Malaysian attire was a smart looking, well-fitting enhancing her body, a cotton blouse of a bright green with, red and yellow Hibiscus flowers. Her matching sarong was tied around her waist and fell to the floor that covered her ankles. She was stunning, unlike the women he saw in Lebanon who wore their black bulky burkas with only slits for their eyes. It was the only part of their body that was not covered. Amirah's soft brown skin and dark eyes were mesmerizing she did not need to wear any make up. Her appearance exuded from her naturally without being pretentious. Cam could not refrain from sneaking looks at her at every opportunity without being rude to his host

"Let's eat" said Colonel Hussein after sitting on a mat of thatched bamboo leaves. Cam and Jack had changed into their sarongs and met the rest of his family. Before eating each one washed their hands because there were no forks or knives. They continued to eat their food with their hands which was placed on dishes while sitting on a thatched mat lit only by candles. Cam caught on very quickly how to eat rice by scooping up a ball of rice with his right hand and then flicking the rice with his thumb as though he was playing marbles into his mouth.

"Where is your family won't they join us?" asked Cam hoping to see Amah again.

"They will eat in the kitchen after we eat first. It is our tradition." said Colonel Hussein. This is the house where I was born and raised, even though I have traveled the world, I have my degrees from Stanford and the War College in England, and I'm a Colonel in the Malaysian Army. I still prefer to come home here in my kampong and live my traditional life as I have known it. My Malay name is Hussein bin Haji Mohammed Noor. Haji because I have already done my pilgrimage to Mecca. I'm very proud of my heritage and my Muslim religion that is why I wear my white skull cap when I am not in uniform. We Malays want to learn and grow with the rest of the world using Allah and the Holy Quran as our guide and the Prophet Mohammad as his messenger. But we must tread carefully as we have Muslim countries in the Middle East who are not as liberal as we are" he said dutifully.

Both Jack and Cam enjoyed the hot and spicy foods. Eating with their hands was awkward at times there was no silverware or napkins. However, sitting in a circle lit by candles brought a sense of intimacy and sharing of stories. It was good to get away from military cooking and military lifestyle. All drank copious amounts of Arabic coffee and coconut milk. Eating Durian was the most exotic fruit they had ever eaten. Colonel Hussein called it, the king of all fruits.

"What do you think of Durian Cam?" said Colonel Hussein.

"Well, the skin smells of thirty-day old dirty sweaty socks or spoiled fruit or something like that, but that soft pasty yellowish meat that covers those large seeds is absolutely fantastic, I have never had anything quite like it," Cam said while licking his fingers of the tasty fruit. Once again Jack looked at Cam in amazement as Cam was rapidly acquiescing into Malaysian culture

"Colonel Hussein," Cam said, "may I use your bathroom?" Cam assumed Colonel Hussein's house had running water and a bathroom to go with it.

"Yes, of course, but I must warn you we do not have running water or electricity you must go outside if you wish to use our bathroom, once outside you must look to the right between all the bamboo trees and then you will see a well beaten path, follow it for about 20 meters. Once you reach the river you will see a wide wooden plank traversing out from the river bank, that is where you will go to the bathroom." said Colonel Hussein.

Cam was confused, but not wishing to seem rude or ignorant, he followed Colonel Hussein's instructions. He made his way to the river's edge through grove of palm trees and found the plank that Colonel Hussein described to him. Not wishing to fall into the river, he carefully and slowly walked to the far end of the plank, lifted up his sarong, and with great relief urinated into the river. Immediately after Cam was finished there came a loud cheer and whistles coming from a group of boys who had followed Cam in secret and silence to see what Cam was up to. They all cheered and shouted in excitement as Cam urinated into the river. Cam hurried back to Colonel Hussein's house, "Colonel, Colonel" he shouted breathlessly, "these kids seem to want my autograph they all have pencil and paper they want me to sign my name, I don't know why but it's like I'm a movie star or something."

"Mengapa ikut orang puteh American?", (why are you following this white American?") asked Colonel Hussein to the group of young boys.

One boy, by the name of Izahar answered, "kaseh kami belum tidak melihat orang puteh buang air cecil. Dia suda baderi, tidak dudo. Dia buang air cecil pandai, steady lah We have never seen a white man urinate before and he did it standing up instead of squatting. His distance was amazing:" said Izahar one of the small boys who followed Cam to the river's edge.

Colonel Hussein could not stop from laughing. "Insallah Cam, you have become a celebrity to these small boys, they have never seen a white man urinate into the river before and you did it standing up instead of squatting, your trajectory and aim must have been spectacular". Both he and Jack laughed out loud, at Cam's sudden rise to fame and popularity.

"Since the British left us in 1948, these boys have never had any live contact with Europeans or Americans, you are the first white man in our small kampong they have seen up close other than in movies Cam," said Colonel Hussein while still laughing at the situation that had just reigned on Cam.

"Then I guess I'm sort of a hero to these boys I had better sign my autograph to my new fans I've never been a celebrity before," said Cam proudly of his new found fame and reflected on the sincere warmth and generous everlasting hospitality he was receiving from these charming and wonderful Malay people.

"Well gentleman, we must get back to the base as it gets dark here at the equator very quickly. Welcome to Malaysian culture gentleman, as long as you are here you still have a lot to learn. Perhaps Cam may even become a Bomoh or a witchdoctor to these boys.

"What's a bomoh?" asked Jack;

"Well, it's like this he is some sort of powerful medicine man or witch doctor who can change things that ordinary men cannot." Colonel Hussein replied.

"Such as?" enquired Cam

"Let's say we have an important soccer match against a rival team, and it looks like the game will be played in a heavy downpour and the match will be postponed. The home team employs a Bomoh to prevent it from raining so the match will be played."

"You mean he can stop it from raining?" asked Jack.

"No, he cannot stop it from raining, but he can move the clouds to the visiting teams, town and make it rain over there, so, it will not interrupt our soccer match." Colonel Hussein replied with a huge grin on his face. "Each one of your professional football, basketball and baseball teams in America should hire a Bomoh to give an edge to the home. team."

Cam's meeting with Amrah never left his mind, in the week that followed Cam finally got up his nerve to ask Colonel Hussein if he could come back to Sungai Karang and get to know Amrah, with all respects intended.

"You cannot, she is a Muslim girl you are a Christian are you not? Eventually she will be betrothed to a Muslim man after she finishes her studies. Even though our country is fairly progressive compared to other Muslim countries we still do not allow our women to freely consort with men as you do in the West. I'm sorry it is forbidden for you to see Amrah. You know nothing of our customs and culture and language." He said with finality. You are here for one thing only, and then you will go back to America, then what? No! I forbid it."

Cam accepted his rejection with silence, but felt he had to somehow prove himself to Colonel Hussain that his intentions with Amrah were sincere.

Several weeks of training of: day flying, night flying, rainy weather flying, five meters above the canopy and skimming the ocean's surface flying, Instrument only flying the training we went by very quickly flight paths usually took them over directly over Kampongs Beserah and Sungai Karang. Cam would deliberately fly his craft lower than Jacks as he would fly over colonel Hussein's house hoping somehow to impress Amrah. However, it was not necessary this time around to refuel in midair. It was not a requirement for this mission. On one occasion Cam and Colonel Hussein flew over a major construction site on the East Coast fifteen kilometers north of Kampong Sungai Karang.

"Say Colonel what' going on down there?"

"Ah that is the Perlabohan Baru or New Harbor It will be the largest seaport on the East Coast of Malaysia and North of Singapore. It will be finished in about two years. We have a Dutch company building it for us with funding from the World Bank. The Dutch do a great job they are great engineers when it comes working with the sea" Colonel Hussein boasted to Cam.

Cam took a closer look at the raw attractive wide open coastal landscape next to the New Harbor as he flew closer and slower. "Jesus look at that raw undeveloped beautiful coast line." he said to himself. He was struck by a powerful epiphany as Cam's brain began to twist and turn with an incredible idea but did not say anything to Colonel Hussein or Jack. His epiphany haunted him he could not sleep; it would not let go of him.

On each training flight Captains Sivasambo and Lee became more involved with handling the aeronautical operations of flying Jack and Cam's crafts and were able to fly their crafts with a certain degree of proficiency. However, Cam could not get Amrah out of his mind but he could not find a means to meet with Amrah face to face. Meanwhile the rest of the team practiced their ground assault tactics.

"Talk softly Botak, how did your bank job go? I read about it in the newspapers how much did you get?" said Ah Hing. Both he and Botak Chin were enjoying tea, noodles and festive cake at the Fook Yu dim sum restaurant in Kuantan. It was August the first day of the August Moon Festival, and as Ah Hing predicted Kuantan would be bustling with Chinese sight seers and tourists.

"Botak, talk in our Hakka dialect so that our conversation cannot be so easily understood if someone might be listening to us."

"That Malay bank girl was so frightened, she began crying while she was handing me my money, she was so frightened she even handed me her purse, there was only MR25 Ringgits in it, so I took it anyway. It was sweet revenge for losing our properties and businesses to the government. I was able to get MR30,000 Malay Ringgits as he patted a leather satchel.

"Good, hand it to me and I'll make sure we can buy some more weapons from our Chinese Brothers in Thailand. Our communist brothers have made contact with the Japanese Red Army. Our Japanese brothers have agreed to storm the AIA building, the American Insurance Associates that houses the Swedish and American embassies in Kuala Lumpur. The Japanese Red Army or JRA plan on taking hostages with the weapons we will provide them from the money you give us.

The hostage situation will be an illustration to free some of our Japanese Communist friends who are held prisoners in Japan. We can also embarrass our government on a world-wide scale. The world will see how futile the Malaysian Government has become. We will make our demands known, that we Chinese Malaysians want the government to relinquish the policies that have made us second class citizens in our own country. We'll show the government the anger we feel towards their policies of taking away our land and businesses and giving it to the Malays. Thanks to you Botak, we can now buy the weapons to give to the JRA so they can accomplish their demands as well," he said gratefully to Botak.

"How will you get the weapons to the JRA?" asked Botak inquisitively.

"We have a base on a small and secluded island just off the coast of Thailand not too far from our border. After the war ended, the Japanese abandoned a large concrete warehouse that had been used as a Japanese supply base. It's not more than 50 meters from the wharf. We took it over and have been using It as a storage and staging area for all of our plots against the government." said Ah Hing with a clever twist in his voice.

"Won't the locals see what you're doing and report you to the authorities.?"

"That's the clever part Botak, we disguise it as a day-to-day fish market, where fishing boats tie up every day, while coming and going with their daily catch of fish. We conceal our cache of weapons and explosives in baskets disguised as a day's catch of fresh fish. No one ever suspects. We blend in with the fishing boats going out to sea and coming back to our small fishing harbor to tie up at the dock. When we want to smuggle arms into Malaysia, we hide them in the bottom of our fishing boats then we cover them with fish. We simply sail down the coast of Malaysia as any fishing boat would and empty our wares at a predetermined pick-up point. Usually, it is a very quiet jetty, upstream on one of the rivers that flow out of the jungle. Tomorrow we will sail down the East Coast on the outgoing tide just like any other fishing boat. Without causing suspicion we'll sail up the Pahang River to a small predominantly Chinese village called Temerloh. We off-load our weapons and smuggle whatever we need overland by car, taxi or bus to Kuala Lumpur not more than fifty kilometers away. The authorities have no idea what we are doing. We will give our weapons to the Japanese Red Army here in Malaysia We will let them do the dirty work for us. We surely will; get worldwide attention and hopefully humiliate the Malaysian Government." said Ah Hing proudly while looking around to see if anybody could understand their Hakka dialect. As usual the restaurant was crowded with clatter of cooking and eating, loud conversations about political issues and about life in general became a noisy din of any typical Chinese restaurant. All seemed normal with no apparent secret service agents. Botak was amazed how simple Ah Hing's plan was constructed. No wonder the Malaysian security forces have not caught on to Ah Hing's subversive plan.

"Next week, I will rob a bank in Kuantan I will find a busy Indian owned bank and rob it of all of its money with my homemade pistol. It will be my biggest haul yet" as he continued to boast to Ah Hing.

August 4th 1976 five members of the JRA stormed the AIA building in Kuala Lumpur with machine guns and light weapons that had been smuggled in to Malaysia by Ah Hing's communist guerilla group. The Japanese communists eventually stormed the AIA building in Kuala Lumpur that housed the Swedish and American embassies. The hostage takers demanded that several of their imprisoned leaders be released from Japanese jails especially the leader of the Japanese Red Army or JRA. Kunio Bandó the leader would be released and the remaining JRA members to be put on a plane to Kuala Lumpur and then on to Libya Otherwise, all fifty-three hostages will be slaughtered. It took four days of negations between Malaysia, Japan and the hostage takers. Americans did not participate as the primary negotiator. On the fourth day, the Japanese government eventually relinquished to the demands of the hostage takers and released five JRA members, placing them on Japanese Airlines DC 8 for Kuala Lumpur. Once in Kula Lumpur the hostage takers were offered safe passage to Libya in exchange for the freedom of the fifty-three hostages. It went smoothly, no one was hurt, no shots were fired, and buildings remained intact. However, the Malaysian Government was deeply chagrined and embarrassed over whole state of affairs.

August 10th found Defense Minister Abdul Taib Mahmud unexpectedly landing at Sultan Haji Ahmad Shah in an old-world war two DC3.

"May I help you?" said a surprised air force Sargant as he rolled up the gantry for any passengers wished to disembark from the plane.

"My name is Defense Minister Abdul Taib Mahmud, I need to see Colonel Hussein immediately, here at my plane. Do you understand Sargent?"

"Yes sir", he saluted and ran off to find Colonel Hussein.

"Peace be with you, Colonel it is good to see your again. I am sorry for dropping in like this unannounced to meet you, but our security needs to remain intact. We have too many probing eyes and ears. Can you to round up your strike team have them meet me here inside my DC3 and bring those two

Americans with you." he said firmly: I'm afraid we have loose lips on our base and so if we meet in my plane, I know no one will be listening. There seems to be too many security leaks in our defense department. these Chinese Communists bastards always seem to be one step ahead of us," he said to Colonel Hussein.

"Peace be with you as well. Defense Minister, yes, I understand, has this something. to do with the hostage taking at the AIA building in Kuala Lumpur this past week?"

"Yes, get your team together Hussein we have a lot of plans to make. Meet us inside the plane. We will have privacy there; I know we have severe security issues in our department. My plane is a secure place as any right now."

"Yes Sir," Colonel Hussein replied.

"Gentleman," as he spoke in English to the assembled team. "We are very embarrassed over this whole state of affairs that just happened in Kuala Lumpur. We know that the hostage taking was the result with those communists in Southern Thailand. Our intelligence sources here and in Thailand, believe they have identified where at least one of their major bases are hidden in Southern Thailand. We have approval from the Thai government to launch a covert assault on their clandestine base. Thailand wants them gone as well. The Thai government has a backup air base at Ubong Air base if you need to use it and a standby American ship called the Baxter if will be stationed just off the Thai coast in the event, we should need to use them. The Philippine Government has seen that our plan is in their mutual interest as well and so they have arranged for the Baxter a medical rescue ship, to stand by off the Thai coast as a courtesy through our mutual defense treaty with the United States. You can use the rescue ship in case we need emergency medical assistance. Let's hope nothing goes wrong so we don't need their services. These Chinese communists are a huge threat and embarrassment to both of our governments. I want your team Hussein, to wipe them out to a man, take no prisoners. Here are your instructions, tomorrow you will launch your raid to a small island called Koh Sumai just of the Southern coast of Thailand. "Selamat Jalan" (safe journey) gentleman" as he said safe journey in Malay."

Ah Hing returned to his base at Koh Sumai after the hostage ordeal was over in Kuala Lumpur. He had been tipped by one of his contacts in Malaysia's defense department that there will be a night time strike using two helicopters against his base at Koh Sumai Island and that he should be ready for the assault. The informant told him that the strike will occur sometime on the night of August 12th.

"Listen you bastards," said Kai Dai in Cantonese after receiving instructions from Ah Hing to his lieutenants while at their warehouse, "I have good information that idiotic Malaysian Government will launch a surprise strike here at our base probably tomorrow night. Bai Dong, take five of the men and as much ammunition and rocket propelled grenades as you can manage and go the West end of the small landing strip at Baan Bang Rak and prepare to ambush them there".

"Why the air strip?" complained Bai Dong, '" Why not stay here?"

"Because they have helicopters and must need a flat surface to land somewhere, we can catch them out the in open where there is little cover, that is why," said Ah Hing impatiently.

"Kai Lan. Take three of your men and go to the South end of the air strip so we can catch them in a cross fire. You bastards had better not shoot each other, aim carefully at your targets.

Kai Dai, you stay with me here at the warehouse and set up a defensive position with grenades in case they get past us and storm our warehouse. They will be here sometime tomorrow night so get yourselves ready." Ah Hing said to his group of militant rebels

"Colonel Hussein," when do you plan to launch our attack, I want to make sure we have enough rest, and fuel so we can make it there and back or onto our back up base in Thailand., said Jack,

"Our defense minister wants it done professionally as soon as quickly as possible, he has given the location and coordinates of the communist base camp at Koh Sumai Island. We will launch about 0200 hours this morning and catch them off guard hopefully sleeping at about 0400 hours."

"Are you going with us Colonel Hussein?" Jack asked curiously.

"Yes of course, I wouldn't miss this, I will ride in Lieutenant Hays's air craft along with Captain Sivasambo and four members of the ranger team. The rest will ride with you and Captain Lee. We're going to Koh Sumai Island gentleman. Let's makan angin" (eat the air) in Malay he said eagerly,

"Bai Dong are you ready and are you still awake it's 4 am?" Ah Hing said over his walk talkie. Make sure you hide your selves well they have some sort of special camera that see in the dark."

"Yes, we are hiding under canvas mats to conceal ourselves from their cameras, but are you sure they'll be coming? It is too quiet right now and it is getting towards dawn and no one is in sight."

"Yes! they will come. Our sources in Kuala Lumpur claim that this is the night, so stay awake. Remember don't open fire until the helicopters and those Malaysian Rangers are on the ground," said Ah Hing to both Bai Dong and Kai Lan over their walkie talkies.

Lift off went smoothly, Colonel Hussain rode with Cam Hayes, Captain Sivasambo and four members of the assault team. Jack's craft carried Captain Lee and the remainder of the squad. The night air was still, with no apparent head wind. Far in the distance Jack saw magnificent sheet lightening dancing in big rolling thunder heads. The illumination lit up each cloud in elaborated shades of purple, pink, orange and yellow hues against an electric blue background. Jack dismissed the idea that the lightening would come closer to his craft. The flight time would be approximately one and half hours to reach Koh Sumia Island. He had plenty of fuel to land the assault team, return to Kuantan and land if necessary, at the closest air base in Thailand. Those thunderheads would not reach him for three to four hours. "This should be a successful mission", he thought to himself "the weather seems good and the assault team is well trained."

Flying low at treetop level concealed their identity from any communist sympathizer. The plan was for Jack to be the lead aircraft to come in from the East and land at Baan Bang Rak airfield. Using his night vision and thermal cameras, he would check for any heat blooms that may indicate hostiles in the area. Once on the ground, Jack would give the OK for Cam to land his craft. The ranger team, led by Colonel Hussein would silently proceed to the warehouse, destroy it and kill any hostiles and return to the waiting air crafts. The raid should take no longer than forty-five minutes if all went well. Jack and Cam as well Captains Lee and Sivasambo were to stay with their respective crafts to be ready for immediate extraction after the completed mission. Before landing, Jack checked out the air field; using his night time cameras and thermal imagining cameras. There was nothing to be seen his night time cameras did not pick up any movement and his thermal cameras did not illuminate any signature heat blooms. All seemed quiet. Jack landed his craft and radioed Cam to come on in and land next to his. Two minutes later Cam landed his craft ten meters away from Jack.

"Get ready to go, steady-lah" shouted Colonel Hussein, as he alighted from the craft and met up rest of his team from the two crafts.

The cross fire was murderous, white hot tracer bullets from the West and South of the airfield caught the team in a deadly crossfire. Immediately Colonel Hussein went down taking a bullet to his shoulder. Four other members of the team were cut down in seconds not to move again.

Cam shouted, "Jack it's a trap I'm going out to get Colonel Hussein."

"No Cam, this is my job" replied Jack over his head set. "I've been through this before I am not going to let this happen again by sitting still. Give me covering fire with your nine-millimeter."

As soon as Jack jumped out his craft a rocket propelled grenade exploded hitting his craft. The explosion instantly killed Captain Lee and set the aircraft on fire. Jack was momentarily knocked down from the concussion but recovered enough to try and retrieve Captain Lee who was already dead. Captain Lee was trapped inside the burning craft. Jack could not extricate Captain Lee who was caught up in the webbing of his seat belt harness. In trying to get Captain Lee out of the burning craft Jack severely burned his hands and arms, however, it was futile attempt as Captain Lee died in the conflagration.

"May day, may day" Cam shouted into his microphone. "We need immediate assistance at Baan Bank Rak air field. Respond ASAP." He repeated over and over again.

"Roger that" said a friendly voice, "this is the rescue ship USS Baxter we have a chopper on the way with an ETA in ten minutes to your location."

The cross fire continued killing two more of the Malaysian Rangers who were huddled next to Cam's craft.

Cam rattled of his nine-millimeter causing a momentary suspension of incoming fire.

By this time Jack with his burned hands, along with a wounded Colonel Hussein, Captain Sivasambo and four surviving members of the assault team formed a defensive perimeter around the one intact air craft.

"Cam! get out of here take Captain Sivasambo, Colonel Hussein and the rest of the rangers back to Kuantan," said Jack over his headset."

"That's a negative Jack, I'm staying until the rescue chopper gets you guys the hell outa of here. Captain Sivasambo and I will lift off and provide covering fire with my nine-millimeter. By this time Cam knew where the incoming fire was coming from. Both he and Captain Sivasambo began to see them clearly in his night vision and thermal cameras. Before he could elevate his crafts nose for takeoff another RPG round exploded in front of him. Bits of shrapnel pierced his windshield wounding Cam's eyes and face.

"Captain Sivasambo take over I can't see right now." He shouted out as he was injured by penetrating glass shards. Captain Sivasambo took over, he was high enough to hover and rotate his craft in various directions to providing covering fire. Captain

Sivasambo did so for five minutes until he was out of ammunition. Landing again he set his craft down by Jack's burning craft. The suppression fire seemed to have worked as incoming fire seemed to have ceased. Ten minutes seemed like a long time but the chopper from the rescue ship Baxter arrived at the air field and sat down close to the burning craft.

"I see you guys need my help" said a medic from the USS Baxter. "We have hospital services on board, I only have room for the injured. Whoever is not hurt will have to wait for my return.

"Captain Sivasambo can you fly Cam's craft back to Kuantan along with the survivors and dead?" said Jack

"I believe I can, you chaps have trained me well enough by now. My concern is the broken windshield. But, If I put my helmet on and pull my visor down, I believe I can do it, and protect myself from the wind blowing in through the broken glass" as the murderous cross fire ceased. The morning sun was just beginning to rise above the horizon. The communist insurgents were pleased with the results of their ambush

"Ok then, Colonel Hussein, Cam and I will go to the Baxter for medical care. Good luck captain, one day we will see each other again in Kuantan. We will go out for some fine Indian curry and maybe quaff some good tasting Indian beer."

"That a roger sir, we'll meet again soon I hope I will pray to my God Lakshmi for good fortune," smiled Captain Sivasambo. The remaining survivors loaded the bodies into the air craft. There was barely enough room for the remaining survivors, but Captain Sivasambo was able to lift off without any further incident and proceeded for the return trip to Kuantan.

"Your colonel is not too bad he has as a shoulder injury, but he needs immediate medical care to stop the bleeding he is unconscious right now; he is going into shock. So is Lieutenant Hays his eyes and face are a mess right now. And you, Lieutenant Garron, have serious third degree burns on both of your hands and arms up to your elbows. All three of you will need immediate medical care on the Baxter," said the medic in a matter-of-fact tone. "Get on board we'll fly to the Baxter which is about ten minutes off shore. Let go. First help me with Colonel Hussein and then we'll fly out of here," he said.

On the Baxter Colonel Hussain Jack and Cam all received medical care in the Baxter's infirmary.

"I guess we messed up this one big time we walked into a trap," said Cam. "The doctor told me I will probably not recover one hundred percent of my vision. He doubts if I will be able to fly again. They plan to discharge me and return me stateside.

"Yeah, we messed up Cam, we failed in our mission again we got half the team killed, lost my craft, and Colonel Hussein is injured. I don't even know if we killed any of the enemy combatants. They're going to fly me to Cebu in the Philippines at a special hospital that specializes in skin grafts and burn treatments at the nearest US base there. I'm not sure if I can fly a craft any more, I don't think I can recover from my burns to handle a ship safely. Besides my mission is over. I'm finished with Captain Winchester and Morley Warburton. I 've had it up to here," gesturing to his chin.

"We taught those Malaysian troops a lesson," said Ah Hing proudly to his lieutenants. We did not lose a single person. You are good fighters he said to Bai Dong and Kai Dai. That helicopter of theirs or whatever it was, began shooting at our positions after we had left, it was fortunate that it was a good time to pull out and return to our warehouse. We'll find another base camp soon and continue our assault on the Malaysian Government. We will have Botak Chin continue to rob banks and supply us with money."

I time after his injuries healed Colonel Hussein eventually met with Defense Minister Abdul Taib Mahmud.

"We flew into a trap sir they were waiting for us. Our mission to knock out that communist base was a complete failure. Half my men were killed before we got one shot off," said Colonel Hussein. "It was lucky we have that rescue ship the Baxter to help with me and the two those American Pilots," he said in an apologetic tone.

"Yes, I know, I read your account of the raid, I'm afraid we have too many leaks in our government, we have too many eyes and ears to wage a successful campaign against these communist insurgents here in our country. I will talk to prime minister Tun Abdul Razak at his cabinet meeting and see what our strategy will be for the future," said the defense Minister sadly.

Well Jack, I guess this is goodbye you're heading off for Cebu at the Army medical burn unit there for medical treatment, and I'm heading stateside" said Cam quietly

"Yeah, that's not too bad, I have grandparents on the island of Bohol. I can see them now. I used to spend many a summer month with them while on summer vacations with my family," he said cheerfully.

"What about you Cam, what are you going to do?"

"I don't know yet, I need to talk to Colonel Hussein first, there's a lot on my mind. I will probably resign my commission once my eye sight improves."

Let's meets again in Kuala Lumpur with Captain Sivasambo at the Coliseum we'll have few beers together when all is well.

"You can bet on that Jack," as he waved goodbye as Jack departed for Cebu. He knew in his heart that this rendezvous would never happen.

Captain Sivasambo flew the one remaining craft back safely to Kuantan in which the windshield was repaired and made ready for flight operations again. President Ford felt that it was cost was prohibitive to ship the aircraft back to Area 51 again and so allowed it to remain in Kuantan as a good will gesture to be used for Malaysian military for security purposes.

True to his word, Botak Chin did rob an Indian owned bank, this time in Kuantan. Using his motorcycle for a quick getaway he rapidly headed up the coast road. He was so pleased with himself.:

"How will those slow-moving Malaysian security forces ever find me.? I am much too fast for them I think I will hide in the Cave of the Reclining Buda for a day or so," he said to himself. I can hide in the rear of the cave and come out for food and drinks. He knew there would be a bountiful supply of food and drinks as offerings to the Buddha left there by devout Buddhists. However, this time Malaysian security forces were instructed to radio the air base in Kuantan to see if Captain Sivasambo could use his air craft to track Botak Chin's escape route. Botak used the coast road for his getaway he did not go into the jungle as he usually did. Not knowing that Captain Sivasambo was a thousand meters above him, Captain Sivasambo followed every move and radioed his position to the ground security forces who were lumbering slowly on the coast road in chase of Botak Chin. Once in the air Captain Sivasambo could easily identify and follow Botak Chin's motorcycle dangerously zigzagging in and out of oncoming logging trucks on the two-lane road. Botak Chin had no idea that he was being followed from above. Even penetrating the jungle to the Cave of The Reclining Buddha Cam could follow him on his infra-red camera as the jungle covered up his visibility. Carelessly he headed for safety to hide in the Cave of The Reclining Buddha where he thought he would be safe for a day or two. Captain Sivasambo continued to radio his position to the slower security forces to where Botak was hiding in the Cave of The Relining Buddha about ten kilometers inland from the coast road. Finally, hours later Malaysian security forces showed up and cornered Botak in his hiding place. With guns drawn, a fierce gun battle erupted inside the cave, wounding Botak Chin in the leg and was subsequently captured and arrested. A swift court trial found him guilty of carrying a weapon and robbing numerous banks. The court magistrate quickly sentenced Botak Chin to hang from the gallows until pronounced dead. Botak Chin was executed two weeks later. Malaysian law is very swift. Captain Sivasambo became a hero to the minority Indian community as the man who helped capture the notorious bank robber and fugitive Botak Chin and enabled Malaysian security forces to return most of the money that Botak had stolen from the Indian Bank in Kuantan. Three years later the Malaysian Government allowed greater Chinese participation in in parliament alleviating the need for a communist insurrection.

Over time the insurgency slowly faded away, Malaysia relinquished its policy of taking away private holdings away from Chinese Citizens. Later the government adopted another social program in which each Chinese company must have at least one Malay person on its board of directors or involved in the ownership of the business. This was much better than before, because the Malaysian Chinese who owned business or land holdings could now pay a Malay person to donate their name on paper as a ghost person in order to meet the new governmental policy. This Malay person had no say so in the running of the business other than in name only. Eventually, this social policy would be scrapped as well. The uprising died out as greater participation in national politics for the Chinese, Tamil Indians along with the Malays began to participate equally.

"Colonel Hussein how are you feeling?" Cam asked politely.

"Much better thanks, I had a couple of blood transfusions, and the doctor did some surgery to repair the wound in my shoulder, I'm almost back to normal. I will be returning back to KL soon I just need to keep my arm in a sling.

"Colonel there is something I need to talk to you about, and please do not say it is forbidden. I have no more use for flying helicopters any more. I plan to resign my commission very soon and return to civilian life. I love the warmth and friendship of your country that Malaysia has offered me. I want to become a Muslim," he said with conviction.

"You are Christian, your faith is Christian why do you want to do this?" Colonel Hussein said incredulously.

"This is my plan colonel, to me God is God whether he is called Allah, Jehovah, Buddha or just plain God. They're all one in the same it is just how we humans interpret the message of God. I want you to sponsor me and coach me. I know I could learn to become a Muslim. I would like to stay here in Malaysia and marry Amrah if she will have me and I get your blessings. I want to buy land on the coast next to the

New Harbor. I believe I can build a beautiful resort hotel right on the beach We can franchise with Club Med, it will turn out beautiful. It's just a matter of time when your government will supply us with running water and electricity. The timing is right Colonel. I know we can cater to the Japanese and Australian tourists who come to Malaysia for your beautiful beaches and warm sunny climate and crystal-clear waters. I have some money saved and I can borrow some from my family to buy the land on the beach. I want Amrah to be my partner. I know she can get a government construction loan under her Islamic name since she is a true Malay woman and not Chinese. It will take three to five years to complete my plan. During this time Amrah can still pursue her degree at the University of Malaya. Between us Colonel Hussein, I know we can make a go of it. What do you say Colonel?"

"I don't know what to say right now, I'm astonished. Your plan is overwhelming to me. You seem to have thought of everything. I have never heard of Americans or white skinned people wanting to convert to Islam." The British when they were here would chastise government workers if they wanted to convert by saying "going native old boy" it was very subtle remark but the consequences were huge. Are you sincere about this?" Are you sure you want to change your life 180 degrees?" he said in amazement".

"Never in my whole life have I been more sincere. It came over me as we flew over the New Harbor. However, I'm not sure Amrah will take me as her husband, but I believe it is written," Cam said.

"My god, you are beginning to sound like a Muslim already. We'll talk it over with my family. Do you understand that you must give up pork and alcohol? Make a journey to Meccas to complete your Haj. During Ramadan you must fast and also give up sex for 30 days," Colonel Hussein said as he was warming up to idea. "By the way have you been circumcised?"

"No, my parents did not believe in it, why?" Cam said curiously.

"Oh, you will see, I think you'll have some interesting moments ahead of you," Colonel Hussein said with a chuckle in his voice.

True to Cam's vision, his plan did come to fruition. After his conversion he did marry Amrah, he chose the name Razak bin Hussein. The idea of a high-class resort was perfect, and as he predicted, the Malaysian Government did supply the area with running water and electricity. Amrah received her degree in business and in doing so she could help run the business, it did not take long for Japanese, Europeans and Australian tourists to find their resort. called "Penyu Pantai Resort", (Turtle Beach Resort) The tourists eventually flocked to the resort to watch the turtles come out under a full moon on the incoming tide to lay their eggs in the soft white sand. Cam's plan was indeed written.

Cebu

Jack arrived at the American Army medical hospital located next to Clark Airforce Base in Cebu. He was at a loss; his hands were severely burned he was not sure but he felt that his flying days were over. He was tired and fed up. During his service to Captain Winchester and Morley Warburton, he had crashed into the med with broken ribs suffered a major concussion, and now third degree burns on his hands. Losing Francine, his baby and François was just as tragic was almost more than he could endure.

"Now what's next for me"? he thought glumly.

True to his word Morley Warburton brought Jack's family up to speed as to Jack's predicament and released Jack from his obligation to the special ops team that he had been assigned to him in Saigon. Depression began to set in as the effects of post-traumatic stress disorder were becoming more pronounced. He felt that his life had become one disaster after another. Once his hands were healed, he would probably go to Loay Bohol to see his grandparents and then head home for Hawaii. There was nothing positive for him to look forward to, the remainder of his life did not look too promising. He felt his military career was over and had no desire to fly helicopters again. He slumped into his hospital bed and went to sleep. His future looked very bleak and dim.

"Well hello soldier, you've been a hard person to find," said a friendly female voice.

Sleepily and slowly, Jack began to wake from his deep sleep, at first, he thought he was dreaming. Who was this person? Rubbing the sleep from his eyes he focused on the face of Mena Delacruz.

"Mena is that you? I can't believe it; how did you get here and why are you here? You are the last I person expected to see," in a surprised voice.

"Yes, it's me Jack After I saw you last in Beirut, I decided I wanted a career in the military as a combat nurse. I joined the Army and received my commission as a lieutenant as a combat field nurse. After my basic training at Fort Benning, I was assigned to the Philippines as part of our Mutual Defense Treaty with the Philippines. Our country and other South East Asian Countries who needed our military assistance so we have joint operations here in the Philippines. I guess because I'm Filipino, born here and can speak Tagalog, the Army sent me here to an Army medical post here in Cebu similar to a MASH unit attached to Clark Air Force Base. We have a special burn unit here to take care of wounded soldiers who might have suffered severe burn wounds from fighting communist and Muslim insurgents in the Southern part of the Philippines. After a while, I was promoted to captain That's how I got here, and that is why you're here Jack. We are trained and equipped to treat your third-degree burns. I can only imagine what your story is Jack," she said smiling while kissing his forehead.

"I don't know if I should kiss you or salute you? You're still the bravest person I have ever met Mena. I've never forgotten you. What you did in Beirut was incredible, saving the lives of those soldiers under heavy fire. I have so much to tell you. Is there a chance I can spend some time with you," he said shyly?

"Of course, we have a lot to catch up on" she said in a joyful tone of voice.

Over the next several weeks Jack's hands began to heal with skin grafts and medicated dressings. During this time, he became more and more acquainted with Mena.

"Jack, there is someone here to see you," Mena said, "I believe you know Captain Winchester." She left to let the two talk alone.

"Jack, you son a bitch you're back in the hospital again how are we going to keep you out?" he said with a smile on his face. "How are you feeling?" he said warmly.

"I'm doing much better, my hands are healing, I can feed myself and bath myself and go to the bathroom by myself now. Captain Delacruz is taking good care of me. What brings you here Capitan Winchester?" Jack said with a sardonic tone in his voice.

"I thought I would bring you up to date Jack. As you know, President Ford assigned me as a special military liaison directly from the White House. Well, I am no longer assigned to the While House. I have been reassigned to a regimental combat team with the 101st airborne. Morley Warburton has a desk job now at Langley, his days for special covert assignments are over for him. And your good friend Cam Hayes resigned his commission and converted to Islam. He plans on marrying a Malay woman and now lives in Malaysia. Go figure that one out Jack, he went native" he said with a frown on his face.

"Yeah, I think I know who she is, she is Colonel Hussein's daughter, he told me about her once," he said in retrospect.

"And that brings me to you Jack. As we promised, you are no longer part of the special ops team as our hot shot pilot. You're still listed as officially being on active duty, you've not officially resigned from the service. Your records have been expunged from your activities in Vietnam, you're clean to do whatever you wish. Your record will also show three Purple Hearts, a Bronze Star and Distinguished Service Cross. Before you make up your mind to resign, I want to consider this Jack."

"What is it now Captain?" as Jack felt something was coming at him again.

"The Army is going to give you a years' time of medical leave to get you well and back on your feet. I would like you to consider being a flight instructor at Fort Rucker, we need a hot shot pilot like yourself to teach those young lieutenants how to fly those crazy looking helicopters coming out of area 51. You will be promoted to captain of course. What do you say Jack?" he said hopefully. "You don't have to tell me now you have a year to consider. The Army wants you to get well first emotionally and physically. I will leave a set of orders with you in case you decide you want to go to Fort Rucker instead of resigning from the service."

"That's a lot for me to chew on Captain, let me think it over and discuss it with my family. They are overly concerned that I keep winding up in the hospital. They will be coming out to see me from Honolulu in three weeks' time."

"Ok Jack it's your call, you can always find me at Fort Benning," as he said goodbye to Jack.

"Mena do you have some leave time coming, I would like to take you to the Island of Bohol to meet my grandparents. My hands are healing well, and I believe I can travel without impairing my healing process," he said hopefully.

"I've not had a break since I have come to Cebu, I would love to go and meet your grandparents. I need a little R and R time as well," she said in excited anticipation.

Two days later, Jack and Mena took the ferry from Cebu to Bohol and then a taxi to Loay where they met Jack's Grandparents Mr. and Mrs. Marapao.

"My family will be coming soon to Cebu to see us," he said to his grandparents after introducing Mena, "we'll have a wonderful homecoming," as he could not contain the excitement inside of him. Later that evening under a full moon Jack took Mena to the ocean's edge to see the natural wonders of a tropical moonlit beach, the quiet rhythms of gently breaking waves on the shoreline disturbing the bioluminescent algae lighting up each incoming wave. Each breaking wave enabled the shoreline to capture its own universe of shooting stars and miniature moonlight. It was breathtaking for Mena she had never seen it before even living in Hawaii. The backdrop of a beautiful tropical balmy evening breeze can easily provide the stage for a romantic prelude. Pulling Mena gently towards him he kissed her on the lips and then moments later with great passion and eagerness kissed her as heatedly as he could. She did not resist, heatedly they both entwined, as they fell on the soft sands of this quiet beach and made love between the twinkling of the stars in the night sky above and the brilliant display of shooting stars and moonlight that were now illuminating the shoreline on the incoming tide of the Bohol Sea.

Mena's passion was equal to his and submitted with eagerness with sexual excitement she had never known before. While lying quietly under a full moon in peaceful bliss that he had not felt for some time, Jack propped himself up onto one elbow.

"Mena" he said," I have a tough decision to make. I've been offered an instructor's position at Fort Rucker; they have given me the rank of captain and a year of medical leave to think about it. Or I can resign and start my life as a civilian. I'm not sure what to do right now. But I do know that I want to marry you and have our wedding in Cebu, will you marry me? Are you catholic?" he said rapidly without thinking in a low tender voice.

"Of course, I will, I thought you would never ask me Jack. Yes, I'm catholic and I've another two years to go when my hitch is over. I also don't know what to do Jack. I can re-up with both of us in the military or return to civilian life as a civilian nurse and have you by my side as my partner," she said to Jack while still embracing him.

"Well then, we will leave it up to time I have a year of medical leave so I can spend time with you here in Loay Bohol and Cebu. We both need time to decide what we need to do next. In the meantime, Mena, it'll be a year of happiness until at that time then we will make a decision. it will be what it will be," he said with calmness and relief in his voice.

"I need to tell my CO first about my marriage to you, I think it'll be OK. Why get married in Cebu?" she said curiously.

"It is because my parents were married in Cebu and they will be here in two weeks. I need to go to St Josephs to talk with Father Silva if he is still there to marry us. What about your family Mena?"

"Well, it'll be quite a surprise when I tell them. We'll have to visit them on the mainland Jack" with a twinkle in her voice.

Jack's family arrived as expected, they were overjoyed as Jack had begun his recovery without complications and at the announcement of marrying Mena. Ligaya's father stood in as the best man as he had done so before with Ron and Ligaya. Tanya was to be Mena's bridesmaid, Monsignor Silva wept for joy as he realized what must have transpired to bring these special people back together again to his church. He was so pleased to recognize Ron and his cousin Ligaya from many years ago, and now he was going to marry their son and is future bride in the same church as he had some thirty odd years ago.

"We have a great and wonderful God," Monsignor Silva would go on to say to everyone.

Two weeks later on December 7, 1975 Jackson Garron married Mena Maria Delacruz in the Church of St Joseph The Patriarch, on the Island of Cebu, Visayas, Philippines.

God surely works in mysterious ways; it truly was a remarkable rendezvous of fates.

272

EPILOG

So how is it, that in a such small event as a marriage in the grand scheme of things did Ron meet Ligaya or Jackson meet Mena? Was it a fate or destiny of war? How could they have ever met in any other way? Historical events that are unforeseen, have an immediate incalculable impact on the players who play out their role in history. Jackson Garron had his own impact on the people around him culminating with his marriage to Mena Delacruz in the same church that his father and mother were once married in a faraway land some thirty odd years later. It came clear to Jackson that his future belonged to those people around him who believed in the beauty of their own dreams.

Was it preordained destiny, karma, chance, the laws of probability, fate, destiny, or just random acts of coincidences that changed the lives of people both good and bad who traverse their time through history.? There is or can be no logical answer, it can only be from the Hand of God that guides all things and shapes the course of mankind.